PSYCHOPATHS
RULE
THE WORLD

ALSO BY MIMA

The Fire Series
Fire
A Spark Before the Fire

The Vampire Series
The Rock Star of Vampires
Her Name is Mariah

Different Shades of the Same Color

The Hernandez Series
We're All Animals
Always be a Wolf
The Devil is Smooth Like Honey
A Devil Named Hernandez
And the Devil Will Laugh
The Devil Will Lie
The Devil and His Legacy
She Was His Angel
We're All Criminals

Learn more at **www.mimaonfire.com**
Also find Mima on Twitter, Facebook and Instagram @mimaonfire

PSYCHOPATHS
RULE
THE WORLD

MIMA

PSYCHOPATHS RULE THE WORLD

iUniverse books may be ordered through booksellers or by contacting:

iUniverse
1663 Liberty Drive
Bloomington, IN 47403
www.iuniverse.com
844-349-9409

Because of the dynamic nature of the Internet, any web addresses or links contained in this book may have changed since publication and may no longer be valid. The views expressed in this work are solely those of the author and do not necessarily reflect the views of the publisher, and the publisher hereby disclaims any responsibility for them.

Any people depicted in stock imagery provided by Getty Images are models, and such images are being used for illustrative purposes only. Certain stock imagery © Getty Images.

ISBN: 978-1-6632-2397-5 (sc)
ISBN: 978-1-6632-2398-2 (e)

Library of Congress Control Number: 2021911080

Print information available on the last page.

iUniverse rev. date: 06/01/2021

CHAPTER 1

The media. It was said to be the truth seeker, the exposer, and the source that showed you an alternate view from what government and corporations wanted you to see. It could've been a newspaper, television, or eventually the internet, but it was there to inspire and intrigue. Ideally, the media gave you an unbiased view of the world, but more importantly, it was there to distribute food for thought. Whether it be a breaking news story or long-term investigation, our media exposed who we really were, and sometimes, it wasn't a pleasant view.

But then people got tired of thinking because they were already overwhelmed by life, and propaganda began to seep in. Eventually, people lost trust in the media. Contradicting ideas were proposed, emotions manipulated, often by reporters, entertainers, and even memes, that it became almost impossible to distinguish truth from fiction. And that's when Jorge Hernandez got into the game.

"Put on the siren!" Jorge screamed, his voice echoing through the SUV as he followed a police car, that in turn, was following a black sedan. "What the fuck you waiting for, Hail?"

"But, I…" Constable Hail attempted to reply before getting cut off by the raging Latino.

"I'm not fucking around, Hail," Jorge yelled back as he looked toward his dash, then back ahead at the traffic moving along the highway. "Do it! Now!"

Without replying, the siren came on as the police car sped up, with Jorge on his tail as they swerved through traffic until the sedan eventually slowed down and eased off the road. The driver, Jameson Field, thought he was only dealing with local police, but he was about to deal with someone much worse. The former Mexican cartel leader made his own rules, and unlike those of the Canadian justice system, his were much more brutal.

Mark Hail approached the car in the usual authoritarian manner while Jorge rushed to the passenger side. While the police officer started to calmly speak through the barely opened window to the man inside, Jorge was pounding on the passenger side. The young, white man inside the car didn't appear concerned with Mark Hail, even though he was a police officer. However, when he turned to see Jorge Hernandez on the other side, fear-filled his eyes, and in an instant, he put the car back into drive and stepped on the gas.

"Get him!" Jorge yelled to Constable Hail as the two men ran back to their vehicles and immediately began to follow the black car as it sped away. With sirens on, the two men flew through traffic, passing everyone on the highway. Jorge hit the call button on his steering wheel, and Hail quickly answered.

"That fucker, he's going to take that off-ramp up ahead. I can see it now," Jorge insisted.

"I'm thinking the same," Hail's voice echoed through the SUV. "He'll be easier to get when there's less traffic."

"And less *eyes, amigo,*" Jorge insisted.

"Look, you gotta…"

"I know," Jorge snapped at the constable. "You will take him away. I will follow you."

Just as Jorge predicted, Jameson Field tuned onto the off-ramp, and both Jorge and Hail were right behind him. Perhaps it was defeat that brought the man to a halt on the side of the road, but Jorge spent many years playing this game and touched his gun inside his leather jacket before getting out of the SUV. He noticed Hail was reaching for his too as he headed toward the car.

Jameson Field looked terrified yet attempted to hide his fear as he barely opened the window. Unfortunately for him, Jorge Hernandez could smell it.

"You, there," Jorge abruptly pointed at the man whose eyes were full of desperation. "Unlock your door, put your hands up where I can see them, and get out of the fucking car."

Without saying a word, the man slowly raised his hands. His sharp blue eyes glanced around his car as if to suddenly find the solution to this problem. There was none.

"Now get out of the car," Jorge barked as Hail stepped back and watched the man, his gun within reach, as Jorge pulled the car door opened.

"Am I under arrest?" Jameson Field asked, appearing confused as he glanced between Jorge Hernandez, the man well-known in the underground community for his brutal styles of retaliation, then back at the local police officer. "Because I have a lawyer, and he…"

"You're under arrest, motherfucker," Jorge sharply cut him off as the man slowly got out of the vehicle. "But unfortunately for you, it's not by this guy," Jorge tilted his head toward Hail. "The Canadian legal system, it is weak beside me."

Halfway out of the vehicle appearing stunned, the man froze.

"Now!" Jorge abruptly grabbed his arm and pulled him out before shoving his body against the car, causing the young man to whimper. "Constable Hail is going to put handcuffs on you, and then you and I, we are going to have a little conversation. And that piece of shit car of yours? It's gonna be towed."

Defeated, the man held a weak pose as Hail quickly cuffed him. Appearing nervous, he exchanged looks with Jorge.

"Meet you there," Hail muttered.

Jorge thought for a moment and nodded.

"Back door."

"Yup."

Hail escorted the man to the police car while Jorge jumped in his SUV. Calming slightly, he took a deep breath before fastening his seat belt and watching Hail push Jameson Field into the back of his car. With a grin, Jorge hit a button on his steering wheel to call his associate.

"Were you successful?" Diego Silva answered abruptly.

"*Si*," Jorge replied as he watched Hail get back into the car and slowly start to move. "Transporting the garbage to the waste facilities as we speak."

There was silence on the other end.

"You there, *amigo?*" Jorge finally asked as he followed the police car as they both moved through traffic.

"Chase was talking to me," Diego referred to the youngest member of the group, a half-indigenous man from Alberta. "We got Andrew on the job."

"*Perfecto.*"

"And Paige?" Diego referred to Jorge's wife.

With some hesitation, Jorge agreed. He was very protective of his wife even though she was one of the best assassins in the world. She had a few close calls in the last few years, and he preferred keeping her in the background as much as possible.

"If you think this is…necessary," Jorge searched for the words. Despite his years in Canada and previously working in the US, he still stumbled on his English from time to time. "I would rather not."

"You know she will want to be there," Diego insisted

"Chase….we need him to…" Jorge considered.

"I was thinking the same," Diego agreed. "We'll be there."

"*Gracias.*"

They ended the call, and Jorge continued to follow Hail as he drove toward his crematorium. It proved a good move when he purchased the business a couple of years earlier. It had helped to eliminate a lot of problems.

He hit a button and listened to the phone ring.

"Hello," His wife's smooth voice filled the car, and he immediately relaxed. "What's going on?"

"Taking out the garbage," Jorge replied as he kept his eyes on the car ahead of him.

"That's what I was hoping you'd say," Paige said in a soft voice. "And…"

"You are welcome to join us, *mi amor*," Jorge cut her off. "Is Juliana there?"

"Yes," Paige replied, as they referred to their live-in nanny. "She's upstairs with Miguel, and Maria is at school."

"Can you call Jolene?" Jorge referred to Diego's sister. "The rest, they will meet us."

"Anything else?"

"Just meet us," Jorge replied. "Andrew will be there, and that is all we need."

"I understand."

"But, *mi amor,* you know, if you do not wish to…"

"I *want* to be there," She spoke with determination this time, and he didn't argue.

"Very well," Jorge backed off. "Then I will see you soon."

"You will."

He ended the call and took a deep breath.

By the time they arrived at the crematorium, Jorge had managed to calm his racing heart, but the fire continued to burn through his veins when he saw Hail get out of the car. He exchange looks with Jorge as he reached for the door handle. Opening it, Hail appeared apathetic as he reached in the back seat and pulled out Jameson Field. That's when Jorge got out of his SUV and silently followed the two men as they walked toward the back door of the crematorium. Ringing a bell, Hail waited while Jorge glared at Field before glancing around to make sure no eyes were on them.

The door swung open, and Diego Silva, a middle-aged Colombian, twisted his lips as he looked at Jameson Field.

"This the guy?" He asked as he moved aside, his question directed at Jorge.

"This is *him.*"

"Take him in," Diego tilted his head and glanced at Hail. "We already got the plastic on the floor."

Jameson Field paled as Jorge closed the door behind them.

As Hail led the frightened man into the next room, Diego raised his eyebrow before following them, and Jorge was left behind. He briefly turned on his phone to check to see if their police chase was on the news. It wasn't. However, there were a few clips on Twitter, some independent recordings.

Searching his contacts, he found the number for Tom Makerson, editor of *Toronto, AM* and called him.

"Hey," Makerson answered. "What's up?"

"There was a police chase. People are commenting on Twitter."

"Yeah?"

"Say it was the Hernandez Production Company that was doing it for an upcoming show or movie," He spoke in his usual, abrupt manner. "And we are sorry if we alarmed anyone."

"But usually when a production company is going…"

"Don't worry about this here," Jorge cut him off. "I will make sure I have the bases covered. We were working on a show."

He ended the call, and a smooth grin crossed his lips as he turned his phone off.

They were all puppets on a string. And Jorge was the devil that controlled them.

CHAPTER 2

"Is this the one?" Paige Hernandez spoke in her usual, calm tone as she pointed at the frightened man lying on the crematorium floor, his hands still handcuffed behind his back. She briefly glanced across the room at Mark Hail, who appeared uncomfortable, then back at her husband.

"He is… the one, *mi amor,*" Jorge nodded, speaking in a gentle tone reserved for only a few. "It was because of him that you and our children were almost murdered."

Paige said nothing but crossed her arms over her chest and nodded. Standing nearby, Jorge noted that Diego had the same pose. He was one of his oldest, dearest friends and associates, a part of the *familia,* therefore, having little patience for those who attempted to hurt anyone in their group.

"*Mi amor,* this is the man who worked at the hotel," Jorge clarified. "The night that we were asked…." Jorge now turned his attention toward Mark Hail. "by the head of the police to take care of the white supremacists that were infiltrating them. It was this one," Jorge returned his attention to the man on the floor. "That tipped off someone in the group."

Jameson Field shrunk back as if to make himself smaller.

"See, it was him that *encouraged* the group to meet at this specific hotel in the first place," Jorge continued. "He wanted to be part of their racist group because his uncle was in it and this was his way of impressing them. He got them a deal."

"So, he suspected something was off..." Paige calmly replied.

"He was an idiot," Jorge insisted. "Who should have kept his fucking mouth shut."

Paige looked away.

"So now, our friend here," Jorge moved closer to the man on the floor as he wriggled on the plastic. "He will learn what happens when you try to hurt my family. No one...*no one* hurts my family."

"But I didn't know!" Jameson suddenly spoke up, his voice full of anxiety. "He didn't tell me what he was going to do. I thought he was going..."

"You know, this here," Jorge cut him off, shaking his head as he glanced at Diego, whose eyes were narrowing. "Does not matter to me. The point is that you were on the wrong side of this here situation. I do not care what you did or did not know."

"I don't believe him," Diego shook his head, wrinkling his nose. "He knew. He's trying to save his ass."

"Well, unfortunately, his ass may be the only thing left when I am finished with him," Jorge sharply replied.

Just then, the door opened, and Andrew Collin walked in, whistling. The skinny twenty-something strolled through the room as if it wasn't out of the ordinary to have a handcuffed man lying on the floor.

"I got the oven heating up," he informed Jorge and glanced toward Jameson Field. "We cooking him dead or alive?"

"No, please!' Jameson started to cry. "No, I will do anything..."

"I do not have anything you can do for me," Jorge reminded him, as he casually shrugged. "You got nothing I want."

"The truth would be nice though," Paige suggested, her eyes on Jorge, not the man on the ground. "I feel like he isn't telling us everything."

"I'll tell you anything..." Jameson continued to sob. "I swear, *anything*."

Jorge appeared bored. He heard something and turned around. Chase Jacobs and Jolene Silva walked into the room. Chase was massive, a trained boxer, half-indigenous man, while beside him, the Colombian wore a skin-tight dress that showed off her curves.

"Why do you talk so much!" Jolene spoke loudly, abruptly as she crossed the floor, her heels clicking on the cement. She stopped and pointed at the man. "You do this every time, Jorge, just kill him. Do not waste time. So dramatic!" The Colombian swung her arms in the air. "Put a bullet in his head because nothing this man says…it will be lies!"

"Is this the shitstain that might've caused Paige and the kids to be killed?" Chase asked while his dark eyes narrowed in anger. "*This….*"

Before Jorge had a chance to reply, Chase rushed toward the man and brought one of his Dr. Martens down on the man's back. Jameson screamed like an animal about to die.

"You are not getting any sympathy from me," Jorge shrugged as he glanced at Jameson, who attempted to wiggle away from Chase as the large, powerful man stood over him. "After all, regardless of what you say, I know you are the reason why my wife, my kids, could have been killed that night. What he just did to you, is *tame* compared to what I am about to do to you."

With that, Chase moved aside. His eyes met with Jorge's. He nodded.

"I do not care what your story is," Jorge continued to speak. "I do not care if you did or did not know what this man came to my house for. The problem is you are a snitch and you should have kept your mouth shut."

"See, when you knew that something was going on," Jorge continued. "This is when you should have walked away. This is when you should have decided that it was not for you to get involved. This was when you learned a lesson and moved forward with your life. But, no, instead, you decide to contact this man to win points with him. And when he learned that it was too late, that all his people were dead, he decided to target my house."

"I didn't know, I thought…" Jameson attempted to explain as he started to cry harder. "I thought…"

"What did you think?" Jorge cut him off. "That he was going to come to find me to have a peaceful conversation? Maybe to swap recipes or talk about the Bible? *What?* What the *fuck* did you think was going to happen?"

The man was silent.

"I suggest you talk!" Jolene's harsh, loud voice took over the room. "We are not patient people!"

"He…." Jameson began to mutter. "He said…."

"Louder!" Jorge's powerful voice rang through the room. "We cannot hear you talk. Be a man, for once in your pathetic life, speak up!"

"He said that he….he knew your house…."

"And?" Jorge prodded.

"He didn't say…." Jameson struggled with his words as his teeth began to chatter, tears ran down his face. "He said he knew where you lived."

"And it did not occur to you that I had a family?" Jorge shot back. "That I had children?"

Jameson cried harder and nodded.

"So, he knew?" Paige spoke up. "That there were children in the house?"

The man hesitated before nodding, his eyes closed, as tears gathered in a puddle on the plastic beneath him.

Jorge and Paige shared a look. They already knew the answers. They just wanted him to say them out loud.

"Back in Mexico," Jorge glanced around the room. "We do not like people who talk so much."

With that, Diego approached him with a knife in hand. He passed it to Jorge. On the floor, Jameson continued to cry with his eyes closed.

"This is where I peace out," Hail suddenly spoke up as tension grew in the room. He walked toward the door. "I don't need to see this."

The constable rushed out of the room while Jorge continued to glare at Jameson Field. Without missing a beat, he continued to speak.

"We find it very….*rude* to gossip as you did, Mr. Field," Jorge approached the man and knelt on the floor. Jameson's eyes sprung open, and he struggled to move away when he saw the knife in Jorge's hand. Chase and Diego immediately rushed over and held the man down as Jorge reached in his mouth and pulled out his tongue. With one quick strike, the knife drove through the man's tongue, cutting it off as blood splattered everywhere, including on Jorge. He dropped it on the plastic and stood up while Chase and Diego stepped back.

"This here," Jorge screamed as the man struggled with shock. "Is what happens when you talk too much. You do *not* get to keep your tongue. My family, they could have been killed that night. My son, he is just a baby. My daughter, she is 14 and very, *very* brave!"

Blood poured out of the man's body, running on the plastic. Jolene looked away while across the room. Andrew appeared intrigued.

"We gonna burn him now?" He called out lazily.

"No, this one here, I plan to torture way more before I put him in the oven," Jorge replied. "Where is the crowbar?"

"This here is messy," Jolene muttered to him as if it was a secret. "You will…"

"Do not worry about me," Jorge insisted as he glanced down at his expensive suit. "The baby, he already puked on this suit. It has never been the same since."

Jolene appeared to accept the answer and nodded before glancing at Paige, who was transfixed.

"Can we get on with this?" Diego pointed toward the man on the floor as he passed him the crowbar. "There's blood all over the Goddam place. It's going to drip off the plastic soon, and this dumb fuck, he ain't worth it."

"I got it," Jorge insisted. "But I need you all to leave."

"But…." Chase started.

"No, I want to do this myself," Jorge insisted. "And I do not want my wife, I do not want any of you to see me lose control with this man because it will not be pretty."

No one replied but started to head toward the door.

"Paige," Jorge glanced at his wife, ignoring the man agonizing on the floor. "I need my other clothes."

"But, you will…"

"I can clean up real good, *mi amor,*" Jorge winked at her. "This is not my first rodeo."

Paige nodded as they looked into each other's eyes. She eventually turned and followed the others out the door.

He was now alone in the small room with the man on the floor.

"You," Jorge began to speak. "You are responsible for someone almost killing my entire family. I will tell you, this here, it would have brought the animal out in me because without my family, I have no reason to keep any level of sanity."

"Unfortunately for you, *amigo,* my conscious it, it is long gone *Tu mueres aqui!*" Jorge lifted the crowbar and brought it down hard on the man on the ground. "Thanks to you, motherfucker…" He continued to speak as he slammed the heavy object into Jameson's legs. "My daughter, who is only 14 fucking years old, had to shoot a man…"

Jorge felt rage erupt inside him at the memory of Maria standing in shock, a gun in her hand, after shooting the man that was about to kill her family. She had nightmares since that day. She would never be the same little girl, and although this briefly brought tears to Jorge's eyes, it created even more fury toward the man on the floor, who was dying before his eyes.

"Do you know what that's like?" Jorge screamed as he brought the crowbar down even harder, this time on the man's torso. "Do you know what it is like to see your child in pain? Do you know what it's like to know your family could've died?"

Without realizing it, Jorge started to beat Jameson faster, with more fury than he started with, even though he no longer struggled. Feeling his anger begin to subside, Jorge felt tears burning his eyes as he thought back to that night. He would never forget the look in his daughter's eyes. It would be something Jorge would carry with him until his dying day. Jorge grew weak and eventually sunk to the ground as he stared at the lifeless body beside him.

His poor Maria.

His poor little girl.

No one hurt his family and got away with it.

No one.

CHAPTER 3

"Are you ok?" Paige gently asked as she walked up behind Jorge. He stood alone in the crematorium office. She placed her hand on his shoulder, and Jorge slowly turned around. Although he had splatters of blood all over him, she didn't even flinch as she looked into his eyes.

"*Mi amor,* I am fine," He shrugged apathetically. "I was thinking."

"You need to get out of those clothes," She gently reminded him as she glanced down at the suit. "Put them in the oven with him."

"I know, you are right," Jorge hesitated for a moment. "I guess this here was too much. We looked so long for this man, trying to connect the dots…"

"We found him," Paige said. "It's over."

"But is it over, *mi amor?*" He quietly asked. "My Maria, she has not been the same since…"

"She'll be ok," Paige reminded him. "I promise. I am working with her. She's stronger than you think."

"I hope you are right, Paige," Jorge spoke with sadness in his voice. "I cannot live with myself if she is…."

"She'll be fine," Paige nodded. "I know it. It's hard for her to understand… everything. But she's coming around. It's a lot to take in. But she needs to see her power rather than her weakness."

"This is a lesson we all must learn," Jorge nodded.

"Go change, and I'll get the clothes," Paige spoke quietly. "Please."

Jorge nodded, and they both left the room. His legs felt heavy as he reached the stairs and made his way down into the dark, dungeon-like basement, passing the room where Andrew worked to find the small bathroom. He had added a shower in recent months, anticipating a day when things got a little messy. And with Jorge Hernandez, things often got messy.

Finding a large garbage bag in a drawer, he removed his clothes, carefully placing each inside until he was naked. Once finished, he tied the bag and set it outside the door before locking it and turning around. Feeling vulnerable, he briefly glanced down at his body before walking toward the mirror, where he studied his face. He was well into his forties and felt every second of it in his soul. His face was starting to show his age, with grey popping up more and more in his hair, but his spirit was still 19-years-old, and ready to take on the world.

In the last few years, Jorge had managed to uproot his life in Mexico to move to Canada, where he married Paige while satisfying his daughter's need to attend a Canadian school. His son was born shortly afterward, just about the same time that Jorge took over the Canadian marijuana industry as the founder of Our House of Pot, a nationwide retail operation. He had later stepped aside as CEO but stayed on as an advisor. He entrusted his associate Diego Silva to look after the business. It was the result of a lot of blood, sweat, and tears. Of course, most of the blood, sweat, or tears that resulted were not his own.

Stepping into the shower, he felt the hot water stream over him as Jorge paused and closed his eyes. He was worried. His recent attempts to mediate with his wife were useless. His mind never stopped. Where he came from, it was too dangerous to have your mind not be on high alert at all times. If you relaxed too long, you found yourself dead. Not that Canada had lessoned those same opportunities. But it was different here. And yet, so many things were the same.

Lathering the soap, he cleaned himself slowly, eventually washing his hair. His mind went through a checklist. There was no proof of this man's disappearance, and his body was currently burning in the cremation oven. The floors would be disinfected with hot water and bleach. The victim's car towed to a chop shop. Mark Hail would never be associated with the arrest because the police department looked after him, and he looked after them. He had power over them as well as the government and the media. It was fine.

Turning off the water, he grabbed a towel and quickly dried off before wrapping it around his hips and stepping out of the stall. Checking outside the bathroom door, he found a fresh, clean suit while the garbage bag was gone. Closing the door again, Jorge quickly dressed. Walking toward the mirror, he wiped away steam to inspect his reflection. Satisfied, he left the bathroom. Someone would be in shortly to clean the entire room with bleach. It was good to be careful.

Paige was waiting for him in the office.

"Where is everybody?"

"Andrew is taking care of the body," Paige gently commented as he reached out to touch her arm. "Chase and Diego are helping him. Jolene is gone back to the production house. Diego picked me up, so I'll need a drive home. You need to take it easy for the rest of the day."

"I must go later to discuss some things with Tony," He referred to a man he had previously worked with on two seasons of *Each the Rich Before the Rich Eat You,* before earning a powerful position at Hernandez Production Company earlier that year. "I have some ideas for shows I would like to present to him."

"He's pretty busy already," Paige reminded him. "You keep him on his toes."

"It is good, Paige, that everybody, they are always on their toes," Jorge reminded her as he leaned in to give her a quick kiss. "I think it is time we leave. Maria, she will be home soon, and I would like her to know."

"Do you think we should tell her?" Paige wondered.

"I think, yes," Jorge nodded. "She knows that there was another man behind this….so yes, it will give her peace of mind that he will not be an issue."

Paige agreed.

"I will, of course, not give her the details," Jorge insisted as they headed toward the door. "But I will give her the comfort of knowing that he will not show up at our door. We wiped them out."

"His family will be looking for him…"

"Let them look," Jorge assured her. "I do not care. They will never find him."

"What if it gets in the media?"

"Not all stories make it to the newspaper," Jorge reminded her. "We have control over the most powerful newspaper in the city, and as for the rest of the country, do you think they care about a man missing in Toronto? Do you know how many go missing that never even get on the news? Trust me, this is not a concern to me. Even if they thought they saw me with him, they got nothing. And of course, the police, I own them."

"That is true," Paige agreed as they made their way toward the exit. "After what you did for them…"

"What I continue to do for them," Jorge reminded her. "And they will do more. Trust me, this here is not a casual relationship. This is a serious commitment, and it goes both ways. I have more plans for them. It does not stop here."

The couple headed outside. Locating the SUV in the parking lot, they exchanged looks as they walked to the vehicle. He breathed in the crisp air, a sign that winter was coming.

"You know, *mi amor,*" Jorge said as he climbed behind the wheel. Paige jumped in the passenger side. "This year, I think we should have a huge family event for Christmas. Each year, we keep things quiet. But this year, maybe we need a party for our *familia.* Maybe, Maria can help plan it. We can do some more traditional things from Mexico. I want her to look forward to something."

"She'd like that," Paige agreed as she fastened her seatbelt. "I think she'll be ok. I know you worry…"

"Oh, *mi amor,* you have no idea how much I worry," Jorge confirmed. "Ever since that night. And even before, there were reasons for concern. But that night, I will never forget the look in her eyes. She was in shock. I remember carrying her to her room, and she was shaking. It broke my heart. I did not want this for my children. I did not want them to see or experience what I have. That is why I leave Mexico. That is why I do so many things."

Paige didn't reply but reached over and touched his arm. They exchanged looks as he started the SUV and slowly eased onto the road. Once in traffic, Jorge turned on his phone, and she did as well.

"I got a message from Makerson," Paige referred to *Toronto AM's* editor. "He said no one is talking about the police chase today other than the videos on Twitter. He responded in a fake account and said it was for a television show and put out the fire."

"This is good," Jorge nodded. "The good thing about people now is they have a short attention span. It does not take them long to forget."

"And everything is entertainment," Paige added. "So it's a pretty convincing story."

"The world, it has gone crazy," Jorge confirmed. "Everything is drama and nothing more."

"So what did you have in mind for Tony?" Paige changed the subject. "Another docuseries? He seems pretty busy overseeing the other shows."

"I want to do a show," Jorge thought for a moment. "Loosely based on my life."

"What?" Paige spoke abruptly. "Are you serious?"

"Very loosely," Jorge confirmed, "fiction."

"That might be getting a little too close to the fire."

"Trust me, I have some good stories," Jorge shrugged. "I do not wish to take them to the grave. I need a writer who will put them on paper, change them up a bit, and you know…"

"This sounds like an ego thing," Paige thought out loud. "You know what I said about your ego getting in the way."

"Trust me, this here is fine," Jorge assured her with laughter in his voice. "I think that people must know the truth."

"By putting it in fiction?"

"People sense the truth from fiction," Jorge assured her. "And sometimes it is a fine line."

Paige didn't respond because she knew he was right.

CHAPTER 4

"Are you sure, *Papá*?" Maria Hernandez asked as she leaned against the back of the couch, raising an eyebrow as if to question her father's words. This made him throw his head back and laugh.

"Maria, do you not trust your *padre?*" He leaned forward and touched her long black hair as she looked at him with her big, brown eyes. For a brief moment, he saw her innocence return, but it was quickly overcast with skepticism. "Of course, I tell you everything is ok, and I mean it. Today I located and took care of the man who caused this here trouble. It is finished, *Princesa*. So, you must not worry."

"*Papá*, I worry," Maria replied with sadness in her eyes. "Our family will always have enemies."

"But Maria," Jorge grew serious and sat up a bit straighter. "We always prove to be stronger than our enemies, and this here is all that matters. You cannot spend your life worrying about the unknown. You will miss so many beautiful things."

"But you say to be vigilant," Maria reminded him as she fixed her skirt and gave him an upward look. "That's what you tell me."

"Vigilant, yes," Jorge suppressed a smile as pride flowed through his body. At 14, his daughter seemed so fragile, and yet, when he least expected it, he saw a power gently burning from beneath the surface. "But Maria, I do not want you to have the same worries as me. I have built this world to accommodate you and Miguel, to make things easier. You must know that. You will always be protected. There will always be people around who will make sure of this."

"I think she has proven she can protect herself," Paige said as she entered the room carrying Miguel, who struggled to get out of her arms and she let him free. The toddler wandered toward Jorge, who reached down and picked him up.

"Ah, but of course," Jorge replied as he pulled his son close and the child snuggled against his chest. "But from time to time, we all need someone watching our back. Even me."

"Even *you?*" Maria giggled, and he realized she was teasing him.

"*Si,* Maria, *even* me," He joined in on the joke. "And Paige is right. You are capable of looking after yourself and, of course, our family. I agree. But what I mean is that you are part of a powerful group of people. You have no reason to be afraid. And today, we assured you of this."

"Did you kill him, *Papá?*" Maria asked with wide eyes.

"Kill!" Miguel repeated his sister's words.

"Maria, this here," Jorge gestured toward his two-and-a-half-year-old and shook his head. "Not here."

"I understand," Maria reached out for Miguel. "I said will…"

"Kill!" The little boy repeated as the doorbell rang.

"Ok, this here is enough," Jorge shook his head and noticed Paige walking toward the door. "I have a meeting now, and you two, you must go upstairs and *unlearn* that word you just say. We do not need him repeating that outside the house,"

Maria grimaced and reached for the baby.

"Come on, Miguel," She sang out. "Let's go upstairs and play."

"*Gracias,* Maria."

"We'll talk more later," She reminded him as she carried her brother toward the stairs. Jorge rose from the couch just as Ronald Evans walked in the room, with Paige behind him.

"We will go to the office," Jorge pointed toward a dark section of the house, his face showing no emotion.

The chief of police didn't reply but nodded. He knew the routine of turning his phone off and leaving it outside the office. However, once behind closed doors, he didn't waste any time speaking up.

"We were lucky this time," Evans said before Jorge had time to cross the room. "This didn't get out in the media, but we can't keep having these things happening in broad daylight."

Jorge didn't reply at first. Walking behind the desk, he calmly sat down.

"You know, I have had a long day," He finally commented and pulled his chair forward. Jorge looked at the older, white man as he sat across from him. "I do not need a lecture from you on keeping things quiet."

The man paled, didn't reply, as he looked down at his lap.

"However, the problem, it has been taken care of," Jorge assured him as the chief of police looked back up with some hesitation. "I have made sure to put out any potential media fires, and by now, I would think that you would know this about me."

Ronald Evans merely nodded. Jorge had taken care of a much big problem for him earlier that year.

"Yes, I know this about you," Ronald finally spoke up. "I just…"

"I will be cautious," Jorge assured him, and the two men exchanged a look of understanding. "But you know, you have it good. You call in a problem, and I fix it. And on occasion, very rare occasions, I borrow your police department to take care of mine. This is pretty good compared to back in Mexico. There, we have what is called *polisicarios* to assist us. Do you know what this here is?"

"I….doesn't *sicarios* mean hitman?" Evans slowly spoke as he leaned forward in his chair. "As in, the police?"

"It does," Jorge nodded. "So, you should be happy that so far, I have not required this service."

"You mean, you would…"

"It means that when I lived in Mexico," Jorge nodded toward a collage over beside his desk that consisted of everything that represented his home country. "I owned the police, but unlike here, they were my hitmen. They worked for *me*. Here, it is more of a partnership. But this is Canada, and I run a clean business, so things are very different."

"I didn't think you could casually leave the…"

"Well, you never fully leave them," Jorge replied but didn't divulge more information. "But, you could say, I have divorced them. But like an ex-wife, they never really go away."

"I hear you there," Evans muttered and shook his head.

"But this is not for you to worry about," Jorge left it at that. "So, is this here why you pay me a visit today?'

"Partially," Evans nodded. "I had some concerns that the department would be tied up in this...situation you dealt with today."

"It has been taken care of," Jorge assured him. "This...situation, it will no longer be a problem for me or anyone else."

"Will I have a missing person case to contend with?"

"You will, I am guessing, if anyone misses this piece of shit," Jorge replied. "I cannot imagine why."

"But still..."

"You will most likely have a missing person case," Jorge confirmed as he leaned back in his chair. "And when you do, he left his work one day and disappeared."

"No trace to Constable Hail?"

"No, and if there ever is," Jorge thought for a moment. "He simply stopped him because he was a little bit drunk...."

"Does this man drink?"

"We know for a fact he does."

"And that's why his car was towed? You do realize there are records of that?"

Jorge shrugged. "There are no records."

"But, we had to..."

"I know," Jorge nodded. "We have reached out to the tow truck operator. There are no records."

"And his car?"

"Chop shop."

"Out of my jurisdiction?"

"Yes, out of Toronto."

Ronald Evans seemed to relax.

"Evans, this here, it is not my first day on the job," Jorge assured him. "Everything is taken care of. It will look as if this man went missing. Sure, if Hail was seen putting him into his car, it was to give him a breathalyzer."

"But, cameras are nearby...

"I have someone who takes care of cameras," Jorge nodded. "There are no records. And no one would record a random police stop. There is only traffic. No pedestrians. No houses. No businesses in this area. On the rare chance someone sees something and makes a stink, well, we will disqualify them immediately. We will make them look like tin foil hat-wearing morons, and that will be that. As I said, this here is not my first rodeo, and I assure you, people are too wrapped up in themselves to notice anything these days unless it is dramatic. There was nothing dramatic about this situation. At least, nothing in the public view."

"But if someone saw you there…"

"I think you do not realize how little most people think about others," Jorge shook his head. "Most people are self-involved. They do not see anything or do not care. Again, if it were dramatic and could be recorded, for extra attention on their social media, then maybe…"

"A police chase isn't dramatic?"

"It wasn't that much of a chase," Jorge reminded him. "Plus, I had Makerson report that we were working on a movie in that area today, so people believe the fantasy much quicker than the reality."

Evans appeared hesitant and finally agreed.

"You worry too much," Jorge reminded him. "This here was the same when I took care of those white supremacists for you. Remember, you worried about every little detail and, here we are. People have forgotten it. There was no trace of who did it. The media, they shit a brick for a week or two, and then what? *What?* Your people gave half-ass answers about carbon monoxide poisoning and put them off. They moved on to the next thing that got their attention. And that there was *much* bigger than this here little police chase."

"That is true," Evans nodded and glanced at the Mexican picture on the wall. "You have a way of covering your tracks."

"This has been my life," Jorge reminded him and decided to change the subject. "So, you say there was another reason to come visit with me today? What can I help you with?"

Appearing apprehensive, Evans began to talk. And Jorge, he listened.

CHAPTER 5

"Yes, Jolene, I *did* put you in charge," Jorge abruptly spoke as he leaned forward in his chair. "But as I stated, *again and again,* it was to dismantle the newspaper that I originally bought *to* create this here media company. I had *you* do this because Jolene, you are good at destroying things, so I thought this was perfect for you."

He delivered his final words with such force that it automatically eliminated any power that Jolene Silva thought she had when speaking up in the meeting. People needed to know their place, and at times, she had a way of stepping out of line.

"I understand," Her voice was small this time but quickly gathered more strength. "But, now…"

"But now nothing," Jorge automatically cut her off as he glanced around his home office, then into the faces of each of his associates. "Tony, he knows what he is doing. You do not. You were there to rip the paper apart, fire people, and now, you still have a job at the media company, but it is not to give Tony orders. He is running things, and you are there to assist him. You are also to make sure that things are going the way you think I want. That is it. I do *not* want to hear one more report where you are trying to tell him what to do, Jolene. I cannot emphasize this enough."

This time, she closed her mouth and nodded.

"Now, we must move on," Jorge swung his hands in the air. "I have a lot to do today. I wanted to meet so we could check on things."

"So yesterday," Diego Silva jumped right in as he sat forward in his chair. "That Jameson Field shitstain was the last link to the white supremacists from the spring?"

"Sir, it does seem so," Marco Rodel Cruz jumped in and raised his hand in the air. The Filipino was technically an IT specialist but was known to slither into some pretty dark places to find information. "Not to say there are no more white supremacists in law enforcement, but...this particular group, they are gone."

Jorge thought back to the bloodbath he had carried out at Ron Evans' request and nodded. The police and RCMP had a brutal way of cutting ties to assure no connection to the racist group, however, both they and the hotel dimmed the details released to the public in hopes it would quickly disappear from the news. They said it was carbon monoxide poisoning that killed those in that particular conference room in hopes of lessening the impact on business. The police took care of funeral expenses, and the hotel went on to do massive renovations with attention to safety. And then the people forgot.

Everyone had a price. Everyone had a short memory.

"But why...that man who come to your house that night?" Jolene spoke up with some hesitation, appearing confused. Beside her, Chase Jacobs rolled his eyes. "Why did he want to kill your family?"

"Pay attention, Jolene," Diego snapped at his sister. "This was months ago, and you keep asking this question."

"But it does not make sense to me!" She snapped back at her brother. "Why was this one man away from the others? How did he find out what we were doing?"

"It doesn't matter *why* he wasn't with the others," Chase informed her. "This Jameson Field asshole worked at the hotel and thought something was up because the doors were locked on the conference room floor. He was trying to sneak in because he wanted to be part of the group."

"And when he couldn't," Paige calmly continued, noticing Chase was getting frustrated. "He thought he'd be a good warrior and get points with the group if he called it into this other guy...."

"That piece of shit that went to Jorge's house," Diego jumped in. "Yeah, he got brownie points all right."

"So, he…he knew this man who came to your house?" Jolene asked Paige.

"He knew he hadn't checked into the hotel yet," Paige replied. "So he called and tipped him off that he thought something was wrong. This man attempted to reach out to people in the group to check-in, but no one was answering."

"So he come here," Jolene swirled her finger around to indicated Jorge and Paige's home. "To kill Jorge's family?"

"Not right away," Marco answered. "There was a series of messages between him and Jameson Field. When no one from the conference answered his messages to them, he started to get nervous. He asked Jameson if he saw Jorge Hernandez around. It seems he heard some rumors."

"People, they should never listen to rumors," Jorge shook his head.

"From the messages I hacked, it would seem that he maybe was hanging around Jorge's house."

"But he knew where you lived?" Jolene was confused.

"He was an RCMP," Diego reminded her. "He can get that info on anyone."

Jolene made a face.

"He was panicking to find out what was wrong," Paige went on to explain. "Then someone in the conference sent him a message."

"What did they say?" Jolene shook her head. "I do not understand."

"Someone in the conference sent a message that said, 'Jorge Hernandez', and 'SOS'," Marco spoke calmly despite the irritation in his eyes. "That was all he needed to react."

"Oh, so he come to kill Jorge's family," Jolene nodded her head. "I did not understand before…"

"Jolene, you got to listen," Diego complained.

"I *do* listen, but my English, it is not always so good," Jolene shot back at her brother. "I am sorry, but I miss things for this reason. I did not have private lessons like you did, and no one explained in Spanish…"

"Ok, enough," Jorge's voice was sharp as he raised his hand in the air. "Jolene, here is the story. The man was late for the conference. Jameson tried to sneak into the meeting. He noticed the doors were locked. He reported this to this here man…..who tried to contact people at the conference. One of them said SOS and my name. He decides to kill me *and* my family."

"And Maria saw him," Chase softly added.

"Yes, Maria, she saw him, called me because she knew something was wrong," Jorge said and looked down.

"And I was giving Miguel a bath," Paige added. "I didn't hear a thing because he was crying."

"*Mi amor,* you cannot hear anything over that child when he cries," Jorge shook his head. "So, Maria, she gets scared, finds a gun…"

"Which was smart," Diego jumped in. "Since the fucker had a gun… he was going to kill the family."

"And Field," Jorge assured them. "He is now *missing.*"

"A lot of people are going missing from Toronto these days," Diego muttered.

"Can we move on now?" Jorge asked Jolene. "Have we answered all your questions?"

"So you do not know why he not at the meeting on time?" Jolene asked.

Jorge gave her a look.

"Does it fucking matter?" Diego jumped in. "Who cares?"

"I just want to understand," Jolene attempted to explain.

"It does not matter," Jorge assured you. "It is done."

"And that is all," Marco tied up the story. "What I am saying is that this group is now silent online. If there is anyone left, I would not worry at this point. A strong message was sent."

"And now, we are done with the police?" Jolene asked.

"We help them when they need us," Jorge replied. "And they help us."

"Like yesterday, they helped us," Diego added. "But me, I don't trust the police and would rather keep away from them if I can."

"We did not have a choice yesterday," Jorge shook his head. "Jameson Field, he was hard to find, but Hail, he spotted him. I have helped him in the past, so he owed me."

"But from now on," Diego added as he shook his head. "That's it!"

"We must help the head of police with something," Jorge informed the group. "That is why we met yesterday…at least, part of the reason."

"What the fuck does he want?" Diego appeared annoyed. "Haven't we done *enough* for him?"

"It is merely an intimidation thing," Jorge said as he glanced toward Jolene and then Paige. "Evans said his son is getting a divorce. His daughter-in-law refuses to let him see the children because there was an affair involved, and well, he needs some help persuading her."

"Do we need to get involved in this?" Chase asked. "I'm just saying…"

"I know, and when he first tell me," Jorge shook his head. "I laughed. I said I was not a marriage counselor."

To this, Jolene laughed loudly.

"But it is an issue because she is threatening to leave the country with this man's children," Jorge continued. "For this, I do have sympathy. I cannot imagine. The children are quite young. I said I would have someone gently persuade her."

"We don't do gentle," Diego reminded him. "This isn't for us….what we going to do?"

"When I said there was an affair involved, you naturally assume I meant him," Jorge reminded Diego, who sat up. "It was not him. It was her. We need proof to hold over her head before they go to divorce court and fight over the children. She is a woman of luxury who thinks that the whole world revolves around her. She never worked a day in her life…"

"Oh God," Jolene rolled her eyes.

"You know the type," Jorge went on. "Big, expensive wedding, everything is for a show on Facebook."

"A Disney Princess," Paige injected. "They aren't only a princess, but they don't even live in the real world."

"This here, it sounds about right," Jorge nodded. "Any thoughts on how to take care of this for our friend Ron Evans?"

"So we gotta catch her screwing someone else?" Diego appeared bored. "It ain't gonna be me. I'm gay and…"

"Diego," Jorge began to laugh. "She's currently having an affair. We gotta catch *them* in the act. Trust me. This will be easy peasy."

He shared a look with his wife, who nodded.

CHAPTER 6

"So, this here is what you call a Disney Princess?" Jorge asked his wife as the two of them watched the club's security cameras from his phone. He wrinkled up his nose and shrugged. "She looks like another soccer mom. I don't get it."

"You will once she comes in," Paige insisted as they watched Chase letting the woman inside the bar while they waited in the VIP room. "Trust me. I deal with these women every time I take Maria to school or Miguel to daycare. They drive me insane."

To this, Jorge laughed as he turned off his phone.

"But, *mi amor,* do we have a leg to stand on here?" Jorge reminded her and waved his arms in the air. "After all, she is meeting us at the *Princesa Maria?*"

"Trust me, when you think of a princess," Paige gently reminded him. "You're thinking of a completely different thing. You'd never let Maria be like this…trust me."

Ron Evans' daughter-in-law was a petite, white woman who appeared skeptical when she entered the VIP room to find Jorge and Paige. They politely rose from their seats to welcome her. As if being a woman somehow gave them a common bond, Madison Evans rushed over to Paige as if Jorge wasn't even in the room.

"Oh my God! I remember when you were popular online," She waved her hand in the air and talked as if they were old friends. "What happened to your little....show thing you used to do online? It was psychic stuff or something...."

Her words dragged on, and Paige stood in stunned disbelief. She was referring to Paige's former life coach cover from years earlier, a method used to launder money made from committing assassinations. It was a clever way to keep the government wolves at bay.

"Life coach," Paige corrected her as her blue eyes widened. "It was self-help and a spiritual website."

"Oh, yes, I always get that stuff mixed up," Madison laughed and rolled her eyes. "It was...*cute.*"

Jorge swallowed back his laughter as he looked away from his wife.

"And I am Jorge Hernandez," He waved his hand toward the conference room table. "If you care to have a seat..."

"Oh, and *you*," She cut him off as her eyes grew in size. "I know *you.* Why did you ever get out of politics? I would've voted for *you.*"

She finished her comment in a slightly flirtatious manner, which caused Paige to cringe.

"It was not for me," Jorge replied calmly, recalling what he had told the press at the time. "I wanted to focus on my family instead."

As if she was starting to understand that they were married, she suddenly seemed to pull away from Paige as a coolness filled the room.

"Now, would you mind having a seat?" Jorge pointed again toward the chairs on the other side of the conference room table as his frustration grew. Ron Evans would really owe him one for this. "This will only take a few minutes."

"I was a little surprised when I got the request to meet with you," Madison headed around the table while her citrusy perfume erupted as she moved through the room. Pushing a strand of blonde hair behind her ears, she pulled out the chair across from Paige while Jorge moved to the head of the table. He took a minute to take her in; Madison wore a white sweater and pricey yoga pants, something he only knew because Maria constantly asked for the same brand. She planted her large, designer bag on the table, as if it was an extension of herself, before plunking down in the chair. Glancing at Paige, he could see she was already irritated. It was not a good start to their meeting.

"So, um…a friend of mine, he asked me to meet with you today," Jorge started but stopped when Madison suddenly had her attention diverted by her phone, which she reached in her bag for and began to study. Jorge and Paige exchanged looks.

"Could you please turn this off?" Jorge shook his head, pointing toward the phone. "This is a meeting. We would ask you to turn off your devices while we speak."

"*We* do," Paige tersely clarified.

"Oh, but if my kids…" Madison started although, when Jorge glanced toward her phone, he noted she was checking a notification on Facebook.

"This here, it will not be long," Jorge leaned forward with a dark glare. "And I am *not* asking you."

As if she finally understood who she was sitting with, Madison turned off her phone and showed them before putting it back in her designer bag. Her expression went flat.

"Now, we are here to discuss something brought to my attention from a concerned party," Jorge started again. "Your father-in-law…"

"He can go to hell," Madison sharply cut him off. "I already told him to keep out of my life and mind his own business. And if a police friend of his…"

"Lady, I am *not* the police," Jorge cut her off, and she sat up straighter. "Now, if you will let me speak. Ron Evans came to see me, and he asked that I talk to you since I am a….how do you say? An unrelated party? This here, it has nothing to do with me."

"Look, I know you are Jorge Hernandez, and I only came here because I thought you were offering me a job or something," The woman said his name with the Spanish pronunciation rather than English, which he hated, causing him to tense up. "You're powerful and stuff, but you can't tell me what to do with my marriage."

"Lady," Jorge's voice grew sharp. "I do not care about your marriage or this here soap opera. I care about none of it. The only reason why I am here is because Ron asked me to suggest to you that you allow his son to see the children. This here is not a suggestion. They are his children. It is his *right*. I am making it easy for you to sort out now because it will not be pretty if you are forced to go to court."

She sat up straighter and didn't reply. However, when it seemed like he had gotten through to her, Madison Evans swung back.

"We broke up, and I have a new boyfriend," She started to speak. "He lives in the United States, and I want to move there to be with him."

"And take the children out of the country of their father?" Jorge countered.

"He *can* come to see them," She insisted. "I don't care, but I'm not staying here because *he's* here. That's his problem. If he wants to be closer to his kids, then he can change his life around."

"How are you going to get into the states that easily?" Paige shook her head. "Immigrating tends to be a long, complicated process."

"Well, it wasn't for him," She pointed toward Jorge. "Isn't he from Mexico?"

"That there, it has nothing to do with you," Jorge leaned against the table. "We are talking about *you*, not me."

"We will sort it out," She replied. "My new boyfriend spends a lot of time here too, so maybe I can arrange to come back frequently, you know, if my schedule permits."

"Permits from what?" Jorge shrugged. "What do you *do*, lady?"

"Well, I don't work outside the house, but…"

"Oh, for fuck sakes!" Jorge finally lost his temper. "This here is making my headache. Lady, you got to find yourself a new boyfriend that lives here, or your boyfriend has to find a way to stay here because Ron Evans, his son, wants to have regular access to the children. That is it. End of story."

With that, he stood up, and Madison quickly did the same.

"You can't tell me what to do!"

"Lady, it is this, or we will drag your skinny white ass through the court system, and we will make your life hell," Jorge countered.

"We have proof you were cheating on your husband," Paige gently commented as she stood up. She reached in her bag and pulled out an iPad. Turning it on, she showed Madison the series of text messages, graphic images, and videos that the two had exchanged and parts of the conversation where she planned her breakup. "This doesn't make you look good."

Madison attempted to rip the device from Paige's hand but greatly underestimated her instincts and fell forward. She steadied herself on the table. It was as if Madison suddenly realized what was going on.

"Ok, this here, it is not up for debate," Jorge spoke abruptly, his words directed at Madison. "We are here to allow you to avoid humiliation and get dragged through the court system. It is easy. You stay in this country and allow Ron Evans and his son, his whole family, to see the children."

"You can't expose that," She shook her head in disbelief. "That's private. How did you get it?'

"Oh, do not worry about me," Jorge shook his head. "I have my ways. I can dig a little deeper, but I suspect that you might not want me to do this."

Stunned, she began to cry.

"Why are you doing this?" She moaned. "You're ruining my life."

"Lady, you have no idea how much I could ruin your fucking life," Jorge shot back. "Believe me, this here is child's play compared to what I could do, so I suggest that you listen to my advice, so you do not have to discover what I'm capable of."

"You're threatening me?" She continued to cry. "I'm a mother! You can't do this."

"I am merely suggesting that you keep the peace by staying here in Toronto," Jorge countered. "Consider me a marriage counselor who doesn't fuck around."

"I'll…I'll think about it…" She sniffed.

"There is nothing here to think about," Jorge insisted as he glared at her. "You and me, we are done talking, and you will do what I say. That is it. I am allowing you to avoid a lot less misery in the long run. Trust me. My wife here," He pointed toward Paige. "She is not a psychic, but she can tell you that this here will not end well for you if you do not listen. Allow the man to have easy access to his children or not only will you go through hell in the court system, but I will also put a red flag on your identity so if you even try to enter the United States, you will not be allowed into the country. Am I making myself clear?"

"I….no, you can't do that," She whined and shook her head. "You…."

"I can lady, and I will," Jorge assured her.

"But, I will lose everything…"

"No, lady, I assure you…." Jorge gave her a long, dark glare. "You do not lose *everything*."

CHAPTER 7

"Wait, so you want me to do a series about a Mexican narco," Tony Allman halted his conversation with Jorge Hernandez in the production company's conference room, briefly exchanging looks with Andrew Collin. "I hope you don't mind me asking this, but is this in any way based on… someone you know?"

Jorge thought for a moment and nodded.

"You might say that."

"He means," Andrew Collin abruptly jumped in. "Is this shit about you?"

"Of course not," Jorge laughed and shrugged. "I do not know what you are talking about."

"Reminding you that I also work occasionally at your crematorium," Andrew interjected. "I see things…."

"Those *things* you think you see, you do *not* see," Jorge reminded him with a dark glare. "And this here isn't about here in Canada, but Mexico. I lived there a long time. I saw things. I heard things as many who have lived there also do. It is normal in Mexico. The cartels are a big part of ours lives and not always for bad things."

"Not usually for good things," Andrew muttered as he looked away, while Tony shot him a dirty look. "I'm just saying."

"There are cartels that help the poor, build churches, help communities," Jorge informed them.

"Kill people, brutally so…" Andrew added as he waved his skinny arm in the air.

"Ok, let's not go there," Tony shot Andrew another look. "I think what Jorge is saying is that he wants to do a series that has a more balanced view of someone in a cartel, a better understanding of how they got there."

"For some, for many, it is about money," Jorge insisted as he leaned back in his chair. "There are sometimes no other opportunities and mouths to feed, and for others, it is greed. But sometimes it is about neither. It's about power. It's about family, connection, which is what a cartel can sometimes be. Although, from what I hear, that might be changing. What I witnessed in my youth, it replaced something many young men did not have at home."

Tony nodded in understanding, and Andrew frowned.

"Weren't you talking about writing a book or something?" Tony asked. "With Makerson from the paper? Didn't you say he wanted to do your life story?"

"My life story, yes," Jorge nodded. "But this here, obviously, will not be *my* life story."

"Ah, gotcha," Tony said and glanced at Andrew. "So we're writing fiction, just from things you heard or saw in Mexico?"

"Like a source, but preferably an anonymous one," Jorge stated. "But also, Diego, Jolene, they can also contribute to ideas, answer questions."

"They'd have to answer a lot because this is certainly out of my area of expertise," Tony admitted. "But you know, you might be onto something. Any shows about mobs, gangsters, or cartels are extremely popular right now."

"Try *always*," Andrew corrected him. "Like *The Godfather* was out long before I was born and people still love that shit."

"That's true," Tony nodded. "Maybe I could…"

"Come to think of it," Andrew cut him off and leaned forward on the table facing Jorge. "*You're* kind of like the Godfather here, in Toronto for sure. You run this shit."

"Well, I don't know…" Tony attempted to cut him off.

"Nah, Nah, I'm telling you," Andrew shook his head. "Jorge Hernandez is like The Godfather, a modern, Mexican version of The Godfather. You watch, when Maria marries someday, we will finally be able to ask him for a favor on her wedding day. Isn't that how that goes?"

"You, you can ask me for a favor anytime," Jorge nodded in his direction. "But I may not say yes."

"You'll say yes," Andrew teased him, waving his hand in the air. "Especially if it allows you to harass someone. You love this shit, man."

"Andrew," Tony attempted to take the meeting back to a more serious tone.

"Tony, I'm telling you," Andrew excitedly pointed toward Jorge. "You do not get on his bad side."

Tony sighed and shook his head.

"At any rate," Jorge cut in and started to stand. "It is something to ponder. Maybe watch some similar shows, read some books as things slow down over the holidays, this kind of thing. See what you think. I am pretty resourceful in this area, you know."

"Oh, we *know*," Andrew grinned. "And who doesn't want to read about murder and mayhem over Christmas?"

"It's still a bit away," Tony reminded them both as he stood. "We just had Halloween a couple of weeks ago. Let's not talk about Christmas just yet."

"What is your favorite part of Christmas?" Andrew directed his question at Jorge. "Carving the turkey?"

To that, he got a humored look.

"We will talk more later," Jorge started toward the door. "And also, we must think of what to do for the next season of *Eat the Rich before the Rich Eat You.*"

"Well, we destroyed Big Pharma and the police in the first two seasons," Andrew said as he and Tony followed Jorge to the door. "What's next?"

"It occurred to me the other night," Jorge paused for a moment. "As I was watching an American news channel that the media, it often gets things wrong. There was a story referencing Mexico, and I shook my head. And the Canadian media, it's too soft. That is why I eventually want to start a news program. But I know that it cannot happen overnight."

"It's a lot, even the few shows we have going on now," Tony shook his head. "And we sell them to streaming sites. I'm not sure about the news."

"It would be online," Jorge suggested. "Something everyone can access for free but with ads, like television…"

Andrew and Tony shared a look.

"But this is not for now," Jorge reminded them. "We are talking the future. For now, continue working on the shows we have here at this company and think about what I suggested today. Think about the next season of *Eat the Rich*. I think we need to examine the media. Who owns what media company? How does it create a slant on their stories? As we do this, we can indicate an interest in creating our news program online, indicate that we want to hire journalists who are tired of being on someone's puppet strings and limited by what they can do, say more investigative. I think that would create some interest."

"So we are preparing people for what is ahead," Tony mused. "Shouldn't we wait till we have more ideas together for a news program?"

"Let us think about that some more," Jorge nodded. "I do not want to wear you out, Tony. Look at all we have done in a few months."

"I do have a lot of irons in the fire."

"We can plan," Jorge reached for the door. "But I am going to speak to Makerson now. I suspect he might want to be involved. If not, he may have some ideas. It is a thought."

With that, Jorge left the building and jumped in his SUV, heading to the coffee shop close to the offices of *Toronto AM*. Tom Makerson was already waiting for him at the back of the room.

"Hey," He looked up from his coffee. "Long time, no see."

"I have been so busy with this new production house," Jorge replied as he sat down and caught the attention of the nearby waitress, indicating he would like a coffee. "It has taken all my time."

"How are things now?"

"We have some shows started," Jorge replied. "We have some more ideas."

"I bet."

"I am thinking of doing a Mexican narco show."

Makerson didn't reply but grinned. The waitress returned with Jorge's coffee. After she left, they continued to speak.

"So, when's this happening?" Makerson asked.

"In the future," Jorge replied as he put some cream in his coffee. "Also, I am doing another season of *Eat the Rich,* and maybe, I think it may center on the media and the misrepresentation it often does. Do you have any ideas on this topic?"

Makerson let out a laugh.

"Yeah, you might say that," he finally replied. "It happens a lot. There's a lot of influence in the media. You can get told to cut a story fast if it pisses off the wrong people."

"I guess I am not one to speak," Jorge replied and nodded. "I do have some influence too."

"Yeah, but your influence is different," Makerson said as he frowned. "There's a lot that we expose that others wouldn't touch."

"There have been things we also do not touch," Jorge reminded him. "Speaking of which, anyone looking for Jameson Field?"

"Not a lot of talk," Makerson replied. "There was a connection to the white supremacist story, and you know the police, they want to keep that on the down-low. If his name comes up, people will start to make the connection, and too many questions will come up. I think it's pretty clear this isn't a topic the police want to resurrect after they finally managed to bury it."

"That is true," Jorge nodded and took a drink of his coffee. "As long as it keeps buried, we will not have any issues."

"I won't be digging it up," Makerson confirmed as he reached for his coffee. "And I'm not even seeing anything coming down the wire."

"This is good," Jorge confirmed as he leaned back in his chair. "But I must change the topic now. I am curious. If I were to one day start an online news program from my media company, how interested would you be in joining?"

"Very interested," Makerson's eyes lit up. "The paper, well, you know…."

"Hey, you hold your own, but it is not the same," Jorge nodded. "And much of what you do now often is live-streamed too so, this here, you are already used to doing."

"I would rather do that than sit down and write a story," Makerson admitted. "The news happens too fast. By the time a story is written, edited, and out there, the public has already moved on. So, yeah, I mean, we have to keep up."

"You know the paper will go to shit without you."

"That's fine by me," Makerson admitted. "I can only hold it up so long."

"Also, one day, we have to write that book," Jorge reminded him as he reached for his phone. "You know, about my life."

"The one you said couldn't be published until you're dead?" Makerson grinned.

"Which, you know, it could be any day," Jorge reminded him with a grin. "One never knows."

Makerson observed with interested.

"Just tell me when to start."

Jorge didn't reply but turned on his phone. As soon as the messages showed up, he frowned. The day wasn't going to go as smoothly as he had hoped,

CHAPTER 8

"No!" Paige shot back as she turned to face Jorge at the conference table in the VIP room at the *Princesa Maria*. "You can't do that! People are going to figure out it's about you, and..."

"Paige, I am not going to be telling my *own* story," He attempted to remind her, reaching for her hands. "This here, it will be completely separate from me, but granted...with some of my knowledge."

"No!" Paige continued to shake her head as her blue eyes expanded in size. "How many times have we talked about staying out of the limelight? How many times have I said I want us to be out of the line of fire? I don't want you to be the center of attention because we never know who's attention you're attracting. Between *Eat the Rich* and now this?"

"*Mi amor,*" He started to grin. "You know, this is not me. I do not hide in the shadows."

"But maybe you should," Paige attempted to negotiate. "Look at everything our family has been through in the last few years. You can't keep attracting attention. It's dangerous. I know you like taking shots at people like the police or Big Pharma, but you need to cool your heels a bit. I don't want you in danger."

Rather than reply, he pulled her hands to his lips and kissed them.

"Jorge...."

"Paige..." He mimicked her. "Come on, you know I will not do anything dangerous."

"I *don't* know that," She argued. "If you get stories from Mexico and the wrong person sees it..."

"I will be careful, Paige and..."

"No!" She shook her head. "I don't want a *sicario* at my door. You forget that I know how this works. When I was an assassin, this is why I refused to work with the cartels, because I know how they operate."

Jorge didn't reply.

"Please, keep away from this one."

"But Paige, if this here is already documented in books," Jorge shrugged. "I will lead them to the water, but I will not drink for them, you know?"

"I don't think that's how that expression goes."

"And it is not like I am allowing Makerson to release the book on my life while I'm still alive."

"Oh my God," Paige shook her head. "Jorge, you can't do *that* either. You have children who will be left behind."

"And I will make sure it is wrote that they did not know the truth," Jorge insisted. "That they are safe, that they will still have my money. I will work out the details."

"I don't..."

There was a knock at the door. Jorge squeezed her hands before letting them go to answer it. He turned to wink at her before opening the door to find Madison Evans on the other side.

"This better be good, lady," Jorge spoke abruptly. "I do not have time for much more of this here soap opera."

"I wanted to come back to negotiate," She spoke with arrogance. Sauntering in the door, she sat in the same chair as their last meeting. Ignoring Paige, who was expressionless, now sitting in her usual seat. "I thought about our conversation the other day, and..."

"Negotiate!" Jorge cut her off, his voice abrupt enough to grab Chase's attention from the main bar area. The two men exchanged looks, and Chase held up a pink cell phone to indicate he had forced Madison to leave it outside the room. That meant he also searched her to make sure she had no listening devices of any kind. Jorge nodded and closed the door. "This here, lady, it is not a negotiation."

"Everything is a negotiation," Madison challenged as Jorge turned to walk into her trail of perfume before taking his seat at the head of the table.

"And where would you learn that?" Jorge snapped at her. "You do not work."

"From my marriage."

"Oh really?" Jorge countered as he glanced at his wife before pointing at the iPad in the middle of the conference room table. "Choking on some other guy's dick was part of your marriage negotiation? And to *think* your marriage did not work out!"

Madison's face turned pink, but Jorge didn't skip a beat.

"Look here, lady, I don't got all day," Jorge snapped as he leaned toward her. "What the fuck do you want?"

"I want something in return for…"

"In return?" Jorge yelled. "Are you fucking kidding me? Get the fuck out of here!"

"I think," Madison countered. "If I stay in Canada, if I do this for *you,* that you should do something for me?"

"What the fuck do you want me to do for you?" Jorge felt infuriated by this woman's nerve. "This I gotta hear."

"Well," Madison cleared her throat, attempting to show her confidence even though it was clearly waning. "I thought that since you have a production company, maybe we could talk about me doing a show for you."

Jorge lowered his head as his eyes continued to glare at her. Paige turned to her with interest.

"In exchange for compliance," Madison continued. "For changing my whole life plan, I would like to have a reality show. Something like the shows about housewives, but I was thinking with more of a…."

"Is this a joke?" Jorge shook his head. "Are you teasing me here, lady?"

"No," She sat up straighter and attempted to make eye contact with Paige, who looked away. "They're popular right now, and…"

"No!" Jorge shot back.

"I don't…"

"No!" Jorge spoke louder.

"Well, you have to give me something," She whined. "I'm changing my whole life plan for…"

"No!" Jorge shouted this time as he leaned forward. "What part of NO do you not fucking understand?"

"Then, I'm going to the states and taking my kids with me. My ex, he will see them when he sees them. You don't have the power to do anything at the border, and you can't release these pictures because then you'll have to say where you got them," Madison's voice rose as she jumped up from the chair and started toward the door. "So fuck you!"

"What did you say?" Jorge roared as he jumped out of his chair and followed her. Stunned, Paige got up and followed them both. "You tell *me* to fuck off, lady? You do not know who you are talking to?"

"A criminal?" She shot back. "Everyone knows who you really are…"

"Can we just…" Paige attempted to intervene but with no success.

"Is that so?" Jorge continued to yell as he pointed at her. "You better…"

"What are you going to do?" Madison screamed. "Hit me? Hit a woman? Because if you do…"

Before she had the chance to say anything, Paige suddenly swung around and backhanded her in the face, causing Madison to lose her balance. With one hand, she reached for the wall to steady herself, while with the other, she touched her nose.

"You broke my nose!" Madison started to cry as she kept touching her face in stunned disbelief as blood dripped off her chin. "What am I going to do?"

"Go fix it with the man who did it the first time," Jorge shot back as he walked back to the table, reaching for a box of tissues. "And stop bleeding all over my Goddam club."

Madison continued to panic about her nose. Beside her, Paige showed no sympathy instead, inspecting her hand as Jorge pushed the box toward the bleeding woman. She reached for a tissue.

"You know, lady," Jorge suddenly saw the humor in the situation. "This here broken nose, it is not a good look for my shows. I do not think your proposition will work however, I have another proposition for you."

Madison backed away as if suddenly realizing she might be in danger.

"You fucking leave here, go to the doctor," Jorge continued. "And you do not tell them what really happened. You ran into a door. You fell downstairs. I do not give a fuck what you tell them, but you never tell anyone it happened here."

Paige turned toward her and calmly shook her head no.

"My wife," Jorge continued. "She can be a very violent woman, and me, I am not much better than her. So it would be my suggestion that you keep out of our way because if I have to have another meeting with you for anything after this, it will be the last."

She nervously shook her head.

"It will be *your* last," Jorge quietly clarified. "We are done negotiating. You will stay in this country so that your children will have access to their father and his family. You will keep your mouth shut, and you will get to keep your life. Do you *finally* understand?"

She nodded and started to cry.

"Because me," Jorge pointed toward himself. "I do not play by the same rules as a Disney Princess. Fuck, I don't play by the same rules as most people. Do we understand each other?"

"I won't talk," She said in a small voice.

"Now, I will have my associate take you to the hospital," Jorge said as he reached for the doorknob. "He will assure you keep your mouth shut too."

"I will, I promise…."

"I do not trust promises," Jorge turned to her before swinging the door open. "People have a way of breaking them."

Chase was at the bar and showed no expression when he saw Madison holding tissues to her nose, with blood all over her face.

"I need you to take this woman to the hospital," Jorge instructed. "She got hit in the face by the door."

Chase nodded in understanding.

"And if she tells a different story," Jorge didn't finish his sentence, but Chase was nodding again.

"I can take care of it," He replied as the broken woman headed toward the door.

"Please do," Jorge nodded. "And I will take care of my wife's hand."

He turned to see Paige behind him and smiled.

CHAPTER 9

"*Now* you're interested in self-defense," Jorge teased his 14-year-old daughter as she sat across from him in his home office. He raised an eyebrow as he watched her cheeks grow pink. "When I try to put you in self-defense or any martial arts, you get bored and drop out, but *now* that Chase is helping to teach women this here, you are suddenly interested."

"But *Papá,*" She quickly jumped back to hide her embarrassment. "He needs help when he goes to these different places, and I would love to do this."

"Right."

"Whaaat?" She shook her head. "It's a good cause. He wants to help indigenous women protect themselves by teaching them self-defense. I think it's a good thing."

"It *is* a good thing," Jorge nodded and grew serious. "These women need to be able to protect themselves because the police and RCMP have proven themselves useless."

Maria gave an enthusiastic nod.

"Just like me, *Papá,*" Maria said in a soft voice. "The police will never help me if I need it. I'm brown."

Her blunt comment affected Jorge, and he looked away. Although he was appreciative that his daughter was aware of the facts, he was heartbroken that she had to learn at such a young age.

"Maria, you know that this here is a lesson, I wish I did not have to teach you," Jorge spoke solemnly. "But unfortunately, we know that it is most likely true. And regardless, it is good to know how to defend yourself."

"I can," She replied in a small voice.

"Yes, of course, you have proven this," Jorge nodded in agreement. "I just wish you didn't have to think of such things."

"I look at other kids at school now," Maria confided. "And I think they're so young and naive."

"Maria, they are *your* age."

"I know, but they're so…ignorant or something," Maria tilted her head. "They have lived a safe and sheltered life and aren't aware of the real dangers in the world."

"That is because a lot of the kids you go to school with are rich," Jorge reminded her. "And never had to worry about anything. And for the most part, you have a pampered life too, Maria, but I do not want you to be spoiled."

"I have a job," Maria reminded him. "At *my* bar with Chase."

Jorge threw his head back in laughter, which made her laugh too.

"Maria, it is not your bar yet, but soon enough," Jorge winked at her. "When you are older, it is yours to do whatever you wish."

"I already have so many plans," She spoke excitedly. "It's going to be so much fun."

"This is good," Jorge smiled. "I am glad you are excited."

"So you don't mind if I go with Chase to the indigenous communities to help him?" Maria asked.

"Of course not," Jorge shook his head. "It will be on weekends. I cannot see an issue."

A knock at the door interrupted them.

"Thank you," Maria slid off her chair. "Is that whoever you have the meeting with?"

"Yes, Maria," Jorge nodded as she walked toward the door. "Can you let him in?"

Ron Evans appeared surprised when the daughter of Jorge Hernandez opened the door. He thanked her, and she disappeared, closing the door behind her.

"I hope this is a good time," Evans asked Jorge as he walked toward the desk.

"Oh yes," Jorge nodded as he watched Evans sit across from him. "My Maria, she is helping one of my associates who plans to go to indigenous communities to teach the women self-defense."

"Wow," Evans seemed genuinely impressed.

"Since you know," Jorge couldn't help but make a jab. "The police, they are useless to the indigenous people."

Evans took the comment with a grain of salt and merely shrugged. It wasn't the first insult Jorge had hurled at the local police, the RCMP, or the police as a whole.

"So, I took care of your issue," Jorge said as he moved his chair ahead.

"I do appreciate it," Evans put his hand up. "However, violence…"

"The violence was unfortunately necessary," Jorge insisted. "And that was my wife, not me…."

"I know but, I thought…"

"This lady," Jorge cut in. "She come to me twice. The first time with an attitude. The second time, demanding we negotiate. She was going to get something in return for her compliance. She wanted a television show produced by my company. You do not come in my office and demand anything."

Evans cringed and shook his head.

"Exactly," Jorge continued. "She is not the easiest woman to deal with."

"I know," Evans agreed. "She was spoiled by her family growing up, and well, I guess my son, he never had much of a backbone."

"I can see that," Jorge nodded. "She practically wears his balls around her neck."

"Well, I can agree with you on that," Evans nodded. "However, we are now on a regular visitation schedule, and Madison seems more reasonable."

"Let's hope that continues," Jorge replied. "Because I do not want to deal with that woman again."

"I can understand that too," Evans replied. "I wish I didn't have to either."

"So, is that what you come to see me about today?" Jorge asked. "Please tell me you do not have another family issue that you need me to take care of."

"No," Evans shook his head. "I wanted to thank you."

"All is running smoothly with work?"

"As smoothly as it ever is," Evans admitted. "We still have a lot of issues, but Athas made some important changes that hold the police by a higher standard, with stiffer punishments. Now they're complaining that they feel their hands are tied in *delicate* situations because the new laws have some harsh penalties if they react with unnecessary violence."

"Keep in mind that the rewards should make the difference."

"The pay increase helped," Athas admitted. "But the public wasn't too happy."

"Well, with that increase, there are added expectations."

"That's what we try to say, but you know the media."

"Well, *we* reported it correctly if not the national news," Jorge reminded him. "And in the future, I want to start an online news program with Makerson to help give people...more reliable news."

"Interesting."

"When I do, he's your primary source when you need something reported," Jorge thought for a moment. "Well, I guess he is now too, but we will reach more people this way. That is my goal."

The two men chatted for a bit longer before the head of police left, and Jorge was alone in his office. However, the silence was short-lived once he turned his phone back on.

The first in a series of messages was from Diego, inquiring about something concerning Our House of Pot, the company Jorge founded a few years earlier. Although he had stepped back on his duties, Jorge still advised the company when needed. It was a huge success with him and now, without him. His focus these days was the Hernandez Production Company.

"Jorge," Paige was standing at the door. "Are you ok to talk now?"

"Of course, *mi amor*," Jorge turned off his phone and sat it down. "I just had some messages from Diego and some others, nothing important."

"I wanted to talk to you about..."

"I know, and *mi amor*," Jorge waved his hand in the air. "I will wait on the book about me. It can be later. As for the show, I do not know. I still think we should do it, but with, of course, fictional cartels."

"I...yeah, I guess as long as you are careful," Paige was hesitant. "I..."

"I know, *mi amor,* I know," Jorge leaned forward on his desk and lowered his voice. "You do not want the family in danger. I have been giving this some thought."

"And?"

"I feel like maybe we should have an escape plan if something…major ever happens," He hesitated for a moment. "I do not want to scare you because I think we are fine, but what if we had some property that was more secluded, rural, in case we suddenly must leave the city."

Paige didn't reply.

"Not that I am saying there is anything that I foresee but," Jorge shrugged. "We have had some close calls over the years. Ramped up security around the house. It only does so much."

"I agree."

"I am not saying that we will need it, and maybe it will simply be a summer home," He replied. "But I do think we need to consider this in case. Somewhere safe."

"I agree," Paige nodded. "That might be a good idea."

"When the kids are a bit older, maybe we will eventually get out of the city and away from the madness."

"Maybe," She agreed.

"I could own a town!" Jorge spoke with enthusiasm. "I practically own this city, so a town should be easy."

Paige laughed.

"Hey, who knows?" Jorge shrugged. "A rich man can do a lot for some of these places. I would be a God."

"What you've always dreamed of," Paige teased.

"But for now," Jorge promised. "I will be careful."

"It's getting to the holiday season," She reminded him. "Maybe we could be careful about the number of corpses we collect right now. Especially when your son's new word is *kill.*"

Jorge laughed.

"Well, Paige, it was only a matter of time before his Hernandez side came out."

"It always does," She spoke gently.

"*Si, mi amor,*" He agreed. "Miguel will one day rule the world."

CHAPTER 10

"So, where is this house?" Jolene asked Jorge, who sat at the head of the table in the VIP room of *Princesa Maria*. All around him sat his *familia,* the most important people in his life outside his children. "Are we all moving? Is this necessary?"

"I would not say it is necessary, however," Jorge thought for a moment. "I will make sure the house is big enough if we all must stay there together."

"Really?" Chase asked from the other side of Jolene. "How big is this house?"

"There's no house yet," Paige reminded them. "It's an idea we are throwing around."

"Do you expect us to be in danger?" Marco spoke up with some concern on his face. "I mean…"

"Marco, you are merely the IT guy, as far as anyone knows," Jorge reminded him. "I believe you would be safe."

"But not the rest of us?" Diego countered, his face full of suspicion as his nose began to twitch.

"Ok, this here, you need to all relax," Jorge reminded them as he reached for his cup of coffee. "I am not saying we are currently in danger. I am not even saying that we will someday be in danger. What I *am* saying is in the case we need to get away, we can. It will be away from the city, out of sight, out of mind, somewhere maybe where tourists go so we blend in easily. It is just an idea."

"Can we pick the place?" Jolene asked with wide eyes, while Diego automatically shot her a dirty look.

"Jolene, it will be *his* house," He reminded her. "Why the hell would you get to pick the place?"

"We will talk about this more later." Jorge cut them off. "But if the day ever arrives, Diego, I assure you there will be room for everyone and even your lime trees."

Everyone laughed, knowing that Diego had a collection of miniature lime trees in his sunroom, something he took great pride in.

"You joke, but you can't get better limes in Toronto," Diego sniffed and looked away.

"At any rate," Jorge continued. "It is something me and Paige, we talk about it and well, it might be a good idea. Although, right now, I do not see any danger unless Marco, something is coming down the wire?"

"Not that I see, sir."

"There's always something coming down the wire with you," Diego reminded him as he reached for the coffee pot in the middle of the table. "You always ruffle someone's feathers."

"That is my role in this world," Jorge grinned. "And right now, it is looking like the next target will be the media."

"You are the media, are you not?" Jolene countered. "So…"

"Like that will stop me, Jolene," Jorge assured her. "Our next season of *Eat the Rich,* I believe it will be about the corrupt media and how it is influenced by advertisers, investors, this kind of thing. Is the news we receive even true? Do we hear all the facts? How many times has Makerson broke a story or dove into something other places were not, at least not until he did. Even after the bloodbath at the hotel. There were reporters around, but they were told to back off, which they did. In this situation, it was to our advantage. But, how many other times are they so easily controlled and by who?"

"Big Pharma strikes again," Chase suggested. "There are channels that have nothing but fucking ads for pills."

"Oh, the side effect list," Jolene began to laugh. "It is always so long!"

"Yeah, we gotta pill that will make you less socially awkward," Chase joked. "But it might give you a heart attack or make your dick stop working."

Everyone laughed.

"That there," Jorge jumped in. "Might make you even more socially awkward."

Everyone continued to laugh.

"Hey, but we got them the first season of the show," Diego reminded the group. "They were hateful about it too."

"The people, they forget fast," Jorge shook his head. "It is almost like they do not want to know the truth sometimes."

"It's, unfortunately, true," Paige shook her head. "Everything is dumbed down. Even television. It's very sad."

"Yeah, like those fucking reality shows," Chase said with a grin. "I was flipping channels the other night and if the aliens ever land, they just gotta see one of these shows, and they'll leave again."

"The people, they will watch what is there," Jorge insisted. "If we had all smart shows, people would watch but, for most, they enjoy watching people more pathetic than themselves. It makes them feel better about who they are."

"I think reality shows make most of us feel better about ourselves," Chase laughed. "Wasn't that woman, the one who Evans sent over…"

"I heard about that," Diego cut in, turning toward Jorge. "Chase was telling me and Jolene. She seriously thought you'd give her *a show*?"

"She mistakenly thought she had the power to tell me what to do," Jorge said, slightly amused. "But she found out, this here is not so."

"When I drove her to the hospital," Chase jumped in with laugher in his voice. "She was not a fan of yours."

"I am not for everyone," Jorge insisted as he lowered his head and nodded. "I am what you would call, a sharp pill to swallow."

"When you're used to getting whatever you want," Paige calmly added. "It tends to be a shock you when someone suddenly says no."

"Paige, she said no with the back of her hand," Jorge said as he turned to wink at his wife. "It got the point across."

Everyone laughed and then fell silent for a moment.

"So, anything else?" Diego asked. "Other than the new rural house you're buying us?"

"Well, that might not be right away," Jorge said. "But it is in the future."

"And the new season of the show," Jolene jumped in. "I plan to help."

"A couple is being worked on," Jorge nodded. "I am thinking of doing a cartel type show since they are popular."

Everyone fell silent.

"Do not worry," Jorge added. "It will be safe. I will not talk about myself in Mexico."

"Yeah, if you don't got that house for us to hide in yet," Diego reminded him. "You might want to be careful."

"So, is there anything else?" Jorge jumped ahead. "Anything we must discuss?"

"Well, Maria and me are starting the self-defense training this weekend with our first indigenous community."

"Make sure to take the company van," Diego jumped in. "It looks good."

"I was going to," Chase nodded. "And Maria is learning this stuff, so that's good too. I think it will be fun."

"Call Makerson, see if he wants to do a story," Jorge suggested.

"Ah, good idea," Chase nodded.

"Do you have many places to go?" Diego asked.

"I have a few lined up, mostly close by, but eventually, I'll have to leave the province," Chase said. "We've contacted various communities to let them know, but if Makerson does a story and it picks up, chances are we will have more interest. I mean, it's free."

"This here is good," Jorge nodded. "I am happy with this program. It is also very good for Maria. She needs this right now."

"It's a good cause," Paige added. "Maybe eventually you can expand it to help other people that come from vulnerable communities or situations."

"That's what I'm thinking," Chase replied. "There's a lot of people who could use some help."

"So," Jorge thought out loud. "Our House of Pot is going strong. The production company is working on some new shows, including one exposing the media. I'm looking for an escape house. What else?"

He turned to Paige.

"There's nothing in the news about Jameson Field," Paige reminded him. "Eventually, the police will likely say that the investigation is open but suspended due to lack of leads. His family is looking for him but think he left town."

"People, they go missing," Jorge said with a shrug. "Happens in my business all the time."

Everyone laughed.

"Sir, will you require me to work at the production house too?" Marco asked. "Doing research?"

"Most likely," Jorge nodded. "Check with Tony."

"Oh, the news thing you mentioned the other day," Paige reminded him.

"Ah yes, I am thinking of starting an online news program," Jorge jumped in. "Kind of like some of the live steams Makerson does now, except a whole show."

"That would be interesting," Diego said. "As part of the production company, you mean?"

"Yes, but we are working out the details."

"A lot going on," Diego shook his head. "Nothing slows down with you."

"Well, Diego, we have a lot of things to contend with," Jorge reminded him as he pushed his chair back and turned his phone back on. "My focus is on the production company right now."

"You know, if you need help finding a safe house," Diego leaned in and muttered as the others started to leave the VIP room. "I could…"

"Oh shit," Paige exclaimed as she looked at her phone than at Jorge. "We have to go to a meeting at the daycare."

"At the daycare?" Jorge wrinkled his nose. "What's going on?"

Paige just gave him a look.

CHAPTER 11

"I do not know where my son would hear such a word," Jorge spoke innocently as his wife's position stiffened beside him, but he pretended not to notice. Across from them sat Mrs. Chen, the daycare owner, with a lot of worry on her face. "I guess because his older sister, she must have been watching something on television?"

"It's hard to say," Paige jumped in with her soft, gentle voice that seemed to bring a sense of calamity to the room. "Maybe Miguel heard the word from another child, here, at daycare."

The Asian lady looked startled by the suggestion but before she could reply, Jorge quickly jumped in.

"This here is possible," He spoke abruptly. "We do not allow Miguel to be exposed to anything other than children's programming. I would say that my son, he has a sheltered life."

"It doesn't matter where he heard it," Mrs. Chen shook her head. "It's not just that he keeps yelling the word 'Kill' all the time that concerns me, but he tends to be a bit…aggressive with other children."

Jorge shared a look with his wife and quickly considered what he was supposed to say in this particular situation.

"Ah, well, you know, kids," He shrugged. "They are full of energy and get a bit crazy when they are put together. Miguel, he gets excited when he has the chance to play with other kids, you know?"

"What do you mean by aggressive?" Paige countered as if she hadn't heard Jorge speak. "He's not even three yet. What kind of bullying can a toddler do?"

"Yes, I would like to hear this answer as well," Jorge jumped in. "This here, I do not understand."

"He has violent tendencies," Mrs. Chen attempted to explain. "Today, I caught him pushing another child. Another day, one of my employees believes she caught him as he was about to bite one of the other children. We didn't report it at the time because we didn't want to cause alarm if she was wrong."

"Bite?" Jorge processed the word slowly. "I have never seen my son hit or bite anyone before. In my house, he is a good-natured, loving little boy. I do not understand where this is coming from. Have you considered that maybe other children at this here daycare might be attacking him first and he is merely reacting?"

"But we've never seen…"

"He does have a point," Paige grew defensive. "I've never seen Miguel do anything like that at all. What if some other child has pushed him first or hurts him in some way? How closely are you watching the children?"

"We have the appropriate staff for this amount of children," Mrs. Chen assured her. "We watch them very closely."

"I saw one of your employees on her phone while she was in the play area earlier," Jorge commented. "Is this here your idea of *watching* carefully, Mrs. Chen?"

"That is rare," Mrs. Chen assured them both. "I do not allow my employees to be on their phones at work. It must have been an emergency."

"It must have," Jorge replied sarcastically and shared a look with his wife. "Lady, the bottom line is that I pay a lot of money for this here daycare. I bring my son here because he can learn, socialize with other children, and it is good for him. We do not need to do this, but you know, we like to do the best for our son. But these accusations!"

"Mr. Hernandez," Mrs. Chen cut in. "If this kind of behavior continues, we will have to remove Miguel from this daycare and…"

"What?" Paige cut her off. "This is the first time we even heard of this! And you're already talking about kicking our son out of daycare? He's just a baby! You make it sound as if…"

"As if he is the devil's child," Jorge cut in with a grin on his face. "Really? Is that what you are saying?"

"I am saying that I have to think of the safety of the other children," Mrs. Chen attempted to explain. "I don't know why your son has behavior issues, but I wanted…"

"Behavior issues?" Paige cut her off again. "He's a little boy!"

"But these issues, they start early," Mrs. Chen attempted to explain. "I've worked with children for…"

"Do you even *have* children?" Jorge countered.

"This has nothing to do with…"

"Because if you do not," Jorge continued, "then this is just you observing other people's children and that there, is not the same."

Paige put a hand to her head and started to cry.

"See, you happy now, lady?" Jorge snapped at Mrs. Chen, "You make my wife cry by saying her child is out of control."

"I didn't say…"

"You, lady, need to rethink your position on this matter," Jorge stood up and reached for his wife's hand as she rose from her chair. "Again, we pay a lot of money to this here place, and I am *not* happy."

She didn't reply but merely nodded, her cheeks turning pink.

"Now, we are going to get my son," Jorge pointed toward the door. "And go home. And tomorrow, we are bringing him back and hope that you will be watching things more carefully in the future."

It wasn't until they were in the SUV and Miguel was tucked safely in his car seat that the two exchanged looks.

"Unbelievable," Paige muttered under her breath as she glanced over her shoulder at Miguel, who was nibbling on a cracker.

"I know, what a crazy lady," Jorge complained.

"But you weren't much better," Paige continued to mutter. "How did you manage to turn this around that it was someone else's fault?"

"Maybe it is."

"You know, I'm not happy that our son might be kicked out of daycare," She continued as she looked out the side window as they drove off the property. "I like this place. It's close, they're good with the kids…"

"Paige, she probably wants to kick him out to get in one of her rich friend's kid in or something," Jorge attempted to reason. "I am sure what she says is not true."

"Really?" Paige countered. "You don't think Miguel has a chance of picking up violent behavior at our house? You don't think he might naturally get a bullying gene?"

To this, Jorge laughed and shrugged.

"I can't believe we are having this problem when he is only..,"

"Kill!" Miguel yelled from the backseat and laughed.

Jorge laughed and glanced in the rearview mirror.

"You know, you're encouraging him when you do that," She quietly suggested. "That's what is going on at the daycare too. They're giving him a lot of attention when he says it, so he keeps saying it."

"Even if they scold him?"

"I think he takes after you in that regard," Paige suggested. "I think he enjoys pissing people off."

"Well, *mi amor,* he does get it naturally."

"That he does," She agreed.

"Oh, Paige, this here is so stupid," Jorge shook his head. "He is a child. Children, they say all kinds of things. Why do they take it so seriously? It seems like they are trying to suggest he is a terrible child for this here reason. I think it is silly."

"I think him pushing and potentially biting other kids is also a factor," Paige reminded him. "Not just yelling that word."

"Well, yes, but maybe he defends himself like I said," Jorge insisted. "And for that, Paige, I will not apologize. I want my child to be able to defend himself, to be strong. I do not like how these schools make children weak and powerless. In the real world, you cannot be that way. You are eaten alive. Children cannot even defend themselves. I had so many issues with Maria and this situation, even before we come to Canada. Bullies could hurt her, but she was not allowed to defend herself."

"Didn't she take a knife to school once?" Paige asked him.

"Well, *mi amor,* it was not as if she used it," Jorge shrugged. "But the other children bullied her all the time, and she wasn't supposed to say anything or fight back? These schools, they do not bring our children up to live in the real world."

"Our world, I must remind you," Paige said. "Is slightly different from other people's world, other children's worlds."

"We are all different," Jorge shrugged. "But we are all the same. I do not care. I want my children to be strong and powerful, however, the schools, they want to make them weak, and they will not win this battle."

"Let's see how it goes," Paige suggested. "I will talk to Juliana too, see if she's ever noticed Miguel being violent with other children. She's with him all the time."

"I think this here is blown *way* out of proportion," Jorge insisted.

"Today, he pushes kids in daycare," Paige said. "And then what? It will only escalate. I'm not saying he has to be weak. What I'm saying is he has to be *careful.*"

"This here, it is a good point," Jorge nodded as they moved through traffic.

Paige fell silent and turned her phone on.

"Anything happen while we turned the world off?" Jorge asked. "Everything is still standing?"

"Seems ok," Paige commented and tapped her phone. "I wanted to message Juliana that we picked up Miguel. I'll talk to her later."

"Maybe we will need our second home to run away from the toddler police," Jorge continued to joke. "Suddenly, our son, he is the baby from *Family Guy.*"

"We have to seem like normal parents," Paige reminded him. "Even though we are not."

"True, *mi amor,* I understand," Jorge replied. "I do."

"Kill!" Miguel yelled from the backseat.

"Ignore him," She muttered, looking down at her phone. "Don't encourage."

Jorge didn't reply but glanced in his rearview mirror and shared a smile with his son.

CHAPTER 12

"So, we have a few ideas we're thinking of for season 3 of *Eat the Rich Before the Rich Eat You*," Tony jumped right in after the three men sat down at the conference room table at the Hernandez Production Company. "Nothing is set in stone yet."

"Not until you say," Andrew jumped in as he waved his hands in the air before reaching for his cup of coffee, "you the boss."

"Well, this is true," Jorge nodded. "But you two are the brains behind this here project, so what you got for me."

"We're thinking of investigating how media and specifically news media started and going through history…"

"I'm already bored," Jorge cut in. "No one will like that. We need to jump in with both feet."

"Exactly what I said," Andrew agreed. "We need to kick ass on episode one."

"Ok, then what do you suggest?" Tony turned the tables on Andrew and sat back. "I want to hear this."

"I think we jump into a scandal and show how the media didn't cover it enough," Andrew suggested as he glanced at Jorge as if to check his reaction. "Maybe a local scandal?"

"Maybe," Jorge thought for a moment. "We are talking about how the media hides things, get things wrong, But first, we need to start with a story that was misrepresented in the media and show the factors that made it so."

"Like when you were running for politics, and people suggested you were a cartel guy," Andrew asked innocently.

"Let us not use me as an example," Jorge shook his head and gave him a warning look. "Let us not stray far from what has occurred recently too. What has been in the media lately that has been hidden or blown out of proportion?"

"Do you *really* want me to answer that?" Andrew replied. "Remember all those cops that died…"

"Yes, we are not talking about this here," Jorge cut him off and gave him another warning look.

"How about we start this off simple," Tony jumped in before Jorge and Andrew started to argue. "We show shots of some of the first tv shows ever made. Maybe, of different legendary or popular moments on television over the years, while a voice-over talks about how things have changed from *The Waltons* and more wholesome television to now and our reality television, and ask what happened? Who makes these decisions? Who's the person behind what you watch?"

Jorge shrugged, appearing skeptical.

"Trust me," Tony continued. "It will be more interesting than it sounds."

"Throw some rock n' roll in there," Jorge suggested. "The whole *MTV* and what is it you had here, in Canada?"

"*Muchmusic*," Andrew replied. "Back when we *had* music television."

"Well, there is no real music now," Jorge reminded him. "It is processed and put in a box, much like some of that garbage on grocery store shelves. I think we should start with rock n' roll. People, they respond to music."

Tony considered his suggestion and nodded as he looked toward Andrew.

"He's on to something," Andrew replied. "Fuck, we could do a whole series on this music industry."

"Maybe this won't be the first episode but we can do shots of stuff that is coming up in the series," Tony suggested with a shrug. "This could be a part of it. I mean, television used to be the whole family sitting down to watch a show together. Does that even happen now?"

"Jorge, you have a family," Andrew turned the tables on him. "You guys sit down to watch…like Mexican murder shows together, or something?"

"Please tell me Clara was in here today to check for listening devices," Jorge glanced around the room and after Tony nodded, he continued. "Do you think people watch shows that demonstrate their own lives? I do not want to watch a Mexican murder show any more than you want to watch a show about some moron who watches porn and jerks off all day, you know?"

"Let's just…" Tony attempted to talk but was cut off by Andrew.

"I don't do it *all* day," Andrew clarified. "Sometimes I also work on shows and burn bodies for this mobster guy."

"Fair enough," Jorge grinned.

"And that *would* be a good show," Andrew insisted. "I'll have you know."

Tony took a deep breath and shook his head.

"Anyway," Jorge cut in. "This here is a start. You'll introduce the season very powerfully so people are intrigued and want to keep watching. Talk about how television has changed. Talk about who owns the channels and how advertising has an effect. This here, I want to step away from and let you do your thing. These are just my ideas. People need to see how they are being manipulated."

"So, the introductory show will jump back and forth to show how media has changed," Tony jotted down something on a notepad. "Then from there, we will tackle the various segments. I think we should start with who owns networks to explain the rest in the following episodes."

"This here is good," Jorge agreed. "Then end the episode with 'so what does this mean to you?' Then give a tease of shots that leave people thinking."

"Then the next show," Andrew continued. "Maybe get some psychologist or something on talking about how certain shows, certain scenes, manipulate us."

"Yes, because it does," Jorge nodded. "But you know something, in Mexico, we see more graphic images on the news than here in Canada or America. We aren't afraid of showing the truth."

"We can talk about that," Tony nodded. "Are we too protected?"

"That is possible," Jorge replied. "I find it interesting how the news and other media decide what we can and cannot see, that is my point."

"And who decides that?" Andrew asked. "And why do they get to decide?"

"We can look at that too," Tony jotted down more notes.

"But keep it fun and interesting," Jorge reminded him. "If you are going to get into things we cannot see, talk about who decides what is obscene and what is not, and why that has changed over the years."

"Good point," Tony continued to write. "I'm also wondering how often news reporters or talk show host or whatever aren't allowed to express what they see or think, to keep their job."

"Find the people who did not go along with this," Jorge suggested. "In the end, the people must see how much they are being controlled and manipulated by the media. How we are fed a narrative and anyone who goes against it is banned, kicked out…."

"Made fun of," Andrew piped up. "Can you imagine if some big shot reporter did a story on fucking aliens? It wouldn't matter if said reporter had proof that they're real, footage, and that shit. They'd be dismissed as being a wacko wearing a tinfoil hat and ripped apart by everyone else. Because, you know, it goes against the narrative."

"There have been worse scenarios than that," Tony reminded him. "When people have been honest and went against the narrative, they're fed to the wolves. Trust me on that. We have to expose who decides on that narrative and why?"

"Maybe we should start with the questions and work our way to the top of the ladder as we go on," Andrew suggested, "building the anticipation."

"This here, it sounds good," Jorge nodded and moved his chair back. "I will trust you with this here. Keep me posted on it, on other shows."

"As you know, we have a few things we're working on," Tony nodded. "Everything is going pretty smoothly. We have a good team here."

"Well, if this is the case," Jorge thought for a moment. "I will keep up to date on things, but I trust you to keep the fires burning. I have some other projects that I am working on now."

"Really?" Andrew cut in. "You just started this company, and you're backing away? That's weird."

"I want to allow you to do your work," Jorge insisted as he stood up, "You two, you have done lots of work for me, and I know it is good. I am just here to brainstorm and sound you out. *Eat the Rich* will always be my favorite project, and the others are merely entertainment."

"Jolene is working with those people more," Tony said as he pointed toward the door. "It keeps her out of our hair, and she has some good ideas. She's helping with casting today."

"Yeah, casting for her bed," Andrew muttered.

"What?" Jorge halted. "Do not tell me…"

"Hey, that's what I hear," Andrew shrugged as he stood up, and Tony did the same, glaring at his coworker. "Not like in the casting couch way, I don't mean that. Just sometimes, these men at the casting auditions also fuck her. Probably because they want a job."

"Jesus Christ," Tony shook his head. "Andrew, we don't know…"

"I do not care," Jorge cut in. "I do not want to be sued. That is all I care about."

"I don't think it's with the promise of getting a job," Tony clarified. "But I will look into it."

"Please do," Jorge insisted. "If you think it is an issue, you talk to me. And I will tell her this here is not going to happen. If I get sued because of Jolene…"

"You'll throw her in the oven," Andrew shrugged. "Just remember you got to keep me alive to run it for you, that's all I'm saying."

Jorge grinned as he walked toward the door.

"I'll let you know," Tony called out. "As soon as I find out."

"We don't want you to step on her toes if I'm wrong," Andrew called out.

"Me," Jorge turned back before opening the door while turning his phone back on. "I like stepping on toes."

He was in the elevator when he found a message from Makerson. He needed to meet with Jorge ASAP.

What is going on?

Remember the book we were talking about writing?

Yes

Looks like someone is trying to beat us to it.

CHAPTER 13

"So, what the hell is going on?" Jorge asked before he sat across from Makerson in the VIP room of *Princesa Maria.* Jorge's heart was already racing with fury, despite the limited information he had so far. "Who is writing this here book?"

"I heard," Makerson said, reaching for his phone to turn it off. "That some guy went to a major publishing house, here in Canada, to propose the idea of writing a book about your life. And my understanding is, it's not going to be flattering."

Jorge felt his blood boiling, his lips tightened, but remained silent.

"I have to find out…"

"You do not know who?" Jorge shook his head, attempting to calm down. "Who is the fucking idiot doing this?"

"No," Makerson shook his head. "I barely heard this much and got to you right away."

"So it has not been written yet?" Jorge asked. "This here man reached out to a publisher?"

"No, not yet," Makerson nodded. "That is my understanding. I have the publishing house name and thought maybe someone who works for you could do some snooping. Of course, I can try too."

"My people, they can hack," Jorge confirmed what Makerson already knew. "This is what I will do."

"I mean, it's kept pretty hush hush," Makerson confirmed. "The only reason why I know is because one of my guys heard and thought it was *me* writing it since I've interviewed you so much."

"But how did he hear?" Jorge was curious. "If it is top secret."

"His buddy or someone works at the publishing house," Makerson shook his head. "He brought it up to my coworker, also thinking it was maybe me writing it."

"So, he did not see?"

"No, like I say," Makerson said. "It's top secret."

"As you can imagine, this here, it concerns me," Jorge said as he reached for his phone and turned it back on. "I must get the others here. You can stay if you wish."

"I gotta get back to the office," Makerson confirmed. "But I'll find out more if I can."

"Tell your source you are also interested in writing a book," Jorge suggested. "Use that as a way to find out who this might be. Maybe even lie and say that you have been working on something but weren't allowed to talk about it, confide this here to your coworker. See what he can find out or if he is trying to bait you."

Makerson nodded as he rose from his chair.

"I plan to find out and put a stop to it regardless," Jorge insisted as he stood up. "Thank you for this information."

"I also wanted to suggest," Makerson hesitated for a moment. "If you think it will help, we *can* write a book too, but have it...cherry-picked, information wise. You tell me the story you want me to write. But that's up to you."

"I will consider it," Jorge nodded and thought for a moment. "And I thank you again."

After Makerson left, Jorge contacted Diego and Marco to come to the bar. Chase was in his office when he found him.

"I have another small meeting," Jorge pointed toward his phone before turning it off. "Diego and Marco are on their way. I do not want to discuss this with Paige yet, but I heard that there might be someone writing a book about me."

Chase made a face.

"Exactly," Jorge nodded. "I must find out who and take it up with them before this here happens."

"Who would know that much about you?" Chase wondered. "And who would be stupid enough to talk?"

"I do not know," Jorge shook his head. "That is my concern, but whoever is doing the talking may have the same treatment as our friend who we recently took care of at the crematorium."

Chase nodded. "It seems to me it would have to be someone privy to what you're doing."

"And that is what concerns me," Jorge confirmed. "That is why I only invite Diego and Marco here. I do not fully trust Jolene, and I never will."

"Do you think…"

"Chase, with so many other things she has done over the years," Jorge shook his head. "I do not trust that woman. It may be her, or it may be her letting information slip to the wrong people, who knows?"

"She *is* a loose wire," Chase confirmed. "We've always seen that about her."

"And now, you know what they tell me earlier today?"Jorge said as he sat on the other side of the desk from Chase. "She has a casting couch at the production company."

"What?" Chase asked in disbelief. "Wha….she can't do that."

"It is not official this here, but it may as well be," Jorge shook his head. "These men are fucking her thinking she will remember them for some show down the road, if not the one they have auditioned for."

"And she is taking full advantage," Chase added. "If it were a man doing that…"

"Yes, I know, it would be a huge story on the entertainment news, and I will be sued," Jorge confirmed. "That is why I am not so sure about Jolene. I cannot take much more of her nonsense, and there has been so much over the years."

"Yes, there has," Chase nodded. "Even teaching Maria to shoot a gun behind your back, I mean I know…"

"Exactly, but that wasn't the point," Jorge agreed. "I was clear that I did not want her to learn at such a young age, and Jolene, she does what she wants. I know she has done good work for me too, and I know she saved Paige once, but at the same time, Chase, I feel like I can never fully trust her."

"I agree," Chase agreed. "I can see why you're concerned."

"But I must talk to Diego," Jorge shook his head. "Even if she is in no way involved, I still have concerns, you know? This woman, she would be dead long ago if it was not for Diego."

"I don't know if she would do this," Chase considered. "But I can see her blabbing to someone as pillow talk if you know what I mean."

"This here sounds about right," Jorge nodded. "I cannot think of many more that would talk. Most that know my secrets are dead, including my own family from Mexico. Many of my former associates are dead. That is the state of this here business."

Chase nodded.

"At any rate," Jorge continued. "I will find out who is behind this book and end it."

"I'm sure Marco can find out everything you need to know," Chase said as he leaned back in his chair. "Find out who you're dealing with and maybe destroy the entire book before it goes anywhere."

"But whoever has it," Jorge said. "He may have it saved in various places, maybe safely tucked away."

"*He* might be safely tucked away if he doesn't tell you where the copies are," Chase suggested. "If he's writing this book, he also knows who he's dealing with and what it means if it's released."

"You would think," Jorge continued. "But many, they do not think they will be caught."

Chase nodded but didn't reply.

"I can have Makerson write a book too. I pick and choose what I wish to have in it," Jorge mulled over the idea. "I do not know."

"It's an option," Chase said as he considered the idea.

"But Paige, she will be mad," Jorge replied. "She does not want attention brought to me. And I was listening. I backed away from the productions, from Our House of Pot, and yet, here I am. She fears that it makes us a target."

"We'll take care of this," Chase assured him. "We always do."

Jorge nodded.

"And not to change the subject," Chase said with a grin on his face. "But Maria and I are going to our first self-defense class this weekend."

"Oh yes, this true," Jorge nodded, relieved to be talking about something else. "I thought it was supposed to be…"

"The dates got mixed up," Chase said as he shook his head. "But now, it's definitely this weekend. I think it's going to be as good for her as the women I'm teaching."

"I like how you have included her in this idea," Jorge grinned. "This here was genius. Plus, she gets to hang out with her favorite person."

"I don't know if I'm necessarily her favorite person," Chase laughed.

"Trust me, Chase, you are her favorite person," Jorge teased. "She always has such a crush on you! But this here is ok. It is very innocent, and it allows you to have a positive influence on her. So I am happy she is joining you on these trips. I know she is excited."

"Look, Maria is a special kid, so I do what I can," Chase smiled, but it quickly faded. "I see her changing a lot since the shooting."

"I am not always sure it is for the better," Jorge frowned. "I worry about my Maria, she is a sensitive child. She's very anxious. I see the weakness of her mother in her, and it worries me. I want her to be strong."

"It's fixable," Chase assured him. "We can make her strong. I think self-defense will help. It works on two levels. I'm teaching it to the women in indigenous communities, which is important to me, and I'm also teaching Maria, but also, it will empower her."

"I'm positive it will be," Jorge agreed as he grew restless in the chair and began to shuffle around. "Now, my son, he is another story."

"I heard," Chase laughed just as someone knocked on the main entrance.

"Paige, she is not happy," Jorge confirmed as he watched Chase head toward the door.

"Well, he's a kid. They pick up everything," Chase replied on his way out of the room. "The legacy continues."

"The devil and his legacy always does," Jorge muttered as he considered his next move. "And always will."

CHAPTER 14

"So fiction?" Paige calmly asked as they huddled together in the kitchen as she glanced toward the next room. "You want to write fiction."

"No, *mi amor*," Jorge laughed at his wife's reaction to the news of Makerson possibly writing a book about him. "It will be true, but it will skip over, you know, many things in my life. He will write what I want people to know. Isn't that what the celebrities do anyway?"

"I see," Paige appeared skeptical. "I thought we agreed to wait on this. That it would be good to avoid attention on you."

"That is the thing," Jorge hesitated for a moment before moving closer to speak low. "I met with Makerson today, and he heard a rumor that someone might already be writing a book on me, so I…"

"Wait, what!" Paige's eyes doubled in size as she leaned in. "Someone's writing a book about you? Are you serious?"

"That is what he heard," Jorge confirmed and watched Paige process the news. "I had a meeting with Diego and Marco to see what they can find out. And trust me, Paige, if this here is the case, it will be dead in the water."

"It will look suspicious if the author suddenly goes missing," She reminded him. "Especially if he or she has already submitted chapters to the publishing house."

"We will find out who is behind this first," Jorge sternly confirmed. "Take care of that person, and then, we will find the publisher and either suggest he take on Makerson's book instead, with me working *with* them. It will be better if it is authorized because it means more money. That is all they care about in the end. That is all any of these companies want. Maybe I can revive the book industry."

Paige thought for a moment.

"Why wasn't I invited to the meeting?"

"I knew it would upset you," Jorge replied to the question he knew was coming. "And I did not want to worry you. I decided I would come to you once I had it figured out. And Diego, Marco, and me, we figured it out. So see, you do not need to worry."

"I don't like the idea of a book about *you* coming out, *period,*" Paige had concern in her eyes. "It brings too much attention to you. Too many people can come forward with their own stories or versions of stories."

"I will try to delay it as much as possible."

"I think you should find the publisher behind it," Paige whispered. "And if he doesn't agree to stop the project, stop *him.*"

"This here, it is an option too."

"No book," Paige insisted, "from anyone."

"But Paige, what if others get the same idea," Jorge asked with a shrug. "I am a rock star among people. It is not outrageous."

"I think the publishing industry in Canada is small enough that word gets around," Paige cut him off. "Spread a rumor that you and Makerson might be working on an autobiography. If people try to write something unauthorized, then it doesn't stand up against something you worked on."

"It could still happen."

"I know," Paige agreed and took a deep breath. "But most people don't know enough about you other than what's in the news, so it would be difficult to get information. And if they're stupid enough to go poking around Mexico…"

"They won't be poking around Mexico too long," Jorge reminded her. "I have people there. They know what to do in that case."

"They wouldn't talk?"

"They know better," Jorge reminded her. "These people get paid well to keep their mouths shut, their ears opened."

"And here," Paige shrugged. "The only people who have something on you, you have something on them."

"That is the thing," Jorge reminded her as he ran a hand over his face. "The people here, they rely on me, so I am good except there is one person I am not sure about."

"Who?" Paige asked as she leaned against the counter.

"Jolene."

"I just…"

"Trust me," Jorge shook his head as he looked over his shoulder before continuing. "She has been on shaky ground for a long time. I do not fully trust her. She knows a lot about me. She has access to people in Mexico."

Paige thought for a moment and frowned.

"Hey, maybe not," Jorge shrugged. "It may not be true, but believe me, I do plan to find out."

"Well, she can barely put a sentence together in English, so we know she isn't writing the book," Paige confirmed. "But she could be consulting."

"That is what I am thinking."

"But I don't know," Paige considered the idea. "She usually wants to keep in good with us, and if she did that, she knows that would be her final ticket out of the group."

"It would be her final ticket *period,*" Jorge confirmed. "There is no way out alive from this deception."

"But we don't know," Paige reminded him. "Let's see what Marco can find out."

"He hopes to have something by tomorrow," Jorge confirmed. "As soon as he does, we will meet and talk. He's hacking, following some emails, this sort of thing."

"He'll get the answers," Paige replied. "You know, we're jumping to conclusions here. It could be some random idiot pulling together what's on the news."

"They want a controversy to sell their books," Jorge reminded her. "So I am not feeling more confident about this here option."

"Well, also…"

"*Papá,*" Maria's voice came from the stairway, and the couple automatically halted the conversation. Paige gave Jorge a warning look as she left the room, just as her step-daughter walked in.

"*Si*, Maria, what can I do for you?" Jorge asked as his daughter sauntered toward him. "I hear you and Chase are going to your first self-defense class this weekend."

"*Papá*, we are hosting it," Maria reminded him. "not *going* to it."

"OK, yes," Jorge grinned. "I understand."

"That's what I wanted to talk to you about," Maria spoke up as her dark eyes widened. "I was thinking maybe your newspaper friend would like to do a story on the work me and Chase are doing. I thought you said he was doing an article on it. I was online, and I don't see anything."

"Well, Maria," Jorge said as he reached for his phone. "I did plan to do this, but I have been busy with other things. I will send him some information and have him add it to the weekend paper."

"I think he should do a bigger story on it," Maria suggested. "Like have a reporter on the scene or whatever."

"Maria, they are far too busy for this here," Jorge grinned. "But what I will do, is make sure the information is sent to media outlets and that Makerson perhaps will do an interview with you two after your first event. Does this here make sense?"

"I think it would be better now," Maria insisted. "Since it is new."

"This is a good point," Jorge admitted as he tapped into his phone. "As I say, I will make sure that the PR department has the information out tomorrow, and I will ask Makerson to have an interview with you and Chase. See what he says."

"That would be perfect!" Maria beamed. "I am very excited. Chase and I have been going over some self-defense moves when I go to work at the bar, sometimes before we start the real work, I mean. I love it."

"Well, Maria, this is important for you to know too," Jorge reminded her. "You must always be strong, powerful, and able to look after yourself. You always have us, but I feel better if you can look after yourself too."

"*Papá*, is that your office phone ringing?" Maria cut him off.

"Yes, Maria," Jorge said as he rushed away, "I have sent the messages. Check with Chase for more."

With that, Jorge rushed to his office. He quickly closied the door and made his way across the room. It was his secure line.

"Hello," He answered the phone as he walked around the desk.

"Hello," Alec Athas, the Canadian prime minister, spoke from the other end of the line. "I heard a rumor you're doing a project, maybe the third season of *Eat the Rich?*"

"*Si,*" Jorge confirmed as he relaxed in his chair. "We are working out the details now."

"I heard it is on the media."

"Yes, this is true."

"I heard it might be controversial."

"Most things I do are," Jorge reminded him. "You know this."

"Are you tackling specific reporters, networks, that kind of thing?" Athas asked, and Jorge grinned.

"That is the plan," Jorge replied. "Although, we will see how things fall into place."

"Well, if you're targeting anyone," Athas replied. "I have some names that I would like to run by you. There are a few reporters that seem to get in my craw a lot."

"Ahh..." Jorge leaned back in his chair and laughed. "And we do not want anyone stuck in your *craw,* do we?"

"They don't make my life or job easier."

"Well, you give me the names, and I will pass them on," Jorge confirmed. "This here season, we will discuss manipulation in the media, how it has changed, who influences it."

"That sounds like it could work for me," Athas replied.

"Finally, Athas, you have come to the dark side," Jorge smiled with satisfaction. "I have always said, if you work for me, then I work for you. This here, it has not changed."

"But your help comes with a price," Athas spoke cooly.

Jorge leaned forward on his desk as a sinister grin spread across his face.

"Everything, *amigo,* it comes with a price. Everything."

CHAPTER 15

"Some *gringo* wants to write a book about me?" Jorge's head fell back, and laughter filled the VIP room of *Princesa Maria,* while others who sat around the table appeared less amused. "This here, it is crazy. How could some *white* man know anything about my life?"

"He is an entertainment reporter, sir," Marco continued to explain what he had learned after hacking both the publisher and the man in question. "He is one of those guys on shows where they talk about movie stars who are divorcing and such silly things."

"Oh yes, my daughter, she watches this stuff," Jorge continued to be amused as he glanced at his wife, who appeared concerned. "I do not care for such programs, myself. I feel they are ridiculous. Why do I care who these celebrities are fucking or marrying or if they got a new haircut? Such silliness these shows are."

"It's fluff," Chase spoke up as he glanced around the table. "Celebrities don't even seem like real people."

"Well, some of them kinda aren't," Diego said as he wrinkled his forehead. "Just, you know, fake."

"Ok, we must stop making fun of celebrities," Jorge shook his head. "Although this here is fun, I do think we need to get back to business."

"So, sir," Marco jumped back in. "This man, he does entertainment reporting, and from what I have found, he decided that you would make for an interesting book."

"Well, this here, I cannot argue with," Jorge winked at his wife, but she continued to look tense.

"He went to this publisher," Marco pointed toward his laptop. "He suggested he write a book, and that is as far as it's got."

"Was he offered money? A contract?" Paige asked. "Anything? Did they agree?"

"They seem to like the idea," Marco nodded as he continued to glance at the screen. "But there is some dispute who should write the book."

"It is about me," Jorge shook his head. "Should I not be writing the book?"

"That was suggested, sir," Marco replied with wide eyes. "However, it seems they are hesitant to work with you."

"Gees, I wonder why," Diego sniffed. "You got a reputation, Hernandez."

"What do you mean?" Jorge teased. "I work well with people."

"They work well with you or…" Diego attempted to reply, but Jorge was already cutting him off.

"This here, it does not worry me," Jorge shook his head. "If I approach them saying I know about the book, they will squirm to explain why I cannot write my own book."

"So, nothing is for sure?" Chase asked. "They're just talking about it?"

"Yes, that is it so far," Marco confirmed. "It seems recent from what I have read. So far, there are no contracts, just interest."

"And the guy wanting to write this?" Diego asked.

"His name is Jordan Patrick," Marco replied. "He has done reporting for various entertainment columns, but now, he is mainly on TV on one of those shows," Marco waved his hand in the air and made a face. "Sir, he is not very old. I see he's only 30." He turned his laptop around, showing the group a picture of a white man wearing a blue suit at a red carpet event.

"He looks vacant," Paige observed. "Like someone who barely reads a book, let alone write one."

"Yet, he plans to write this here book about me," Jorge shook his head. "I am not a member of a boy band or some pop tart on daytime TV. This here does not make sense. Why a fan of me?"

"He's a fan of money," Marco insisted. "He likes buying things and showing off his wealth even though he does not have a lot for a man on TV."

"Is this so?" Jorge asked with interest.

"Yes, sir, he most likely sees this as a way to make a lot of money," Marco shrugged. "Maybe because he is only planning to report information that was already published."

"He doesn't seem like someone with his nose to the grindstone," Diego shook his head while making a face. "I don't get it."

"None of us do, Diego," Chase said and took a deep breath. "So, what we gonna do?"

"Wait," Paige put her hand up. "Do you think maybe he is working for someone else? Like maybe someone is giving him information and using his celebrity to get the book out there?"

"That there is possible," Jorge spoke abruptly. "Does Jolene know this man?"

"Not that I can see, sir," Marco shook his head. "I thought of that too, but no, no connection."

"He's talking to someone," Paige insisted. "I don't see him being interested in what Jorge is doing."

"That is the part I'm stuck on," Marco admitted. "I am trying to research both him and the publisher."

"In the end," Jorge thought for a moment. "It does not matter. We have to cut this off now."

"How do we do that?" Diego asked.

"I think that this man, I will talk to myself," Jorge pointed toward the screen. "He and I are going to have a conversation, and that is when I will find out everything I must know. As for the publisher, I think I will talk to Makerson. Maybe he can approach them with his idea and suggest that they will get more out of writing an authorized book about me. Then we put them off."

"I think we need to kill this idea altogether," Paige shook her head, "start with the Jordan guy and take it from there. First, we need to know where this came from, and then take care of the publisher. We need to understand what's going on to make a stronger plan."

"So, Jordan Patrick," Jorge glanced at the young man on Marco's screen. "You and I will be having a little meeting."

"Should I set up something?" Chase asked.

"No," Jorge shook his head. "I prefer the element of surprise. Do we know where this man lives?"

"I have an address, sir," Marco said. "And I looked at his schedule. He has a wife and…"

"Oh, is this so?" Jorge perked up and grinned. "Well, then this here will be easy. We have something to fall back on if he won't agree with my strong argument for not pursuing this idea."

"But sir," Marco continued. "If you want to get him alone, it seems he has an office he works out of. It is sort of in an unusual place. Not the best area of Toronto."

"Really?" Chase asked and glanced at Jorge. "He might have something to hide."

"What?" Diego asked. "Other women he's whoring around with. He looks like the type."

"He looks like someone who would *whore around,* is this so, Diego?" Jorge teased.

"I know the look," Diego said and twisted his lips. "And he's got it."

"It is weird," Marco continued. "I do not understand this. His office is located in a strange place. For a man who is about prestige, it is in a rundown building, and it almost seems like no one in his close connections knows about it."

"He's a whore," Diego continued to insist. "I knew it!"

"I do not care," Jorge shook his head. "But he's getting a surprise visit from me. I got to know when he will be there. I might need someone with me as a backup."

"I'm free," Chase jumped in. "Diego?"

"I barely got time to be here now," Diego shook his head. "Things are busy at work, but I can make time."

"I think Chase will do," Jorge nodded. "If we need extra help, we will call you in. Just say something like…."

"A bar emergency?" Chase suggested.

"Sure," Jorge nodded. "We will visit him. Marco, any thoughts when he is usually there."

"I hacked his camera, sir," Marco said as he turned the laptop around and hit a few keys, swinging it back around to show an empty office. "He isn't there now, but when he is, I can call you."

"This here is perfect," Jorge replied. "Now, I must meet with Jolene. I want to discuss this casting couch situation."

"Oh, God!" Diego hung his head while shaking it. "Jolene…"

"At any rate," Jorge continued. "I will resolve this right away, and at the same time, I will hint around about the book and see her reaction. Jolene, she is not good at hiding secrets."

"This is to our benefit," Paige nodded. "Do you want me to come too?"

"No, you can stay here with Diego," Jorge rose from his seat. "She is at the production house. I must drop in to check on things, and then I will go home."

The meeting ended with everyone going their own way and Marco's assurance that he would see what else he could find.

Back in the SUV, Jorge thought about the book. He thought about Jolene. Was she behind this? It seemed like a mess she'd get involved in but yet, something wasn't ringing true.

Jorge had no trouble finding Jolene upon arrival at the production house. As soon as he walked into the building, he could hear her loud voice from down the hallway as she argued with Tony.

"You do not listen," She was complaining. "I say…"

"Jolene," Jorge walked into Tony's office, alarming her. "We gotta talk."

Suddenly, her demeanor changed as she deflated under his dark glare.

"I can…we can talk," She began to stutter while Tony jumped out of his chair behind the desk.

"You can have my office," He volunteered as he headed for the door.

"You stay," Jorge instructed Tony, who nodded and returned to his seat. "I need you to hear this too."

"But I did not do…" She started to speak.

"The casting couch," Jorge shot back. "It ends here. If you want to give someone a tongue bath, find them on a dating app or at the bar, or I don't give a fuck where, but it ain't going to be here."

"I was not, I just…"

"I don't want to hear it," Jorge cut her off. "I got other problems now, and I don't got time for this, but I will tell you this, Jolene. I am not getting sued because you can't keep your legs together."

"It is not like that," She attempted to explain.

"I do not care what it is like," Jorge snapped and turned his attention to Tony, who appeared uncomfortable with this conversation. "And you, do you know a Jordan Patrick?"

"Isn't he on one of those terrible shows?" Tony began, and Jorge glanced toward Jolene, who looked like she was still grappling with their conversation.

"Jolene, you know him?" Jorge shot at her while her defenses were down.

"No? What?" Jolene shook his head. "I do not know…is he important, this man?"

Jorge studied her face.

"Jorge, I promise," Jolene jumped back in. "I will do better. But you do not understand, that man was not casting, it was just…"

"That's all I need," Jorge cut her off and turned his attention to Tony, who was listening carefully. "I got to be somewhere. We will talk more later."

Tony calmly nodded, while a glance at Jolene told him that she was still upset over his earlier comment, as she nervously wrung her hands. Rushing out of the office, Jorge headed for the main exit, stopping briefly to message Paige.

Jolene isn't involved.

CHAPTER 16

"This place here is a dump," Jorge commented as the two men walked into the building that seemed abandoned. The carpet smelled of urine and the walls were in disrepair; including one with a hole in it. Glancing at Chase, Jorge gestured toward a stairway. "Be careful, you never know what you might step on in this fucking place."

"My guess is that some pretty seedy things have happened here," Chase muttered back as he looked around with interest as they started up the stairs. "If walls could talk"

"Yeah, well thankfully for us, they cannot," Jorge reminded him as they made their way upstairs. "I am surprised there are no homeless person passed out on these here steps."

"Or worse," Chase replied as they arrived at the top step. He glanced down the hallway. "I think that's the office there."

Jorge nodded as the two men headed toward the closed door. The building was relatively quiet despite being located in the notorious Jane and Finch area of the city. Most people avoided this part of Toronto, especially at that time in the evening. To Jorge Hernandez, this was irrelevant.

Locating the door, the two men exchanged looks, and without hesitation, Jorge reached for the knob and barged in. A man sat behind a desk, someone Jorge recognized as a local television personality most known to report on who pop stars were dating or what celebrities would be attending the Toronto Film Festival. However, at that moment, his face was full of disbelief as he looked at Jorge, temporarily distracted from the lines of cocaine that awaited his attention.

"Ah! *Cocaina!*" Jorge pointed toward the desk as he closed the door behind him and Chase. "This here, it was always my drug of choice too. You know, back when I was much younger of course. These days, the heart, it does not like me to do such things."

Jordan Patrick continued to look shocked as he sat back in his chair. His appearance was much more disheveled than on television; He had removed his tie, and his hair was in disarray. Dark circles were prevalent under his eyes, while his skin was pale. He was broken.

"You look like a man who has just crawled out of bed," Jorge remarked as he boldly walked across the room, and sat on the other side of the desk. Chase did the same, remaining stoic as he stared at Jordan Patrick. "But that is what cocaine does to a person. I have seen it many times. You start off as Snow White and end up as one of those creepy little dwarfs. So where's it from?"

"What?" Jordan finally spoke, his voice shaking.

"The cocaine?" Jorge pointed toward the desk. "Where is that from? The good stuff from Colombia or what?"

"I...I...."

"You really should know these things here," Jorge insisted. "I mean, there is a difference in quality, but today, with Fentanyl out there, you never know what kind of poison you are putting into your body."

"I...I guess it..."

"And the problem with that," Jorge continued, this time speaking toward Chase. "Is you could just drop dead. The heart, it can only take so much, you know. Someone, they could find you on the floor, cold as ice. This has happened to a lot of people."

"I...well, I..."

"They must get paid good," Jorge pointed toward the cocaine, his eyes on Jordan again. "You know, to afford this habit and to what? Get an office to partake in such behaviors. I guess that is good. The wife, she probably would not like this here much."

"She doesn't like it," Jordan spoke in a small voice.

"He finally speaks in a full sentence," Jorge commented to Chase. "This here is good. I was so worried about how the book about me would turn out if he could not even say a full fucking sentence. This here could be a major problem."

"How did you…" Jordan nervously started but was quickly cut off when Jorge lurched forward and pounded his fist on the desk.

"I know everything *motherfucker,*" Jorge yelled at him. "Did you think I would *not* know about this? That I would not find out? That I would be ok with it? Did you think…you would slip away with a handful of money? What did you think? Tell me!"

"I thought that I would…"

"Who told you to write this book?" Jorge continued to yell as his dark eyes darted at the man behind the desk. "Who had this here idea?"

"No one!" Jordan put his hands in the air as if to defend himself. "You're always in the news and…."

"That doesn't sound right," Chase cut in, his comment directed at Jorge. "There's something not right here."

"I agree," Jorge nodded toward the desk. "Although, he might have wanted money for his expensive habit. I would think there are easier people to write about."

"It was my wife," Jordan said with a shaking voice as tears formed in his eyes. "Please don't kill her. I…"

"Who says anything about killing?" Jorge glared at him but was suddenly calm. "Tell me everything and tell me *now* because I will not be making a return visit. At least not to you."

"It wasn't…it was because…." Jordan nervously stammered along as his face turned red. "She said I should do a book and….you would be easy because you're well known…"

"What was going to be in this here book?" Jorge asked as he relaxed back in the chair. "I am curious."

"The stuff in the news….I don't know," Jordan replied.

"Nothing else?" Jorge asked again.

"No," Jordan shook his head. "But I can…I can stop…"

"You *will* stop," Jorge corrected him.

"Is there anyone else talking about doing this?" Chase asked.

"I...I don't know," Jordan shook his head and cleared his throat. "I don't think the publisher took me seriously anyway. They liked the idea but...I don't know if they wanted me to write it. They expressed concerns. I think they were only considering me because I'm in the public eye."

"So, you decided to write a book on me because your wife said so?" Jorge asked skeptically. "Why do I feel like I am missing..."

"We're in debt," Jordan cut him off. "We had to find fast money. She saw where some other entertainment guy did a book on someone...there's usually an advance for these things..."

Jorge nodded.

"You might want to stop snorting that shit if you're broke," Chase nodded toward the desk then turned to Jorge. "We done here?"

"I think so," Jorge stood up then leaned over the desk. "This here is our last conversation. If I hear you are going ahead with this book, the next time....there will be *no* conversation. Is this here clear?"

Jordan nodded as tears welled in his eyes again.

"How much in debt are you?"

"Like 60 grand," Jordan said and cleared his throat. "Student loans, car....it adds up...."

"Keep your fucking mouth shut about this, and I might pay this for you," Jorge said and noted a look of surprise on the young man's face. "*But* there better be no book. If you find out someone else is writing one, I want you to tell me. If I find out there is, or you ever get in my crosshairs again...."

"I...I won't, I promise," Jordan nodded. "I...would I...how do I..."

"You can contact my associate here," Jorge glanced at Chase who nodded and reached in his pocket, pulling out a card and tossing it on the desk. "He will, in turn, be in contact with me."

"Yes," Jordan jumped up with a mixture of relief and gratitude in his eyes. "You'll pay..."

Jorge shrugged. "I am a wealthy man. I will do this....*once,* and only *once,* but you are loyal to me. There are no exceptions to this rule."

"I can...yes, I can do that..."

"Ok, we will be in touch," Jorge replied as he turned toward the door.

"Do you want...do you need my number or something?" Jordan asked nervously.

"I got that," Jorge commented as he turned back, and Chase headed for the door. "We got everything on you."

With that, the two men left the office and headed toward the stairs.

"You're going to pay his bills?" Chase appeared surprised.

"That man there," Jorge tilted his head. "I can control. If you swoop in and play God, then they will pray to you. That has been my experience."

Chase nodded as the two men left the building. After Jorge saw his associate take off, he turned on his SUV and followed him. Eventually, Chase turned his vehicle in a homebound direction while Jorge drove on. He had one more meeting for the day.

He found Makerson at a quiet coffee shop in the downtown area. Grabbing a bottle of juice, he headed to the back of the room where he sat.

"You don't seem like a juice guy," Makerson commented as Jorge sat across from him. "Let alone this pure, natural, non-GMO guy."

"My wife, she wants to be healthier," Jorge grinned. "But hey, at least I am not snorting cocaine off the desk, like the man I just visit."

"Who's that?" Makerson appeared humored.

"Jordan Patrick."

"Oh, yeah, I could've told you that," Makerson raised an eyebrow. "The guy is on his way to being fired."

"Is that so?"

"Yeah, he's kind of a fuck up."

"That was who wanted to write a book about me," Jorge spoke in a low voice, leaning in as he opened his bottle of juice.

"He just wanted a big name," Makerson waved his hand in the air. "He wouldn't get much about you other than what is already out there. He certainly wouldn't be roaming the streets of Mexico."

"He would not be there for long if he did," Jorge shrugged. "He wanted money. I say, if you back off and work with me, I will pay your fucking debt. I am feeling generous with the holidays coming."

"I can't see him going against you," Makerson said as he leaned in.

"We have already established what would happen if he did but chances are, I will never hear from him again," Jorge said and Makerson nodded in understanding. "He was, you know, a pathetic man."

"That wasn't always the case," Makerson informed him. "He's smart, but I dunno…something happened to him. He could've been more."

"So now, I must address this matter with the publisher," Jorge shook his head. "My wife, she does not want such a book out about me."

"Once the publisher gets the taste of blood…" Makerson warned Jorge.

"I know," Jorge nodded and glanced toward the window. "That is why I must perhaps suggest you as the author if they insist."

"We can carefully craft this book," Makerson reminded him as Jorge looked out the window at Christmas lights across the street. "We can tell whatever story you want. But there's a chance that it will provoke others to start digging, especially if our book is a success."

"We will see," Jorge replied. "I am hoping the people who know of this are few. I can contain a small fire much easier than one that has already got out of control."

"I haven't heard anything else," Makerson assured him. "But the publisher isn't going to get the word out so that other companies don't jump in and steal their idea. It's a smaller publishing house, so…"

"Really?" Jorge raised an eyebrow. "Well, then this will be easy."

"But what if other companies…."

"First we must deal with this one," Jorge thought for a moment. "I may have an idea."

CHAPTER 17

"But Maria, come on, you were featured with Chase in the newspaper on Saturday," Jorge gestured toward the weekend copy of *Toronto AM,* sitting on the nearby table. "You should be happy. I do not understand."

"But *Papá,* I was doing something useful there," Maria shook her head, causing her long, dark ponytail to bop around. She stood over her backpack that sat in the middle of the kitchen floor. "I was helping women learn to protect themselves, but now I'm back to real life. School is a waste of time."

"Maria, school is not a waste of time," Jorge sternly corrected her. "You need an education. You need to learn. Take that article to your teachers, show them you are capable of learning things outside of school. Did they not allow you to write a project about the club at one time? Maybe this can be another of those things, you know?"

"I don't know," Maria sighed. "School is boring."

"Maria, enjoy it, please," Jorge said as he stood up and approached her. Kissing her on the top of the head, he hugged her. "I pay a lot of money for you to have the best education. Take advantage. Do not be like me and have to learn through life."

"But you didn't finish school…"

"Yes, Maria, this is true," Jorge acknowledged but quickly continued. "But it has made life more difficult when it comes to things like business, you know? I wish I had known more. It would have made things a bit easier, and that is what I wish for you."

Maria considered what he said but didn't look convinced.

"Now, *Princesa,* Juliana, and Miguel are waiting outside," Jorge pointed toward the door. "You must get out there or you will be late."

"Ok, *Papá,*" She spoke with reluctance as she picked up her backpack and headed toward the door. "I will see you tonight."

"Be good, Maria.*"*

"*Papá,*" She turned around with a stern look on her face. "I'm not the one running around yelling *kill* all day and bullying other kids."

"Maria, he is a little boy," Jorge corrected her. "He does not know any better."

"Still...."

"Go to school, Maria."

"*Besos!*" She called out as she walked out the door.

"*Besos,* Maria," He replied with a grin as he watched her leave.

Grabbing his phone, he glanced at it briefly before leaving the house and getting into his SUV. He felt guilty for not saying goodbye to Paige, but she was in her meditation room again, her anxieties building over the possibility of someone writing a book about him. She had so many fears about the family becoming a target, and Jorge was well aware he hadn't stepped out of the spotlight, which only made matters worse. He had to find a way to satisfy everybody.

On a whim, he called Marco.

"Good morning, sir."

"Marco, I am wondering if you have any more news for me?"

"No, sir," Marco's voice seemed full of regret. "I was looking this weekend, but I was not able to find out more. I even checked other... sources, but I did not find anything."

"Maybe this here is a good sign?" Jorge suggested.

"I am hoping so, sir."

"We will talk later."

The call ended. Jorge thought about the whole situation more carefully as he made his way across town. He was ready for a fight. Any publisher who had the nerve to take on Jorge Hernandez knew what they were getting into and clearly, thought they had the proper amount of ammunition to fight back. However, they had greatly overestimated their power because he would feed them to the wolves without a second thought.

As soon as he walked through the doors of McMaster and Hopings Publishing, Jorge halted in stunned disbelief. Rather than the more sterile and dreary atmosphere he was expecting, Jorge instead discovered something that reminded him more of a fertility clinic or a yoga studio. The walls were a soft pink, with images of various book covers carefully displayed, each demonstrating titles that represented everything from reproductive health to bringing up children. There was a lemon scent that filled the room. Jorge felt all his original defenses stuck in neutral.

Behind the desk, a young Asian receptionist's head bobbed up from behind the keyboard. She was so small that Jorge almost missed her.

"Can I help you?" She spoke with a friendly tone, pushing her glasses closer to her eyes. "Do you have an appointment?"

"I'm here to meet.....ah..." Jorge thought for a moment. "You know, I think I have the wrong place."

"Are you looking for McMaster and Hopings Publishing?"

"*Si.*"

"Then you have the right place."

Jorge wanted to laugh but instead nodded.

"Who are you meeting with? Tonya or Sylvia?"

"I honestly have no clue," Jorge decided to move closer to the desk, a smooth grin curving his lips. "My associate made this here appointment. I did not get a name. I am Jorge Hernandez."

"Oh yes, I see here that you're here to meet *both* of them," She stood up, and Jorge was surprised to see that the receptionist was even shorter than his teenage daughter. "Come with me to the conference room."

Jorge didn't reply. He followed the miniature lady down the hallway. The theme that he discovered in the entranceway continued through the office, with more images representing maternal titles: everything from breastfeeding to dealing with temper tantrums. It took everything in his power not to laugh. He felt like he was in a twisted dream rather than having a serious business meeting.

"Right here, Mr. Hernandez," The tiny woman pointed into a small conference room where two white women sat. One was older with glasses and smooth blonde hair. The other was young, pretty with huge eyes, and dressed very professionally. Jorge turned and nodded at the receptionist, who smiled and walked away while he entered the office.

"Mr. Hernandez," The younger one stood up and gestured toward a chair, an overly zealous smile on her face. "Please come in and sit down."

"Thank you," Jorge remained courteous as he summed up the two women. This would be easy.

"I guess we should introduce ourselves," The younger one was nervous. Jorge could smell it. "I'm Tonya McMaster, and this is my mother, Sylvia Hopings."

"Ah yes," Jorge reached out to shake each of their hands. He noted both had a soft handshake, but the older woman was studying him carefully. "Nice to meet you both."

"We were happy to have you request a meeting with us," Tonya continued as they all sat down. "As you probably know, we had Jordan Patrick approach us about…."

"Excuse me," Jorge found his voice as he glanced around the conference room at more pictures that indicated that their books were not exactly in the same vein as his story. "I am a little confused. This here, it seems like you publish very different books than ah…let's say, biography or autobiography."

"We're trying to expand our titles," Tonya nodded, her expression growing serious. "I know, I can imagine what you must've thought walking into here…"

Jorge grinned and raised an eyebrow.

"We started in books about women, for women," Tonya continued. "But we want to get into different areas. We were considering some Canadian personalities, and Jordan's agent heard and…"

"Look, I am going to cut you off right there," Jorge put his hand in the air and noted both women sat up straighter when he started to speak. "I do not want this man writing about me, and I have already spoken to him. He will no longer be doing a book on me."

"Oh," Tonya's face flushed. "I thought maybe you…"

"You thought wrong," Jorge replied. "As a businessman, I do not think that this here would fit with your audience, and if it does, *my* story will probably not."

"Why is that, Mr. Hernandez?" Sylvia spoke up for the first time. "Women like various topics. We aren't just about children and families."

"Really?" Jorge waved his hand around to indicate the book covers in the office. "Is this something you have just figured out?"

"Granted," Sylvia continued while Tonya looked defeated. "It isn't our usual topic, but as she said, we wish to expand. You're a very colorful man, Mr. Hernandez. We're certain that people would enjoy learning about your life…where you come from, how you got here."

There was something in her tone that Jorge didn't like as he gave her a long look.

"Look, lady," Jorge leaned forward. "I have no interest in doing this here, silly book. I do not believe that anybody is interested in *where I come from* or *how I got here*. It is simple, I worked hard. That is all. It is not the exciting story of a celebrity that you may crave. My life is boring. I worked for my father for many years in Mexico. I come here to Canada. I marry my wife, and we bring up children together. As I said, that is all."

"That isn't all, Mr. Hernandez," Sylvia continued. "You're a strong businessman who has brought jobs here. You do a lot for immigrants…"

"Yes," Jorge nodded. "This here is a newspaper article at best. Not a book. As I said, my life is not that interesting."

"I think readers would think it is," Tonya jumped in. "People are fascinated with powerful people. They would love to hear your story. If you don't wish Jordan write this story…"

"This here, it is not a good time," Jorge cut her off. "Maybe later, in the future."

"But Mr. Hernandez," Sylvia jumped in. "If we don't write it here, someone else will."

"There's already talk," Tonya added.

"Is there?" Jorge was interested. "Who?"

"Once word got out…." Tonya attempted to explain.

"Look, there is only one way I would write this here book," Jorge spoke calmly, even though he was growing angry. "It is if Tom Makerson would write it. He and I have discussed it before, but it was never the right time. However, I do not want attention brought to my family. It causes unnecessary stress. This is why I left politics."

"It's impossible," Tonya shook her head. "You're very well known…"

"Lots of other people are," Jorge reminded her.

"But not like you," Sylvia spoke in a confident voice. "And there are a lot of stories."

"There are a lot of stories about a lot of people," Jorge reminded her as he shot her a warning look. "This here, it does not mean there must be a book too."

"We can write it any way you want," Tonya spoke with desperation in her voice. "You can write it yourself or Tom…"

"Look," Jorge cut her off. "I must think about this here."

"Of course," Sylvia nodded.

"But if we do it," Jorge looked between them as he stood up. He was silent for a long time, studying both. "We play by my rules."

"That is no problem," Tonya spoke with relief on her face, while Sylvia looked less at ease.

"Ah, but I would suggest you think about this some more," Jorge suggested as he waved a finger in the air as an awkwardness filled the room. "This here publishing house may never be the same again."

With that, he turned and walked out the door.

CHAPTER 18

"It was strange," Jorge confirmed as he laughed and glanced at his wife, followed by Makerson and Marco, who sat around him in the VIP room at *Princesa Maria*. "It was like I was walking into *The Wizard of Oz* or something, including the…you know, the little people."

"Were they all….little people?" Paige appeared surprised. "Like, the women you met too?"

"Well, no, they were not," Jorge laughed. "But what I mean is the receptionist, she was shorter than Maria and the office, it looked like a business for women. Pink walls, you know, pictures of book covers about having babies and other things like this. Not exactly what I was expecting when I go to see a publisher who wants to write about Jorge Hernandez."

Marco was the first to laugh while Paige merely grinned and looked away.

"Oh yeah, that's right," Makerson jumped in. "McMaster and Hopings are more…I don't want to say *women's* books, but you know…."

"Well, it's fair to say books about having babies might be considered women's books," Paige jumped in with a shrug then turned to her husband. "But I can only imagine your reaction walking in there."

"I thought this here must be a joke," Jorge laughed. "My life, it is a million miles away from what they normally publish."

"I heard they wanted to become more diverse to increase their audience," Makerson recalled. "Yes, someone was talking about that at work. I think they sent out a press release, but no one cared. They want to increase their sales, and this seems like the best way to do it."

"Well, a book about me, it would increase their sales," Jorge spoke matter of factly, while beside him, his wife laughed.

"Egos are included…"

"Well, *mi amor,*" Jorge raised his hands in the air. "I would like to think I am more interesting than books about children with temper tantrums and such things, you know."

"You might want to look into picking up a copy of that one while you're there," Paige reminded him. "See what they say about a child that is already a bully at age 2."

Marco laughed again.

"He is a Hernandez," Jorge spoke to Paige. "He is merely showing his dominance."

"Funny how they don't see it that way at the daycare," Paige spoke smoothly.

"Yeah, well, what do they know?" Jorge shrugged. "These days, everyone wants to bring their kids up to be weak, to be powerless, to not fight back. This here, it is not realistic in the world."

"It is true," Marco spoke with wide eyes. "My kids, they are in martial arts. You cannot have it any other way at this time. They need to protect themselves."

"Yes, from kids like mine," Paige laughed, and Marco joined in. Jorge shrugged as if he didn't understand the issue.

"So, they still want to do the book about you," Makerson asked as he leaned back in his chair. "Even after your…conversation?"

"Yes, well, apparently, they believe others are going to write the book if we don't," Jorge told him. "This here, I do not like."

"This could be them saying shit to get you to do what they want," Makerson suggested. "That's the first I heard of it."

"Sir, I am looking at many publishers in Canada," Marco confirmed. "I do not see where any others are talking about this, but it does not mean it's not being discussed in person."

"At least if we do the book," Makerson suggested. "Then we can write it how you want it. Create the narrative."

"But the only problem is that if others jump on the bandwagon," Paige shook her head. "What if more start digging? What are we supposed to do? We can't always monitor every publishing house."

"And there's self-publishing too," Makerson reminded them. "Someone else can write a book and get it out there, without anyone knowing…"

"If only I were not so interesting to the people," Jorge shook his head with false modesty. "But I am very exciting, I guess."

"Jorge, come on if the wrong person…" Paige started.

"If the wrong person, he writes a book about me and says too much," Jorge cut her off. "You know that it will be the last book he writes that I can promise you. I do not feel, however, that anyone here has access to this here information from my past."

"Well, it's not just your past," Paige reminded him. "Since coming to Canada…"

"Too many people, *mi amor,* they will fall with me if I am pushed to the ground," Jorge muttered. "That, you know."

"You know," Makerson jumped in. "I think if you work with me to write this, then clarify to the public that it is the *only* book with the whole, true story, publishers won't be as inclined to revisit it. It sends a message to the industry as a whole, that it's not worth the money they'd invest. People want to read about you, but they want the truth. There's a shame factor that comes with reading or writing tabloid kind of crap."

"Yeah, if you get that message out there," Paige said with reluctance in her voice. "It might help, but I'm just not so sure."

"The publisher you were talking to today seems to have their ear to the ground," Makerson reminded him. "It's not in their best interest that someone puts out another book to compete, so they will let you know if there's an issue."

"They already know that I talked to Jordan Patrick," Jorge confirmed. "So I think they may see that I am a man who can stop things."

"Exactly," Makerson nodded. "You could work together on that. As I said, it's in both your best interest."

"Sir, I can also keep on top of things," Marco confirmed. "Also, I have looked. There are rumors on the internet that you are involved in some.... shall we say, criminal activity, but most sound like conspiracy theories."

"We can address that in the book," Makerson jumped in. "Talk about how there have always been rumors swirling around about you, and suggest that it stems from racist views of Mexicans. We can dive into that but, at the same time, find the things they might associate you with and find a way to explain it within the book. I mean, so it's not obvious."

"Sir, there is talk online that you are associated with the cartel," Marco confirmed. "But most people step on such rumors saying that cartel people, they do not move to another country and start a legal business."

"Is that all?" Paige cringed a bit, and Jorge placed his hand on her back.

"There are also rumors about the sex clubs."

"I was an investor at that time, nothing more."

"Yes, but they say there were drugs you brought in."

"This could be those rumors I talked about," Makerson shook his head. "There are drugs in every club, come on, you can't seriously tie the two, I don't think."

"There are others, sir," Marco continued. "But they are insinuations. Mostly that you run Alec Athas, that you have control over the police and others. But again, there is no proof. Just a few voices, which no one takes seriously."

"I don't like this," Paige shook her head. "I wish people could forget about us."

"Wishes, they do not happen, just because we hope," Jorge calmly reminded her as his hand continued to rub her back. "But we have some control, and that is what we are talking about here."

"The thing is books can take a long time to write," Makerson continued. "Which is good because we can put them off, but it might also be bad because someone might try to beat us to be the first one out."

Paige shook her head. She appeared defeated.

"Look, I do not know what the solution is here," Jorge replied. "I would like to say that this here is easy to fix, but it is not."

"You have a lot of power," Makerson reminded him. "And you have a lot of money. Let people know that any false stories that come out about you will result in a lawsuit. None of these publishers want that shit at their door."

Paige appeared hopeful.

"You know, I got no problem issuing a threat."

Marco laughed.

"That's what I mean," Makerson replied. "I can't see anyone going up against you. I don't think anyone would be that stupid."

"If they believe these rumors, sir," Marco reminded him. "They will know better."

Jorge said nothing but nodded.

"Sir, I will continue to monitor this situation," Marco reminded him. "But I will also counter anyone who speaks against you and try to create more intrigue around the positive things you do."

"This here, it should make you feel better," Jorge turned to his wife. "I know you do not want this attention on our family, but it appears it is already happening."

"I suppose," She still appeared hesitant. "I'm scared that…"

"It will be fine," He assured her. "This will be ok. We have people who are on top of everything."

"I think you and I should meet this publisher together next time," Makerson said as he glanced around the table, "Maybe you too, Paige."

"Maybe," She spoke softly, which tweaked something deep inside Jorge. Suddenly his thoughts were not on the book.

"I think we can control this," Makerson nodded. "I think between us all, we can make sure things stay on track. We write the book that you want Jorge, and then move on."

"But will it be that easy?" Paige didn't appear to be reassured.

"It will have to be, *mi amor,*" Jorge assured her. "Because if it is not easy for me, then it will be *hell* for them. That is a promise."

CHAPTER 19

"I thought this time," Jorge spoke across the conference room table to both Tonya McMaster and Sylvia Hopings. "I would bring Tom Makerson since he is the only person I trust to write this here book."

"So, you've decided to do it?" Tonya spoke enthusiastically, leaning forward on the table. "That's great because…"

"Well, no, I did not say that either," Jorge cut her off and shook his head, glancing at Makerson, who showed no expression. "What I am saying is that *if* I decide to do this, that it will be on my terms. There is no other way."

"That would be fine," Tonya sat back and nodded. "Reasonable. After all, Tom is the editor for a major paper but, will that mean you'll be taking time off?"

"I hadn't thought that far yet," Makerson replied and glanced at Jorge.

"There will be a timeline," Tonya attempted to explain, and Tom cut her off.

"*I'm* aware of timelines. I deal with them every day."

"I don't think anyone disputes that you can do this," Sylvia finally spoke. "But we need to know that this is a priority, not just a side project."

"When I said things would have to be on my terms," Jorge sternly reminded her. "I meant it. That includes how Makerson gets the work done. This will take time. I have over 40 years to remember. It will not happen fast."

The women exchanged looks, and neither said a thing.

"This here is new to you," Jorge continued. "Writing a biography, there are a lot of details to put together."

"This isn't our first rodeo," Sylvia spoke bluntly, and Jorge noticed Makerson tensed. "We're aware that things take time, but we also can't have them stretching out too long. We need to see results."

"Even if it's a chapter at a time," Tonya attempted to smooth things over. "That's reasonable, right?"

"Sure," Makerson nodded. "But my concern is that I'll start this book, and others will jump in to do the same."

"We don't want that any more than you," Tonya assured him. "We're trying to expand our titles, so we are already out on a limb."

"Then would we keep this quiet," Jorge asked. "Or would we let the world know, and also let them know it will be the only...ah...what you call it?"

"Authorized," Makerson nodded. "We don't need copycats, and if we do, we have to make sure that people know they are crap."

"We will keep our ears to the ground," Sylvia assured them.

"And if you hear of anything," Jorge said. "You would need to tell me right away."

"But, you can't...." Tonya shook her head.

"I can, and I will stop them," Jorge cut her off. "I have no problem suing anyone who has false information about me, and from what I understand, there is a lot of false information out there. I cut that off at the knees."

Tonya nodded while Sylvia studied him.

"We would need a press release," Sylvia stated. "With our company name put out there. We hope to bring attention to our brand and maybe bring along similar projects in the future. Perhaps we can do that once we have the details ironed out, along with whatever you see fit to do to keep the foxes out of the henhouse."

"The foxes, they will keep away from *my* henhouse," Jorge said as he exchanged looks with Makerson. "We could make a video, do an interview, whatever is needed. We would be on the same timeline for this here."

"So we have a deal?" Tonya's face lit up.

"I must talk to my lawyer, of course, but it appears so," Jorge was hesitant. "But I will tell you now that this book, it will most likely be boring. My life, it is not that interesting."

"People are interested, though," Sylvia reminded him. "And that is the main thing. A book that talks about your struggles, your family, something relatable to the average reader are often the best fit. Controversial books rarely have the same amount of substance."

"We want to keep our reputation," Tonya added.

"So do I," Jorge replied as he stood up to let them know that the meeting was over. "I will talk to my lawyer, who will be in touch. Please let Makerson know where we are at too."

The meeting ended shortly after, as Jorge and Makerson made their way out of the building in silence, only speaking once outside.

"Do you really have someone to take on some of your duties?" Jorge asked as they walked down the sidewalk.

"I hope so," Makerson muttered. "I can't let go of the reins completely, but…"

"Would it help if I wrote out what I remembered?" Jorge asked. "Or should we talk?"

"Both," Makerson confirmed. "But if you write down or record your memories and a timeline for each chapter, it would help. The first chapter being about your parents. Maybe some of their history, and your birth, then we will get together to talk about it in more detail, or for you to answer any questions. I want to keep the vibe of this book very grounded. I'm leaning toward the theme being that we're more powerful than we think."

"Makerson," Jorge shook his head. "The problem here is that most people do not think they are powerful. How many times do you hear people say that there's nothing they can do about some specific situation? This here, it is all the time. People take the easy way out, but me, I have never taken the easy way out."

"Right there," Makerson said just as the men were about to go their separate ways. "Is exactly why this book is going to be amazing. People need to hear that. We live in a compliant society, where we're trained to make as little noise as possible. And you go against the grain."

"I always will, *amigo,*" Jorge grinned. "That, you can count on."

The men ended their exchange on a positive note. Jorge rushed to his SUV, noting that the winter winds were creeping in. As he drove along the Toronto streets, he glanced around at Christmas decorations already out, sparkling and full of light, but unfortunately, Jorge carried a dark spot in his heart for the holiday season. He attempted to put up a good front for his family, but his childhood had been grim, so the automatic joy of a holiday was foreign to him. He played the role for his children, but Jorge knew from how Paige looked at him, she recognized the bitter memories that never disappeared.

Arriving at the production house, he found Tony in his office. Jolene sat beside him, causing Jorge to grow angry even before he entered the room.

"Jolene, why are you here?" Jorge asked as soon as he walked through the doors. "I did not invite you to this here meeting."

"I am a big part of this company, and I want to be here," She pushed her breasts out as her face hardened. "I have a right to…"

"The casting couch, Jolene, you…"

"I do not have a casting couch," She argued back, cutting off Jorge's words. "Whoever tell you that is a liar. There was one man and one man only, and that is all. He wasn't even in the auditions."

Jorge took a deep breath. Not in the mood to argue with Jolene, he sat down and said nothing.

"Anyway," Tony cut in before the two of them could potentially go at it again. "I have some news. I think I have a writer for the cartel show you want to do, and also, I got the outline for the first show of season three of *Eat the Rich*, I thought you might like to see."

"This here, it is perfect," Jorge nodded, starting to calm down while on the other side of the table, Jolene stood her ground, glaring at him. "Tell me more."

"Well, we found a seasoned writer to work on the series," Tony started as he reached for his cup of coffee. "I knew her way back when and…"

"And you have a woman writing a show about cartels?" Jorge asked with laughter in his voice. "This here, I must see."

"Why?" Jolene shot out at him. "You think a woman cannot write about such things? You are such a sexist…"

"Jolene, calm yourself down," Jorge put his hand in the air. "I cannot deal with fighting with you. If you want to be part of this here meeting, do not get on my nerves. I was not saying this…"

"It was implied," Jolene complained.

"I only laugh because I just visit with a publisher who wants to do a book about me," Jorge attempted to explain. "I think, you know, they must already write this kind of book, but then I walk in and the office is pink, with pictures of covers about pregnancy and children…."

"Really?" Tony appeared surprised. "I thought you were only contemplating this. So, you're doing it?"

"Yes, it appears if I do not," Jorge raised an eyebrow. "Someone else will."

"You?" Jolene leaned in. "You are writing a book about your life? Is this a good idea?"

"It will be written carefully," Jorge clarified to them both. "By Makerson."

"Oh," Jolene appeared to approve.

"Can we do something in the production house, maybe around the same time?" Tony suggested. "Like a documentary. Maybe I can work with Makerson?"

"Well, yes, I mean, if he agrees," Jorge shrugged. "I do not see why not."

"Oh, Paige she will not like this," Jolene shook her head. "none of this."

"She is not happy about it," Jorge agreed. "But if the book is going to be written, then at least, I can make sure it is done right."

"Oh, I do not like," Jolene shook her head. "The more I think…"

"Anyway," Jorge cut her off and turned toward Tony. "So, you got a writer?"

"Yes, we discussed some famous cartels, and she's going to write something based on information already out there," Tony nodded. "It will take some time to research, but she already has some ideas. Jolene will work closely with her."

"*Perfecto,*" He nodded at the Colombian, and she started to let her guard down.

"And of course, if we can do this biography based on the book," Tony continued. "That would be great for all of us. As for *Eat the Rich,* I'm doing as you suggested and having the first show focus on changes in the media.

It will be the then and now. Concerns regarding advertising dollars. I have lots of ideas."

"I like this."

"I also have the other shows outlined," Tony reached for an iPad and tapped on it for a minute before turning it around for Jorge. "I have different people assigned to different episodes in hopes of putting it together quickly."

Jorge nodded and sat back and nodded. Everything was coming together.

CHAPTER 20

"So, we will start by talking about the Hernandez Production Company," Makerson jotted down some notes. Beside him, Jorge nodded in agreement. "Specifically the new season of *Eat the Rich,* then go to the book."

"Wait, I just think," Paige spoke up from across the room where she had been nervously pacing. "Maybe this isn't a good idea. Maybe we should wait until…"

"Paige, we cannot wait," Jorge shook his head. "The publishers, they are releasing a press release, and we agree…"

"I know but," Paige shook her head and walked toward them. "What if….what if some unsavory characters come out of the woodwork, thinking that you are going to reveal names? I don't want a surprise on my doorstep."

"Paige, calm down," Jorge spoke gently. "I promise you, I think of all these things. We will take care of it."

"Yes, we will dive into how his life is supposedly boring," Makerson grinned. "He'll elaborate how he's a run-of-the mill businessman coming from Mexico."

"You know, the truth, Paige," Jorge teased her and winked but noted that she still appeared anxious. "You do not have to worry. I know what I am doing."

She didn't look convinced.

"I can give you a minute," Makerson stood up and sat his notes on the chair. "I have to go check on something anyway. You two talk."

Paige didn't reply, and Jorge gave him a nod. Neither said a word until he left, and the door was closed.

"You know how I feel," Paige shook her head defiantly. "So there's nothing to talk about. You've already made up your mind."

"Paige, if we do not do this," Jorge stood up and crossed the room to where she stood. "Then someone else will."

"But we can find that person and…"

"Yes, but then another person will replace that person," Jorge attempted to show the logic. "It is not that simple. If we write this book, we have control."

"But a documentary too?"

"It will reflect that book," Jorge assure her. "It will be harmless, and it does make sense since I do own the production house, *si?*"

"I just," Paige's voice grew emotional, and Jorge pulled her into a hug.

"*Mi amor,* this here, it will be ok," Jorge assured her as he breathed in the flowery scent she wore. "We are safe. This here, it will be fine."

"If I find out anyone else is writing…." She began to pull away.

"You do what you want to do," Jorge nodded as he looked into her eyes. "You know me. I find it sexy when you defend my honor."

She grinned but looked away as if wanting to hide it.

"Trust me," Jorge leaned in and kissed the top of her head. "I know what I am doing."

A few minutes later, Jorge was seated beside Makerson as they started their interview. Jorge noted that they already had a vast amount of viewers for the live stream, even though it was in the middle of a weekday. People were paying attention.

After a short introduction to Jorge and mentioning his new production house, Makerson jumped right into the interview.

"My understanding is you have lots of projects coming up," Makerson spoke more toward the camera but turned his attention back to Jorge. "Including a new season of *Eat the Rich before the Rich Eat You.* This season, dealing with the media and how it has changed. Would you like to elaborate on that?"

"Yes, thank you," Jorge spoke graciously. "We decided to focus on the media for this season because there is often distrust for it. People are not sure if they believe what they see in the news. They worry that they are not getting the whole story or that in some cases, not the story at all."

"Is it just on the news?" Makerson asked.

"No, that is one element," Jorge confirmed. "I do not want to get into a lot of details yet, but we will focus on how the media has changed overall, how advertisers have influenced what we see, how music channels have disappeared. So many things that are being analyzed by my team."

"That sounds interesting," Makerson spoke with sincerity in his voice, followed by a joke. "As a newspaper editor, should I be worried?"

Jorge grinned and clapped his hands together.

"Well, I cannot give everything away, can I?" He teased.

Makerson laughed, carefully glancing at the number of people watching. Jorge noted it too. They purposely started light, waiting for a larger viewership before making the announcement. Across the room, Jorge could see that his wife still had a look of concern on her face.

"I guess we may as well jump into the main topic we're here to talk about today," Makerson spoke brightly toward the camera, then returned his gaze to Jorge. "We both have an announcement"

"Yes, we do," Jorge nodded. "I recently met with the McMaster and Hopings publishing, here in Toronto, and they asked if I would be interested in writing an autobiography about my life. To this," Jorge looked directly at the camera. "I was surprised because my life is quite boring." He stopped to laugh and returned his attention to Makerson, showing his modesty. "However, I did say yes, if they do feel that people want to read my book. I would say that would be fine."

"I think there's an interest," Makerson confirmed. "After all, you're an immigrant, a businessman, someone who has worked hard to make your dreams come true. That's inspiring to people."

"Well, my hope," Jorge continued to speak in a toned-down voice. "Is to give inspiration to other immigrants who have come to this country. You know, English is my second language. I can relate to their dreams, fears, but with the inspiration to do something wonderful. I want to show that it is possible. At least, this here is my hope for the book."

"Was this something you were thinking about doing before?" Makerson asked as he tilted his head and looked at Jorge.

"No," He lied but spoke so earnestly that no one would ever know that the two men had discussed it many times. "It never did occur to me that people would find this interesting."

Makerson smiled. "I think you're modest."

"But, my English skills, they are not wonderful," Jorge grinned, showing the camera a slightly bashful side as if this was a sincere concern to him. "So, of course, no one would want me to write this myself. The poor ladies at McMaster and Hopings would lose their minds fixing my English. So I decide instead to ask someone I trust to write it for me, and since you are such a wonderful journalist, Tom, I thought that you would be ideal for this project."

"I guess that's the other part of the news," Makerson laughed and gestured toward the camera. "Although, I heard a rumor earlier today that it was already common knowledge."

"Rumors," Jorge confirmed with a smooth grin. "They spread fast."

"Well, I'm honored that you asked," Makerson replied as he placed a hand on his chest. "This is new to me, but of course, I'm excited about the challenge."

"It is new to me as well," Jorge confirmed. "It is not something I thought I would ever do."

"How do you feel about this project?" Makerson followed up with a grin. "Hopefully, you have a great memory."

"Honestly, I do not even know where to start," Jorge shook his head. "I mean, it is hard to remember so many things and, as I say, the early years of my life were quite…uneventful. Just working at my father's company in Mexico and learning about business."

"That was in the coffee business?"

"*Si*, we started small but eventually grew."

"You learned a lot there?"

"Everything I know about business," Jorge nodded as he thought about the actual events of his youth. Most of which involved murder, torture, and intimidation. "There are some things you simply cannot learn in business school."

"I see people are asking when the book will be out?"

"It will take some time," Jorge replied. "I have started many notes, but it is difficult to remember everything. I will do the best I can. After all, as my daughter says, '*Papá*, you are old!'."

The two men laughed.

"It's going to be fun," Makerson spoke sincerely. "I certainly look forward to it."

"Me, as well," Jorge nodded. "I do think it is good to go down memory lane from time to time. It is good to reflect, to remember where we come from and what we have experienced. No matter how young or *old* we are."

"This is true," Makerson shifted gears. "I also wanted to stress that you'll be fully involved in writing this book so it will be authorized. People will know they'll be reading the truth."

"Tom, the people in my circle," Jorge pulled his arms out to indicate an amount. "There are few people who know me or my life's story. People have unfortunately made up stories, which is entertainment, but it is not factual. This book that you and I will work on together, it will be the truth."

"Do you anticipate others trying to do the same?"

"Not necessarily, because as I say," Jorge waved his hand around. "No others will have my approval. Therefore you might be reading fiction, not fact."

"Yes, I agree," Makerson nodded. "This is a concern of mine as well. I hope that people realize that there is a lot of fake news out there. Our book will hopefully alleviate false information."

"Yes, I agree," Jorge nodded as he spoke toward the camera. "The truth, it is important to me. If I learn of any copycats that wish to write about me, then I must make sure that this misinformation does *not* get out there."

To most, it was a simple, fair statement. But to those who knew Jorge Hernandez, they knew this statement carried a powerful punch that would knock any opponents out.

CHAPTER 21

"Sir, we might have a problem," Marco said as soon as Jorge answered the phone. "Where and when can I meet you, please?"

Jorge glanced at his wife, who sat on the passenger side of his SUV. Concerned filled her eyes.

"*Amigo,* I am on my way to the bar right now," Jorge replied as he glanced ahead at the traffic. "I…"

"I will meet you," Marco automatically cut him off.

"Ok," Jorge replied. "See you soon."

As soon as the call ended, he reached out and touched his wife's hand.

"You, you worry too much," Jorge insisted. "This here, it will be fine."

"I feel like you're putting yourself out there too much," Paige reminded him. "I don't want to seem like I'm nagging, but…"

"*Mi amor,*" Jorge spoke gently. "If anyone decides to write a book about me, then chances are they are already aware of what I am capable of."

She nodded but didn't look convinced.

"Trust me," Jorge insisted as he looked ahead at traffic. "My reputation, it proceeds me."

The couple shared a look, and he winked at her, then with a grin on his face, focused on the traffic ahead.

Jorge was parking the SUV when Marco sped around the corner on his bicycle. By the time the couple reached the bar's entrance, the IT specialist was already walking beside the bike, his helmet in hand, a laptop bag swung over his shoulder.

"Sir, I was doing some research," Marco began as Jorge unlocked the bar's main entrance, nodding as he listened. "and I see that…

A loud smash from inside the bar alerted everyone's attention. Jorge reached inside his leather jacket for a gun. Marco fell behind as Jorge and Paige rushed in to find Chase standing in the middle of the floor, his face red with fury. The remainder of a barstool was scattered throughout the room.

"I do not know what you were trying to hit with that there stool," Jorge pointed to the middle of the room as Marco walked in with a shocked expression, pulling his bike beside him, and Paige locked the door. "But I do not think it lived."

Chase didn't say anything at first, shaking his head.

"Should we talk?" Jorge pointed toward the office. "Or?"

"No, it's fine," Chase swung his hand in the air, his face flustered. "I may as well tell all of you."

"What happened?" Paige asked in a soft voice.

"I was talking to my ex," Chase said as he took a deep breath. "We…. there's been some issues with the boys. You know, they talk to me less and less as they get older. Her new husband is their 'father' in their eyes, and I'm just some guy."

"I don't think that's true," Paige tried to assure him, but Jorge didn't appear so convinced.

"This here, it is not right," Jorge said in a quiet voice.

"I can't do anything about it," Chase shook his head. "The kids want Audrey's husband to adopt them. They want me out of their life."

"What?" Paige was surprised and shook her head.

"This is not right, sir," Marco said as he stepped ahead. "You are still their father."

"It doesn't matter," Chase shook his head. "Audrey wanted to do this before."

Jorge and Chase shared a knowing look.

"But now it's the boys asking," Chase took another deep breath, his eyes full of sadness. "They want to change their last name to his, and

Audrey is pregnant with another baby, and…the kids want them to all have the same last name."

"But can they not *just* change the last name?" Jorge was confused.

"I don't think that's what they mean," Chase gently replied. "They asked, and I couldn't say no. Then Audrey got on the phone and said, 'I know what kind of lifestyle you have now, and I think it's better the kids not be a part of it.'"

"Oh, is that so?" Jorge grew defensive. "How would she *know* anything?"

"She knows I work for you," Chase replied honestly. "She's heard rumors."

"These are the rumors I worry about," Paige replied as she touched Jorge's arm. "I'm worried that they will grow."

"Sir, this is what I wanted to talk to you about," Marco grew concerned. "I have been doing some research…"

"And?" Jorge felt torn between this new information and what Chase had just told him. "Please tell me that there's not another book."

"I do not see that, no," Marco shook his head. "But what I do see isn't good either, sir."

"Maybe we should go into Chase's office," Jorge pointed behind the bar. "Before staff comes in."

"I should throw out this broken stool," Chase shook his head.

"No, leave it for now," Jorge insisted. "We all need to calm down. Let us go in there and…sort this out."

Jorge pointed toward Chase's office, and they made their way into the cramped room. On the desk sat a picture of Chase's sons: a reminder of what should be the first matter that needed attention. Everything else could wait.

Jorge turned his phone off, and the others followed as they all sat in their usual seats.

"Now," Jorge said and took a deep breath. "Let us start from the beginning. Chase, what is it you want to do here."

"I don't think I can do anything," Chase shook his head as he sat behind the desk. "This is my kids asking."

"Are you sure your ex didn't encourage it?" Paige asked.

Chase shrugged.

"You will still be in their lives, no?" Jorge was confused.

"The truth is that things have been falling apart for a long time," Chase confirmed. "Less FaceTime, fewer visits in the summer. They were young when I left Hennessey, and I guess…."

"I blame the mother," Jorge cut him off. "It is her job to encourage them to see you, to talk to you."

"She does try," Chase shook his head. "In fairness, I know she does, but it's the distance thing."

"Chase," Jorge spoke solemnly as he carefully chose his words. "I do believe you will stay in their lives, but the fact is that they have developed a close relationship with this here other man. As much as it may not be what you wish for unless you move back and are in their lives regularly, I do not see what else you can do. But this here does not mean that it will always be this way. Kids, they change. As they get older and become teenagers, they may feel differently. You may have more to offer than that sleepy, redneck town."

"It's true," Paige agreed. "Just stay in their lives, be there for them, and things will fall into place as they get older."

"I don't think I have a choice." Chase quietly replied.

"I'm sorry," Paige shook her head. "I know this is hard."

Chase nodded and looked down.

"Ok, well, we can and will talk more about this later," Jorge said and took a deep breath. "Meanwhile, if there is anything we can do, Chase?"

Now resembling the wide-eyed teenager Jorge had met many years ago, his defenses on the ground, the strong, powerful man suddenly appeared weak and defenseless. He looked lost in thought as he shook his head no.

"Sir, I do need to speak to you," Marco began and glanced at Chase. "We can talk in the other room. Perhaps that is better."

"No," Chase shook his head. "That's fine."

"Ok," Marco hesitated and returned his attention to Jorge. "Sir, I do not see where anyone else is writing a book or planning to…so this is good news."

"Yet," Paige reminded them.

"I did see a few emails between major publishers," Marco admitted. "And most people, they want to keep out of this completely. They say Jorge will 'lawyer up'. They say the topic is 'too dicey'. They think it is too much for a book, but there is other talk."

"Oh?" Jorge asked as he leaned toward Marco.

"When I hacked emails within these publishing houses," Marco continued. "I saw where a man was telling his coworker that his friend, who has a YouTube show, plans to address the 'truth' about you. He plans to talk about it in an upcoming episode. He talks on his show about true crime, corruption, government, that kind of thing."

"Oh, does he?" Jorge took this in stride. "Does anyone watch this here show?"

"Yes, sir," Marco nodded. "He has quite a following."

"Is there a way we can get him removed from YouTube?" Paige asked. "I know that it's been known to happen…"

"He will go to another platform," Marco reminded them. "His main show is YouTube, but he has other places where he also places these videos."

"So, it's not the show," Paige replied. "It's the person."

"And who is this man?"

"He goes by the name Sonny McTea."

"This here, it is a real name?" Jorge was confused.

"I think his real first name is Sonny, sir," Marco shook his head. "But I think his last name is Mac…something else. He's in his twenties, somewhat flamboyant."

"A white boy?" Jorge asked with a raised eyebrow.

"Yes, sir," Marco nodded. "Let me show you."

Within minutes, Marco had his laptop turned on. All four watched Sonny McTea talking about local politics, rumors surrounding Alec Athas, and he ended the show by talking about future topics. He had dark-rimmed glasses that were too big for his face, while he wore bright clothes that were somewhat distracting as he spoke excitedly about each subject.

"And of course, Jorge Hernandez is telling his life story," Sonny McTea announced. "Will it be the boring, predictable book he claims, or will it be a page out of the Mexican mafia's playbook? I will have the full story in the next episode."

Jorge felt anger shooting through his veins as his heart began to race.

"Sir, I am wondering if Andrew, he might know more about this man," Marco suggested as he closed the laptop and attempted to get Jorge's attention. "I see where he follows him."

"I will call him," Jorge turned his phone back on. "This here, it ends now."

"I have looked into him more, sir," Marco nervously continued. "He is researching the rumors about your online."

"Hello," Andrew's voice echoed over the phone. Jorge put it on speaker.

"Andrew, I got a question for you," Jorge spoke sharply. "Do you know some *gringo* named Sonny McTea?"

"That greasy motherfucker," Andrew spoke dryly. "Yeah, I know him. Why?"

"He does this here show," Jorge replied. "And I'm the next topic."

"He's in the Toronto area. I know where he lives," Andrew said with laughter in his voice. "And I can't wait till he meets you!"

CHAPTER 22

"So, this is where the magic happens?" Jorge spoke with sarcasm in his voice after barging into Sonny McTea's apartment, with Chase, Andrew, and Paige in tow. He glanced around the cramped space and shook his head. He turned toward Andrew. "This better be good to drag me to this here, *shitty* part of the city."

"This is where he records his show," Andrew spoke calmly, pointing toward a blue screen that sat behind a small kitchen table, a light hung over the area in an amateur fashion. "Just some shitty little apartment in the dirtiest part of the city."

"Somehow, this here makes sense," Jorge glanced toward Sonny McTea, who appeared slightly unnerved as he stood aside. Wearing dirty pants and an old hoodie, he wasn't presenting the same professional look that he demonstrated in his shows. "And you, you are the man who wants to do a show about me? Is this here true?"

Sonny nodded and opened his mouth to say something but stopped. Nearby, Chase had his arms crossed over his chest, glaring at the little man, while Paige remained poised, quiet.

"For a talk show host," Jorge nodded in his direction and glanced back at Andrew. "He don't do much talking."

"Oh, but he's got lots to say when he gets in front of the camera," Andrew reminded him, as he gestured toward the home studio in the kitchen area. "Trust me. He got lots to say."

"I hope this here does not include me," Jorge glanced toward Sonny, his hand in the air. "Because if you got something to say, then maybe we should discuss it first. I can tell you the facts."

Sonny appeared hesitant under his glare.

"Do you speak?" Jorge pushed as he moved forward. "Because this here is fortunate for you. See I heard you were going to discuss me in an upcoming episode of your little pretend show on the internet, and I thought, at least I can come over and sort your information out first."

"I…" Sonny nervously started as Jorge moved closer, staring at him.

"Because misinformation may lead to other problems," Jorge continued. "This way, I give you the…opportunity to not make these errors."

"I was going to talk about some stuff I found online," Sonny finally spoke but his face grew pale. "I…"

"Tread fucking carefully," Jorge said in a quiet yet, strong voice. "It is important that you get your facts straight. People, they get very angry when you make mistakes. It causes them not to trust you, to walk away. And it causes them to shoot and ask questions later. Metaphorically speaking, of course."

Sonny nodded as he stepped back from Jorge, who in turn, stepped ahead.

"And," Jorge continued. "We do not want to do this."

"No," Sonny's voice was barely audible.

"There is already so much misinformation online," Paige spoke calmly from behind. "And when you have kids, you can't be too careful."

"Do you have kids, *Mr. McTea*?" Jorge asked, mimicking his name.

"No," Sonny shook his head.

"Parents?" Jorge pushed as he moved closer to the anxious, young man.

"No…I mean, yes…." Sonny answered nervously. "I…"

"Exactly," Jorge cut him off. "So you understand that protecting your *familia,* it is important, am I right?"

Jorge stared down the sheepish Youtube star until he could almost smell his fear.

"You don't want to fuck around with this guy," Andrew pointed out as he casually looked around Sonny's apartment. "He ain't joking."

"I....I understand...."

"Good," Jorge nodded. "This here, it is good. We have an understanding."

"I won't do..." Sonny began.

"Oh no, you will do the show," Jorge shook his head as he shoved his hands in his leather jacket pocket, causing Sonny to tense up. "But you will do it *my* way."

"Yes, I will, I..."

"And you will do it while I am here," Jorge continued. "Just to make sure there are no...misunderstandings."

"Yeah, but when he gets on there live," Andrew shook his head, pointing to the makeshift studio. "He can say any goddam shit he wants."

"Oh, I am pretty sure he will not be doing that," Jorge assured Andrew. "This here, it would not be a good look for him."

"What...what do you want me to say?" Sonny stumbled. "I can say whatever..."

"Oh, you *will* say what I want," Jorge assured him. "I am thinking, we should have an interview. Right here. Right now. Live. You and I will talk about what you have heard, and I will correct you. I tell you now, and this here will be the last you talk of it because, if you do, again...."

"I...no, I won't," Sonny started to cough nervously.

"You better fix that up," Jorge pointed toward his throat. "Because you need to be asking me some questions, and we are doing it soon."

"Maybe we should tell him the questions to ask," Paige suggested. "Just to make sure there is no confusion."

"Mi amor," Jorge commented. "It will be simple. He will mention rumors he saw online, and I will correct him."

"That's it?" Paige asked as she shook his head.

"We will talk about my new book," Jorge shrugged. "A few quick questions. This here, it gives him what he wants because *mi amor,* all he wants is attention."

"I...I need to fix my hair, put on a shirt...."

"Andrew," Jorge glanced toward the scrawny kid, who continued to snoop around the apartment. "Watch him."

Andrew nodded as he fixated his attention on Sonny.

"We don't got all day," He pointed toward the next room. "Go pretty up."

Sonny followed orders, heading toward his bedroom with Andrew in tow.

Chase moved closer to Jorge.

"I don't know," He shook his head, speaking in a low voice. "He's going to be live, so he can turn this shit around on a dime."

"He won't if he has guns pointed toward his head," Jorge commented as he glanced between Chase and his wife. "And he *will* have a couple."

"He knows you won't shoot him live," Chase pointed out.

"We have Andrew ready to turn off the internet."

Chase appeared satisfied as he nodded.

A few minutes later, Sonny emerged from his room with Andrew behind him, appearing bored.

"We got a plan," Jorge said as Sonny moved toward the makeshift studio. "Andrew, you get near the modem. If we suddenly need to have things shut down, you do it."

Andrew nodded and glanced across the room, finding the small, plastic box in question.

"Chase, Paige, you know what to do," Jorge said as he fixed his tie and headed toward the table where the laptop sat. Sonny reluctantly did the same. "Now, my friend, you will do your job and do it well because if not, see that beautiful woman there…"

Sonny looked toward Paige.

"She is a terrific shot," Jorge said in a low voice as his wife took out her gun and pointed it in Sonny's direction. Chase did the same. "And that man beside her, he does not even need a gun to fuck you up."

"I won't…..I…"

"Oh, I know you will not," Jorge assured him. "This here will be your last show if you do…"

Sonny nodded and cleared his throat, taking a deep breath as he turned on his computer and began to set things up, under Jorge's watchful eyes. After a few minutes, he finally nodded and cleared his throat again.

"It's ready," Sonny said as he sat up a bit straighter. "I posted that I'm going live shortly."

"Very good," Jorge leaned back. "Now, you will introduce me, talk about how you got me rather than to speculate. You will ask about rumors you saw online, and I will squash them, one by one."

"And if not," Andrew muttered from the other side of the room. "He will squash you."

"I…I understand…"

"At the end of the day," Jorge pointed out. "You want ratings. This here, it will get your ratings."

Sonny nodded and cleared his throat again.

After making some adjustments, Sonny said he was ready to go live. After doing his introduction flawlessly, if not slightly tense, he went on to introduce his guest.

"I was saying that I wanted to talk *about* Jorge Hernandez in the next episode," Sonny spoke brightly into the camera. "And I pulled some strings and was lucky enough to get him as a guest on my show."

"Thank you for having me," Jorge spoke courteously, vastly different from the intimidating man from earlier. "I do appreciate the invitation."

"I thought it would be the perfect way to learn about your new book," Sonny became more at ease, despite the two guns pointed in his direction. "Maybe clear up some rumors."

"*Si*, there are so many terrible rumors," Jorge nodded his head, sincerity filled his eyes. "It breaks my heart because my children learn of this stuff, and well, I do not want to see my family hurt, you know?"

Jorge gave Sonny a quick warning look, his lips curved in a smile.

"I understand," Sonny nodded. "Your children are quite young."

"Well, my daughter is 14 going on 35," Jorge joked, and Sonny managed to laugh. "My son, he is almost 3. So, I do what I can to protect them."

"Then let's clear things up right now," Sonny spoke with enthusiasm.

"Yes, let's." Jorge nodded.

CHAPTER 23

"Let us just say that I got my point across," Jorge commented with a tense smile, his head was tilted forward slightly as he looked across the table at Makerson, who nodded in understanding. "I let him have his interview, and he, in turn, got to keep his…"

"More coffee, sir?" A waitress interrupted the two men, and Makerson jumped slightly while Jorge calmly turned in her direction and shook his head.

"I'm fine," Makerson spoke in a quiet voice and nodded his head. After she moved on, he returned his attention to Jorge. "Are you shitting me? He was going to talk about the stuff he found online?"

"*Si*," Jorge nodded as he reached for his cup of coffee, his eyes scanning the area before continuing. "I changed his mind."

"I was wondering what that was about," Makerson nodded in understanding. "I saw the interview, and it seemed…strange that you'd be talking to that kid."

"Yeah, well, now you know," Jorge replied as he took a drink of his coffee and made a face. "Let us hope that he gets the word out to his little internet friends to keep their fucking mouths shut."

"I'm pretty sure that message is received," Makerson replied. "Consequently, it has increased his ratings and followers on YouTube."

"Then that should be enough to keep him out of my business," Jorge insisted. "Or at the very least, report what I say."

"In the end, that's what some of these independent journalists want," Makerson insisted. "Instant fame, attention, money to sit at home and sleep in every day."

"Ah....we do not like these here people, do we?" Jorge teased.

"I went to school to get the title journalist," Makerson reminded him with a grin on his lips. "I didn't just start a YouTube channel and call myself one."

"I understand," Jorge nodded. "But that is the only reason why I talk to him. Who knows, he may become useful in the future, and if not, well, that is fine too. I will cross that bridge when I come to it."

"Now, regarding the book," Makerson shifted gears as he sat back in his chair. "I used the notes you gave me to write the first chapter. I'm not sure I'm happy with it. I need more information about Mexico during that time, about where you grew up, have a feel for it."

"That, I can do," Jorge nodded. "Where I lived, it was quite poor."

"Then, I have to ask, how did your father start a coffee business?"

"He started small," Jorge said and thought for a moment. "You know, my father, he had always grown his own coffee as did his parents, and so on. It was out of necessity more than anything, but this here is fine. Over time, he grew more and more, local people would ask to buy it, and eventually, he decided to expand his business until we finally had a nice little company. It was not overnight, but it worked. We had great coffee, and that is how this here started."

"Is there anything I should know?" Makerson leaned forward. "That I can't put in the book."

"No," Jorge shook his head. "My father, he was an honest man, at least when it come to business."

"And your parent's relationship," Makerson continued. "I need to get a feel for that."

"They were together," Jorge replied. "That is all."

"Happy?"

"Neither of my parents was ever happy," Jorge insisted. "Especially after my brother, he died."

Makerson nodded.

"But not before either," Jorge continued. "There was always tension, unhappiness in my home. I got the feeling it was a marriage of convenience, not love. That is why I did not marry for many years. I did not want the same."

Makerson didn't reply.

"As for my community, I can send you some pictures, some more information tonight," Jorge said as he glanced toward the window. "I believe we are putting up a Christmas tree when I get home. So, it will be after that."

"And that's fine, no rush," Makerson nodded. "Like I said, I wanted to get a better feel for what it was like growing up in your home. It sounds very...grim."

"It was," Jorge nodded. "There was not so much happiness in my childhood."

"How do you think it affected you?"

"It made me want to do anything to be happy," Jorge sighed. "Unfortunately, we are trained as children on how to see the world. If you have misery burning into your soul, it is hard to get it out."

Makerson gave Jorge a sad look.

"It was a long, hard road," Jorge continued. "But I think I made it."

"That....that sounds terrible," Makerson shook his head. "I mean, my family wasn't great but, my parents at least tried."

"It was a different time," Jorge reminded him. "Mexico, it is also a different country. We do not have the programs you have here in Canada to help people, so life is often a struggle. That is why so many love this here country. But also you have to know that my parents, they came from a long line of misery. So it was their way."

"And they both died?"

Jorge nodded.

"Your mother was here, in Toronto," Makerson remembered. "And your father?"

"Around the time I move here," Jorge replied. "We did not have a good relationship. But for the book purposes, we got along, and I was part of his company as an international salesman. I traveled a lot."

The two men ended their meeting shortly after, Makerson with a lot to think about while Jorge attempting to not think at all. He decided to drop by the *Princesa Maria* on the way home for a drink. He was surprised to find Diego at the bar.

"You are not supposed to be at work?" Jorge teased. "Running my company?"

Much to his surprise, Diego was drunk. Glancing at his phone, Jorge noted it was 4 p.m. The bar had just opened.

"Yeah, well, it's been a day," Diego shook his head and returned his focus on the drink.

"Diego, you are worrying me here," Jorge sat beside him. "This is not like you. What happened?"

"Life," Diego shook his head. "That's what happened."

Jorge looked up to see Chase. The men exchanged looks, and Chase went into his office.

"Stay here," Jorge instructed Diego as he stood up. "I got a meeting with Chase. Then we will talk."

Diego appeared uninterested as Jorge made his way toward the office. Once inside, he closed the door, and the two men exchanged looks.

"What the fuck is that?" Jorge pointed toward the door.

"Exactly what I was thinking," Chase said as he sat behind the desk. "I messaged Paige to see if she could come and talk to him because he's not talking to me."

"Me neither," Jorge added as he sat across from Chase. "This is not like him."

"Not often," Chase shrugged. "Christmas season doesn't always bring out the best in people."

Jorge nodded, thinking about his recent conversation with Chase regarding his sons.

"It is….difficult for those without family," Jorge shook his head. "But we are family…his family. You know, Paige and me were talking about having everyone over for dinner this year. The whole thing. Christmas Eve, and the next day. All of it. You, Diego, maybe even Jolene…."

Chase perked up a bit.

"I think this here would be nice," Jorge said as he noted Chase's expression. "Jolene can stay at Diego's, though."

Chase laughed.

"You can stay at our house or whatever you wish," Jorge shrugged. "It will be nice. We will do the family thing."

"I like that idea," Chase nodded, then pointed toward the door. "But I'm not sure if that's what's going on with him. He got here, was quiet, started drinking…"

"Maybe something at the office?"

Chase shrugged.

"He gave no clue?"

"Nope."

Jorge's phone beeped.

"Paige is telling me about this," Jorge said.

I'm here. He won't talk.

"He might tell her what's going on," Chase said. "Look, everyone is busy lately. You're busy with your book, with the production house, and I get that."

"But?"

Chase turned his phone off, and Jorge did the same.

"Diego, I think he's at work all the time," Chase said as he moved his chair forward. "Marco commented on that the other day. I was thinking about it later, and you know, he's never around anymore. He hasn't been here in ages. You live next door, so…"

"No, I do not see him often," Jorge nodded in understanding. "What do you think is wrong?"

Chase shook his head.

"Why do I feel there is more?"

"Jolene, she's acting weird too," Chase continued. "She was here yesterday going on about some church, a religious thing she's getting involved in."

"Church?" Jorge began to laugh. "Jolene?"

"I know, that's what I was thinking too," Chase shrugged. "I'm sure it will be short-lived. But then, Diego's acting weird. I've been tied up with the self-defense thing I'm doing with Maria, and now this shit with Audrey, so I haven't been keeping up on things."

Jorge took a deep breath and nodded.

"We're just so busy," Chase continued.

"Let Paige talk to Diego," Jorge finally replied. "As for Jolene and this religious thing, it better not make her confess her sins. Maybe it is not that serious, you know?"

"Should I call her in?"

Jorge thought a moment.

"No, I would rather talk to Marco."

Chase nodded his head and reached for his phone.

"Jolene, she will tell us half-truths but Marco," Jorge leaned forward. "He will find out everything."

CHAPTER 24

"Sir, I do not see anything," Marco commented as he scratched his bald head and leaned toward his laptop. "Jolene, she is not around the office much, so this religious thing, it is new."

"Probably a man," Chase leaned back in his chair as he looked across his desk at the others. "Isn't it always a man with Jolene?"

"I do see her talking to a man in her texts," Marco agreed. "But there is nothing here about religion."

"Hmm…" Jorge raised an eyebrow. "Me, I do not care as long as she keeps her mouth shut. She can go see the pope, for all I care."

"Oh, sir, I do not think the pope would want to see *her*," Marco muttered as he looked down at his laptop.

Both Chase and Marco laughed, just as there was a knock at the door.

"Yeah?" Chase called out.

The door opened, and Diego and Paige walked in. Jorge glanced at his wife, who gave him a wide-eyed look, which in turn caused him to look at Diego.

"Well, my friend, are you finished with your late afternoon drinking?" Jorge asked as Paige closed the door, and Diego headed to a chair. Paige did the same, still giving Jorge a look.

"He's finished drinking for today," Paige sternly commented as she sat beside him. "And everything is fine."

"So, what is going on?" Jorge asked. "This here, it is not like you, Diego. You know, we are *familia* here. There are no secrets and nothing you cannot share."

Everyone's attention was on Diego, who appeared skeptical, but then his defenses seem to fall.

"I got a problem."

"Ok," Jorge nodded as he turned toward Diego, looking past Paige, who was between them. "What is it? I am sure we can solve it. You got someone that needs to be taken care of? A person giving you problems? You know we can look after anything."

"Clara was in?" Paige interrupted, referring to the Latina that scoured their offices and homes for listening devices.

Chase nodded, and all attention was back on Diego.

"It's more of a....personal thing."

"Oh, well," Jorge hesitated and shrugged. "You got a boyfriend we need to take care of? I...you know, these here same rules apply."

"No, it's not like that."

"It's Christmas time," Chase jumped in. "I get it. It's not a great time to be single."

"No, that's not it either," Diego shook his head. "It's embarrassing."

"Ok," Jorge shared a look with Paige and attempted to read her eyes. "We are family, Diego, so please tell us what happened."

"I went out last night."

"Ok," Jorge replied. "You drank too much?"

"No," Diego shook his head, making a face. "I mean, yeah, maybe, but that's not what I'm talking about."

"Ok," Jorge said. "Diego, I do not mean to be insensitive, but can you tell us already. We got other things to take care of here today."

On his other side, Jorge could hear Marco snicker.

"I kissed a girl, and I liked it," Diego burst out with his comment, which caused surprise in the room, followed by a ripple of laughter.

"Was it the taste of her cherry chapstick?" Chase asked, attempting to hide the grin behind his hand.

"What?" Diego didn't seem to clue in right away, causing the others to laugh harder. "I don't think she was wearing chapstick, it was more of a..."

"It is a song, Diego," Jorge said as he attempted to stop laughing. "Very popular? Although I must say, I like the fantasy of it more than, well...."

This comment caused Marco to laugh harder beside him.

"Guys, this is serious," Diego complained, his dark eyes shooting around the room. "I'm having an identity crisis. I've been a gay man for my entire life."

"Diego, this is hardly an identity crisis," Jorge corrected him, while across the desk, Chase broke out in laughter again. "So what? You liked it. This here is not terrible. But you know, maybe you should stop spending so much time with my wife now."

With this, Jorge's head fell back in laughter.

"I'm glad you're enjoying this so much," Diego leaned toward Jorge, but Paige put her hand on his shoulder to calm him. "This would be like if you kissed a man and liked it. At your *age!* And you're *way* older than me."

"Ok, let's calm down," Paige instructed.

"And I would not be kissing men," Jorge continued to laugh. "And...

"Ok, let's relax," Paige cut him off. "Diego, it's ok. It happened. It's not the end of world. It was just a kiss. You were drinking. Things happen."

"Maybe, Diego, you should give it a whirl," Jorge continued to tease. "You might like."

Once again, Jorge's head fell back in laughter, and Marco did the same, while Chase merely grinned and shook his head.

"This is serious," Diego insisted.

"Is it, Diego?" Jorge asked. "Is it *really?*"

"You weren't hurting anyone," Paige reminded Diego. "It's not like you have a boyfriend at home that you cheated on."

"No, then there's that," Diego shrugged. "That's why I was out. I should've gone to a gay club, but it's the same people there all the time. I thought I might meet someone who's out with his girlfriends, dancing, you know."

"Why would you want to meet someone at a club at all?" Chase asked. "I mean, really?"

"I hate dating apps."

"Everyone hates dating apps," Chase corrected him. "They're all full of fake profiles and bullshit."

"Ok, this here," Jorge shook his head. "I am not trying to be insensitive, and yes, I have said this already, but this here, Diego, this is not a huge problem. You are the CEO of my company, which has prestige. I would think this here would help."

"Not really," Diego shook his head.

"How about we talk about this more later?" Paige asked. "When you're sober?"

"Good point, Paige," Jorge nodded. "Diego, you are not in your right mind now."

"I can't believe this made you leave work and drink," Chase said. "That's not like you."

"It's been a stressful week, overall," Diego complained, and he turned to Jorge. "I need an assistant."

"You have an assistant."

"That's a secretary," Diego complained. "I need an assistant."

"Whatever, Diego, you are looking after the company," Jorge shrugged. "You do as you wish. You know I do not care as long as it is run well."

"He worries about what you think," Paige jumped in.

"Diego, do not worry," Jorge shook his head. "I do not care if you hire an assistant or kiss a girl or whatever. Just do not feel like you have to hide things from me."

"I don't," Diego insisted with wide eyes.

"Then what's going on with Jolene and the religious thing?"

"What?" Diego made a face. "Jolene is religious now?"

"This is what I hear," Jorge glanced toward Chase.

"She was here the other day talking about some church she was going to," Chase said as he leaned back in his chair. "Said it 'changed her life' and shit."

"If it changed her life so much," Diego made a face. "How come the rest of us didn't know."

"I dunno," Chase shook his head. "She talked about how it saved her."

"Oh fuck," Diego shook his head. "She's done this before. She tries to redeem herself every once in a while, but it don't go nowhere."

"Yeah, but is she going to start confessing her sins?" Jorge asked. "That's my concern."

"We need to talk to her," Paige said. "Just see what's going on."

"Why must she give me headaches?" Jorge shook his head. "It is always something with Jolene."

"Well, we are going to decorate with the kids tonight," Paige said as she glanced around the room. "Maybe order some pizzas, have people over to help out, have snacks. Invite her, see what she has to say for herself. Plus, it might be good if we all get together for a change. We never have time lately."

"Oh, that sounds fun!" Diego slapped his hands together. "I love to decorate."

"*Perfecto!*" Jorge spoke dramatically. "Because I hate it."

"The kids will love having everyone over to help," Paige said to Chase. "If you all want? There's no pressure to come over or to decorate even."

"I'll go," Chase nodded. "I got nothing on the agenda tonight. I like pizza. I'm not much of a decorator, though."

"You're tall. We might need your height," Paige said with laughter in her voice. "And besides, Maria will be excited to have you over."

"Marco," Jorge turned toward his IT Specialist. "You should bring your family over as well. The kids, they will have fun."

"I will check, sir," Marco nodded. "The kids love going to your house. I do not think any of the children have any activities tonight."

"Then this here is good," Jorge nodded. "We will also invite Jolene, and that is when I will talk to her. I do not care what she does, but she has to keep our business here, quiet."

"If she doesn't know that now," Diego shook his head. "She never will."

Jorge exchanged looks with his wife, but neither said a word.

CHAPTER 25

Christmas music filled the large living room where the *familia* gathered to decorate the tree. There were some discussions of adding more trees throughout the house, but Jorge thought that was too much; however, decorations in every room would be reasonable. He had never been much of a holiday person, but he went along for his family. He could see the excitement in Maria's face, something she desperately needed after the last couple of years of her life. She was a young lady, yet still a child in many ways.

Miguel was another story. The site of the tree caused him to be awestruck, but yet, not excited. He turned and gave his father a wide-eyed look before he started to cry.

"Oh, my," Paige swooped in and picked him up. "I think the tree is scaring him."

"Sometimes, it is because the trees are so large," Marco attempted to explain. "My youngest, he was also scared of Christmas trees."

"Until it is decorated," Marco's wife quickly jumped in with a warm smile. "It is good. He will be fine once we have decorated it."

Jorge made a face, unsure.

"Oh, *el bebe!*" Jorge heard Jolene rushing into the room with a gift in her hand. She sat it down and rushed toward Miguel, leaning in to kiss him. "My Godson! You have scared him, Jorge."

The room filled with laughter, while Jorge merely shrugged.

"I did not do that, Jolene," he corrected her and shook his head. "It is the tree. It scared him."

"It is big and," Jolene made a face and shook her head. "Ugly!"

"Jolene," Diego rushed over with a box of decorations in his hand, which he sat on a small table. "We haven't decorated it yet. That's what this whole party is about. So that Jorge don't got to do it."

Laughter filled the room again, and Jorge merely shrugged.

"Hey, some people, they like to decorate," Jorge said. "Who am I to take that joy away from them?"

Glancing toward his wife, he saw that his son was calmed down and was staring at his father.

"Once he sees the gifts under the tree," Jorge pointed toward his son. "He will not be scared of it. I promise you."

The party continued as the group worked together, with the promise of pizza being on the way. Jorge watched everyone jump in, while Chase stood back with a solemn look on his face. Jorge was about to approach him when suddenly, Jolene was in front of him and shoving a gift in his hands.

"This, this is for you," Jolene was saying. "It is for your decorating."

"Is this here going to blow up when I open it?" Jorge muttered and watched Jolene make a face.

"You know, I would not do," She appeared irritated.

"Maria," Jorge called out, interrupting his young daughter from helping one of Marco's children put a decoration on the tree. "Come here. I need you to open this here gift."

"Is it for me, *Papá?*" Maria seemed hesitant. "It isn't good luck to open other people's gifts."

"What?" Jorge was confused. "Maria, this here is not true."

"It is for you all," Jolene corrected her. "Not for Jorge. You can open it."

Maria shrugged and dug into the gift, carefully removing the paper as if it was the most delicate object. The box was from a pricey store, not that this impressed Jorge much, but his daughter gasped when she saw the prestigious label. Gently opening the lid, she reached inside and pulled out a little figurine.

"What's this?" Maria appeared puzzled.

"It's the baby Jesus!" Jolene's face lit up. "You know, this is a nativity set."

"Oh," Maria's voice lacked its original enthusiasm.

"It is why we celebrate Christmas." Jolene reminded them.

Maria seemed bored, and Jorge was annoyed.

"Oh, thank you," Paige said as she moved closer with Miguel reaching out, as if wanting to see what his sister had in his hand. She passed it to him, and the toddler automatically put it in his mouth.

"No, Miguel," Jolene insisted as she reached forward and pulled it out, causing him to cry. "You cannot eat the baby Jesus!"

Maria made a face while Paige rushed away with the little boy, taking him into the next room.

"Are you happy now, Jolene?" Jorge complained. "You have made the baby cry."

"It was the baby Jesus!" Jolene shook her head. "He has some teeth so he would've…"

"I would be more worried about the toxic chemicals in it," Maria dramatically cut in as she inspected the rest of the manger set in the box, "the paint or whatever."

"Oh, put it on the fireplace," Jolene pointed toward the other side of the room and started to walk in that direction.

"Or *in* the fireplace," Jorge joked with his daughter, who giggled.

"No, *Papá,*" She shook her head. "There are toxic chemicals. It would make us sick."

Jorge grinned at his daughter's wide-eyed answer just as Paige returned to the room with Miguel, who was eating a cookie.

Jorge watched everybody decorate the tree from a dark corner. Maria was helping Marco's children and wife with the tree, while Miguel was falling asleep in his mother's arms. Chase was having a conversation with Marco while Diego was attempting to take over the whole project. Jorge decided it was the perfect time to talk to Jolene. Grabbing her attention, he pointed toward the office while Paige raised an eyebrow as he passed her.

Once inside the room, Jorge waited for Jolene to trot in, her heels loudly hitting the floor.

"What did I do?" She asked before Jorge even had time to close the door. "I always do wrong."

"I will get right to the point," Jorge abruptly spoke as he headed behind the desk. "What is with the religion thing, Jolene?"

"Just because I get you the nativity set for…" Jolene started, but Jorge quickly cut her off as he sat down.

"I am not playing games here, Jolene," He leaned ahead on his desk, his dark eyes darting. "Tell me what is going on. Are you confessing your sins to a man hiding in the closet?"

"It is not a closet," Jolene corrected him. "It is.."

"I do not care, Jolene," Jorge snapped. "Chase, he says you are religious now, and it saved your life. You better keep quiet about what we do."

"Of course!" Aghast, Jolene sat back in her chair. "I would not tell this. Why do you think that because I now go to church that I will tell everything?"

"Because confessing is part of this here church thing," Jorge reminded her. "And I know you."

"I will not tell!" Jolene insisted with worry in her eyes. "I go to church. It is something new. I wanted to try. For me and it is a different church. You do not confess your sins. You try to live a better life."

"Jolene," Jorge shook his head. "You cannot go to church on Sunday and shoot someone on Monday. This here, it does not work."

"Maybe it can work for me," Jolene sat up straighter. "You do not know."

Jorge sighed loudly.

"I promise," Jolene insisted. "I will not talk. You know that I do not."

Jorge gave her a dark glare.

"I make mistakes," Jolene went on. "I know this, but this time, I will not. This will not hurt the *familia*. It will make it seem like I am a different kind of person to the world. Maybe your family should…"

"Let us not push it, Jolene," Jorge cut her off. "So where did this come from? Is it a man?"

Jolene was sheepish, and before she could answer, Jorge nodded.

"This is what I thought."

"It is not like that!"

"I do not care, Jolene," Jorge shook his head. "Just do not talk. Not to the religious people. Not to your new boyfriend. Not to anyone. That is it."

"I will not," She said. "Jorge, I do not do this."

"Let's keep it that way," he gave her another dark look. "As far as the world knows, you work at a production house, and that is all you do."

"That is all I do."

"Good," Jorge replied. "Let us keep it that way."

Jolene nodded.

"Do me a favor," Jorge said as he gestured toward the door. "On your way out, can you please shut the door."

"Are you not coming back to the party?" Jolene asked as she stood up.

"In a minute."

She didn't reply but stood up and headed for the door. Stopping briefly, she turned to look at Jorge. "I am praying for you."

He didn't reply as she left the room, closing the door behind her.

Sitting alone in the room, he closed his eyes as waves of anxiety filled him; his heart raced, and he began to sweat. He moved his chair away from the desk and leaned over. Calming himself, he slowly set upright to see Paige standing in the doorway.

CHAPTER 26

"Paige, I do not think you are reasonable here," Jorge shook his head, attempting to make light of the situation. The two walked out of the empty living room, which was now overflowing in decorations. He didn't want to deal with this topic. "As I said earlier, I am fine. But you know, Jolene, she brings out the worst in me."

"That's not an excuse," Paige followed him. "You have to…"

"Paige, please!" Jorge turned to her, quickly seeing the hurt in her eyes. He took a deep breath. "*Mi amor,* I know you only worry for me, but I am fine. I tell you this all evening. I was having…you know, an overwhelming moment."

"In the past, when you had…"

"But this here, it is not the past," He attempted to explain, feeling his heart pounding as he did. "I am fine. I promise you this. I feel it was a long day, and maybe I am tired."

"I think you need to stop taking so much on," Paige spoke in her usual, calm voice as she touched his arm. "You're running all these businesses, and I…."

"Paige, no, I do not run that much, really," Jorge shrugged. "Diego, he is looking after Our House of Pot, you know, when he is not having an identity crisis." Jorge paused to share a smile with his wife. "And the rest, I mean, Tony looks after the production house, him and Andrew. I just step in with some ideas or to check in. That is what I like. The crematorium it is being run and same with the bar. Chase, he is back and forth between the two and me? I do not do much of the work."

"Yes, but now with the book," Paige stepped closer and looked into his eyes. "I'm still not sure it is a good idea."

"Paige, it will not be my true story," Jorge gently reminded her. "You know this."

"But what if it causes someone else to pop up with the real story," She challenged.

"As I said before, Paige," Jorge shook his head. "Then, that person, him, and the book will be done. I have Marco on this, you know, you worry too much."

"I don't have a good feeling," She admitted as her hand ran up his arm, and he didn't argue. "I feel like you need to step back a bit."

"Paige, I barely have a foot in the door now," He reminded her. "And my health, I feel fine. I think tonight was…."

"I wish you would have gone to the hospital," Paige gently pushed. "To make sure."

"Paige, this here, it is ok," Jorge smiled. "I love how you look after me, but I promise, I am fine. I am still walking. I am not on the ground…or *in* the ground."

"Don't even joke about that," Paige said, her cheeks turning pink.

"I am fine, *mi amor,*" Jorge leaned in and kissed the top of her head. "I can take care of all of this."

"But the *familia,*" Paige said as he moved away from her. "There's always so much drama and problems. You take them all on. You can't do that. You need Chase and Diego, and even Jolene, figuring things out on their own. And be there for them."

"Well, Jolene, she is another matter," Jorge shook his head as he started for the kitchen. "That one, I do not always trust. She is a loose….cannon or bullet, or whatever."

"Keep Marco on her," Paige followed him into the kitchen. "But step back. I can step up."

"Paige," Jorge laughed. "If I do not have these things to keep me busy, what will I do all day? Learn how to knit? Watch terrible daytime television? What is it you wish me to do, live in a cage?"

"I think...you have too many balls in the air," Paige attempted to explain. "Maybe...maybe you need Chase or me to step up more with the day-to-day."

"He is not ready," Jorge shook his head. "No one is ready. It is not time."

"What about me?"

Jorge heard the question and took a minute to realize that it wasn't Paige asking but Maria. Tensing up, he exchanged looks with his wife.

"Maria," Paige turned around to see her step-daughter. "Were you eavesdropping?"

"I didn't mean to," Maria said in a small voice. "I came downstairs to get a drink."

"Maria, it is nothing," Jorge assured her. "Paige and I, we sometimes have this disagreement. It is fine."

"*Papá,* why do you need someone to take over the *familia?*" Maria asked in a voice that caused his defenses to fall to the ground. "Are you ok?"

Jorge shot Paige a look. His eyes returned to his daughter.

"Maria, I am fine," Jorge insisted with strength in his voice. "There is nothing for you to worry about. No one is taking over anything. Paige, she worries that maybe I have too many things...you know, too many balls in the air. But this is not true. I can handle it."

Paige appeared skeptical but didn't reply. Maria tilted her head to the side.

"But *Papá,* eventually, you need someone to take over everything you created," Maria spoke logically, her eyes growing in size. "I want it to be me."

"Maria..." Jorge shook his head.

"I can do it," She assured him, her eyes widened more. "I have proven to you that I can when I...."

"Maria," Jorge solemnly spoke as he shook his head. "That never should have happened. You never should have had to step up in this way. You are still so young. And you know, I do not wish this life for you."

"I want it though," She moved closer and touched his hand. "I want to learn how to lead."

"Oh, Maria," Jorge shook his head and squeezed her hand. "My wish is to leave my companies for you and your brother to one day be wealthy.

And with that wealth, you will have power and the ability to do whatever it is you want. But this lifestyle, I do not wish for you."

"*Papá,*" Maria shrugged, then shook her head. "Is it really that simple?"

Jorge thought for a moment and looked away.

"It will be, Maria," Jorge assured her. "I am working on it. When this here book comes out, it will stop the rumors about my past. I am hoping. I will continue to have companies, but Maria, I do not want this same life for you and Miguel. I want you both to be safe and to be happy. I am working hard so that you do not have the same struggles as me."

"But wouldn't it be better if I was prepared?" Maria asked as she let go of his hand and leaned against the counter, her fingers sweeping over the top of it. "I mean, like when you didn't want me to learn how to shoot a gun, and you were mad when Jolene taught me, but if I didn't know how to do it...."

Her sentence drifted off, and Jorge looked away, feeling anxiety sweep through him. His daughter had saved the family that night, for which he was full of pride, but it had also ripped away her innocence at the same time. It killed a part of him that night too.

"Maria," Paige was speaking, and Jorge took a deep breath and looked up. "We were proud of you for protecting the family that night, but you shouldn't have had to, and...."

"Maria," Jorge cut off his wife as she paused for a moment. "We love you and are proud of you for this, and yes, you are right, it was good that you could use a gun when it was necessary, but my hope for you is that this will not be necessary again."

"*Papá,* you can't be sure of that," Maria suddenly stood taller despite her petite frame. She looked powerful. "The right thing to do is to teach me how to protect myself and this family. Teach me what you do, from day-to-day. How do you deal with things if someone...isn't listening? Like, you know, this book thing, for example. What if someone else wanted to write a book about you and it talked about your past in Mexico? Like, how would you handle that?"

"Well, I would call a lawyer," Jorge attempted to explain while avoiding his daughter's eyes.

"*Papá,* I know that's not true," Maria sharply cut him off. "Please stop trying to protect me. Would you kill him?"

"Maria," Paige jumped in. "Can we leave this alone for tonight? It's been a long day."

"Stop trying to protect him!" Maria shot back. "Will you *both* stop trying to hide the truth about this family? I know who you are, *Papá*. You hide it from other people, but why are you hiding it from me?"

Jorge opened his mouth to speak. So many times he looked at Maria and could see her departed mother in her eyes, but this time, Jorge saw himself. It surprised him.

"You are right, *hija,*" Jorge slowly replied, noting his wife's surprise while his daughter watched him carefully as she stood strong. "This is true. You do know who I am. I wish you did not, but I cannot turn back time. You are not a little girl anymore. I know this. And I know you protected this here family when we needed it."

"And I can again..."

"And I also know," Jorge cut her off, speaking with emotion in his voice. "That night, when you shot the intruder, that broke you."

Maria did not speak but gulped back her tears. She looked away.

"And that is what scares me," Jorge continued. "We do not talk about this, but we should. Maria, that night, you were shaking. You shook in my arms. You were crying. This here is why I am hesitant to teach you more."

"I'm sorry, *Papá* I...."

"Maria," Jorge walked toward her. "I do not say this to shame you. I say this to show I worry about you. This here lifestyle, it is not for everyone."

"I'm not weak," She blinked back her tears as Jorge reached out and touched her shoulder.

"I know, Maria," Jorge assured her. "I know."

"If I were a boy," Maria quietly asked. "Would it be different?"

"Maybe," Jorge hesitated and finally nodded. "Yes, I cannot lie. Maria, if you were a boy, it would be."

"That's not fair," She sniffed. "You can't..."

"I know," Jorge cut her off and squeezed her shoulder. "It is the sexist, old man who says this. It is not because I do not believe in you, Maria. It is because I want you to have a lavish lifestyle, to want for nothing. To be honored and appreciated and looked after like a queen, but...I know you are right."

"Don't you want me to be independent?"

Jorge thought for a moment. "Yes, of course. You cannot rely on anyone in this world."

"Then please," Maria begged, then paused before continuing. "Let me learn how to run this family. Let me learn how to be like you."

CHAPTER 27

"Why did you have to put her here?" Andrew complained to Jorge before he even had a chance to sit down. "I mean, you have all these companies. Why can't you stick Jolene like, anywhere but here?"

"I know," Jorge nodded his head as he sat across the desk from Tony and next to Andrew. "I do understand, but with Jolene, you need to give her something to do and send her on her way. It is the easiest thing."

"Please," Andrew was now directing his attention on Tony. "Find her *something* to do."

"I will, I will," Tony put a hand in the air. "I have some ideas."

"Because if I have to hear about her religious shit anymore," Andrew shook her head. "She's almost as bad as those guys that come preaching at your door. I don't need her to say a prayer for me or whatever the fuck, man. Send her to the crematorium. She can't annoy the dead people."

Jorge took a deep breath feeling a heaviness in his chest. He suddenly understood why Paige was concerned for his health.

"I got it," Tony stated. "I have a project for her...a research project for *Eat the Rich.* Just relax, Andrew."

"Look, I only have a few minutes," Jorge cut in as he glanced between the two men. "I am here to tell you that I will be...stepping back on things some more. I am having some stress issues lately. So, in the future, keep me posted on things, but I will be less actively involved."

"I feel like we've done this before," Andrew said as his eyes shifted toward Jorge. "Like, are you sick or some shit?"

"I am fine," Jorge assured him. "I have too much right now, along with the book."

"We're going to do that bio on you," Tony reminded him. "If that's still ok?"

"Yes," Jorge nodded. "This here, it is fine. You can talk to Makerson about that."

Satisfied, Tony nodded. "I'm ok here. Like, I'm overseeing everything, and I know how you want things done. I know the tone, all of that, so I'm fine. I'll send you the final products to view."

"You spending time at *Our House of Pot?*" Andrew wondered out loud.

"Nah, they got things under control."

"And the crematorium is good," Andrew added. "Buddy, who runs it now, he don't worry about what I'm doing on my end of things since I freelance. He only worries about the customers."

"This here, it is perfect," Jorge nodded. "So, I will be focusing on my book for now. Unless, of course, any emergencies come up."

No one responded. They knew the kind of emergencies Jorge Hernandez was talking about and how he usually dealt with them.

"Let's hope it doesn't come to that," Tony finally replied.

"*Si,*" Jorge agreed as he stood up. "Let us hope."

Shortly after, he was back on the road and heading to the bar. Despite his insistence to Paige that he could handle everything, he did feel calmer, more relaxed, now that he stepped back from some of his projects. Maybe, he decided, she was right. Maybe, he was taking on too much. However, this had been his entire life, so he didn't know any other way to live. Perhaps, it was time he learned.

Jorge found Chase alone at the bar, the doors still closed to customers. Staff wouldn't be arriving for some time yet.

"Hey," Chase was writing on a clipboard when Jorge arrived. "I was about to text you. I have plans to go to some out-of-province indigenous communities next year but wasn't sure if you'd mind Maria coming with me. So far, I think I can drive there and back the same day, but the further out they are, there's a chance it will be overnight."

"If Maria wishes to go and it does not interrupt her school," Jorge shrugged. "This is fine. This self-defense program means a lot to her."

"I'm not sure yet," Chase admitted as he set the clipboard down. "Things are going fine, but it's a lot of time. I'm also thinking of streaming it online but, I'm just playing around with the idea so far."

"I would think being there would seem more personal," Jorge thought as he sat at the bar and ran a hand over his face, yawning. "You know, so they feel like you are focused on them."

"Well, my idea was to stream is to try to make it personal," Chase thought for a moment. "Talk to everyone involved, but yeah, sometimes you have to be there in person to make sure the moves are done correctly. I'll have to think about it."

Jorge nodded and didn't say anything.

"So, how's the book going?"

"It is going," Jorge nodded. "But for me, I gotta cut back on stuff. Paige, she worries I am taking too much on."

"That tends to be your MO," Chase nodded.

"But you know," Jorge shrugged. "I like that. I like the chaos. But I was just at the production house, and I say, you can look after this without me. I will focus on my book, and I have some…other things."

Chase raised an eyebrow. He took out his phone and turned it off.

"We should talk in the office," Jorge said as he pointed behind Chase while taking out his phone and turned it off. "There are some things that we need to discuss."

It wasn't until they were behind closed doors that Jorge spoke again.

"There has been…some concerns for me," He started to speak slowly. "As you know, with Maria."

Chase gave a knowing nod.

"She has seen and had to deal with so much in her young life," Jorge said and took a deep breath before continuing. "And this here, it concerns me."

"I think she's resilient," Chase commented. "But at the same time, I understand why you're worried."

"I am," Jorge nodded. "She causes me a great deal of worry. I want her to have a normal life, but I fear that this may not be possible. I have done what I could to make her life better, to shelter her from my reality, but unfortunately, this has not always been possible."

"I know," Chase nodded. "But for what it's worth, she does seem to be getting stronger. I can see that in her."

"Yes, and you have known my daughter for some years now," Jorge said and briefly paused. "I think she would tell you anything, and this is good because I know you will always protect her."

"Of course."

"But at the same time," Jorge shook his head. "I cannot deny that she knows more than I would like her to know. I wish she had never learned that I was...who I am, you know."

Chase nodded.

"And the other day," Jorge continued as he stared into space. "She overheard me and Paige talk. Paige worries that I am taking on too much. That is why, of course, I am only focusing on the book at this time. But also, we talk about me stepping back more, in general, and Maria, she walked in while we had this conversation."

Chase didn't reply but continued to listen.

"And she said," Jorge paused again before finally continuing. "She would like to take over the family someday in the future. She said....she said she wanted to be like me."

Chase's eyes widened.

"I know, this here, it did surprise me," Jorge admitted. "And I must say that I do have mixed feelings. My heart is full of pride, but more than that, it is full of fear. I do not want my daughter to have the life I have. I want her to have a, what you say, normal life compared to me. I do not want her in danger. I want her to go to school, to get married, have a family."

Chase didn't reply. Concern filled his eyes.

"And I realize," Jorge continued. "This is the same for all parents. But, my life, my legacy, it is much different from most."

"I think the key," Chase finally spoke. "Isn't to necessarily assume she will do the same as you but prepare her for any potential dangers. Make her strong, powerful, but at the same time, let her know that the way we do things may not be for her."

"That is what I think too," Jorge cleared his throat. "Me and Paige, we talk about this, you know...a lot. She says the same. But I cannot know what will happen in the future. People may try to take advantage of her. I cannot have this."

"Teach her how to protect herself," Chase said. "That's all you can do."

"But she asks," Jorge made a face. "How we handle certain things, and I do not want her to know the whole truth."

"Maybe it's how you tell her," Chase suggested. "Maybe don't get into details, but tell her…in a general way. Even better yet, take it as it comes."

"If only she knew," Jorge raised an eyebrow and Chase mirrored him. "It is not glamorous. It is not clean."

"But there will be others around to protect her," Chase reminded him. "She won't be on her own."

"I know this," Jorge leaned back in his chair. "But I worry. I would worry if she were a boy, but honestly, not as much. I would worry if she did not have emotional problems, but not as much. This here….it is dicey. I guess I am an overprotected father."

"You can't hide the truth," Chase reminded him. "She knows…"

"I know," Jorge agreed. "But how much more can I tell her?

Chase didn't reply.

"But I do have an idea," Jorge continued. "She will soon have an assignment."

CHAPTER 28

She sat up straight and smoothed out her skirt. Glancing around her father's office, Maria felt unexpected nervousness as she awaited their meeting. She had been in this room a million times, but never in this capacity. Today, Maria wasn't meeting her loving *Papá* who would always protect her, but the notorious Jorge Hernandez. She asked to step up, to honor her father in a position that would allow her to one day lead the *familia,* but as she looked down at her skinny legs and Mary Jane shoes, she started to doubt her power.

"*Princesa!*" Jorge's voice came booming from behind her, causing Maria to jump. Quickly she attempted to hide her nervousness, fearful that this would be considered a weakness. "I see you are early. This here is good!"

Maria turned around to see her father close the door, and she gave him an apprehensive smile as he walked toward his desk.

"This here, it shows you take things very seriously," Her father remarked as he sat behind his desk, carefully inspecting her. "Maria, you do not have to look so scared. I am not sending you to the dungeon."

"We have a dungeon?" She heard the shock in her own voice as her heart raced.

Jorge's head fell back in laugher.

"Maria," he finally contained himself. "This here, it was a joke. No, we do *not* have a dungeon. Where do you think it would be? Juliana has her apartment in the basement, and last time I look, it was pretty lavish. I did not see a dungeon."

"Well, I don't know," Maria spoke sheepishly. "Diego has a secret room."

"Yes," Jorge grew serious and nodded. "And that is a secret from everyone outside this here *familia*."

"Oh, I know," Maria perked up. "I just meant…"

"This here, it is fine," Jorge shook his head and continued to study his daughter. "So, Maria, I have thought a lot about what you say recently. I have discussed it with Paige, with Chase…"

Maria felt her face grow warm but didn't say anything.

"And now, I will talk to you about it again," Jorge continued, noting her expression. "Because I have a few thoughts."

Maria held her breath. Her heart furiously pounded as she listened.

"Maria, I was proud of you when you said you wanted to head this family someday," Jorge continued as he leaned back in his chair. "Very proud. I could not have asked for more but, I will be honest, I do have concerns. I have said many times that I want you to have a good, happy life, and this here, Maria, is not always easy. There is danger involved. You must always be one step ahead and looking over your shoulder. You must have sharp instincts and know who you can and cannot trust. There are so many things that you must know, and although you can learn it, I also think you would be much happier to have a normal life."

"No, I really want to do what you do." She insisted and sat up straighter, looking into her father's eyes.

"But Maria," Jorge leaned on his desk, his voice softened. "What is it you think I do?"

She hesitated.

"There is a lot more to my world than you may know," Jorge continued. "But I do understand and admire your dedication, and you have proven to me, more than once, that you are a smart, young lady who is capable. Maria, I do not want you to be in danger however, as Paige pointed out, this might not be something we can control."

Maria nodded, her eyes widening.

"So, what I have decided," Jorge started slowly, glancing at his desk, as if in hesitation before looking back into her eyes. "That we will start slow. *Very* slow. You are like Miguel when he started to walk. You know, wobbly, falling, but now he can run. This here is normal. My point, Maria, is that you must learn some basics, have some simple assignments to help, but nothing must interfere with your schoolwork."

"I understand," Maria nodded.

"I want you to take your studies seriously," Jorge insisted. "Because you will need them. There is much to know about the world and life to be where I am today. Look at all my businesses. These are things I had to learn. You are in school. Look at everything you learn as something you might someday need in this life because you probably will. Even working with Chase, you have learned some on business, expenses, that kind of thing. You can see how those classes of yours are important because you apply them to real life. This is the same as what I do. I want your grades at the top, Maria. No more messing around. If you want to run this here organization, you have to be smart. Very smart. You cannot just get by in my business."

"Yes, I understand," Maria nodded nervously. "I promise, I will do better, *Papá.*"

"You will continue shooting lessons," Jorge said and Maria briefly looked away. "As you know, I did not like this idea originally. But in the end, it was good that Jolene showed you, but I was *very* angry with both of you when I found out you had secretly convinced her to do this. You, because I had said no and her because she was supposed to know better."

Maria fought back the tears and bit her lip.

"But," Jorge continued as he glanced up at the ceiling. "I do have to admit, you were persistent, which I like. And you followed your instincts, which I also admire. Maybe, I am too protective of you."

Maria didn't respond but noted that her father was once again looking her in the eyes. She gave him a small smile.

"So, as much as I did not agree with this decision at the time," Jorge shrugged. "It was a good one. Maybe you knew better than your *Papá* that time."

"I wanted to protect the family," She spoke in a small voice. "That's all I wanted."

"I know this, Maria," Jorge nodded. "I never doubted this about you and again, this fills me with pride but, I also worry about you. But this here, it is my job."

"I know," Maria said in a small voice. "I promise to be careful."

"You will be," Jorge nodded. "But my thoughts are that we will focus on your education, that we will continue to teach you how to shoot, and Chase will work with you with self-defense."

Maria nodded, her heart dropped. He didn't take her seriously.

"But," Jorge continued, and Maria perked up. "We will take it up a notch. So, with self-defense, Paige she knows someone who was an army seal that can teach you. I actually would like Chase to learn too. He is a strong man, and he knows some basics, but Paige pointed out you could both benefit from more intense training. I must admit, Maria, this is something I do not have, so you might be able to throw your *Papá* around a room when you have this training."

Maria giggled at the idea.

"Also, we will have some assignments for you," Jorge continued. "But Maria, you must be careful. You must never cause suspicion. In some cases, this here could be dangerous."

"I know."

"Paige will help you with this more," Jorge continued. "You will work with her a lot in the upcoming weeks, but Maria, schoolwork, it comes first."

"I understand," Maria nodded.

Jorge studied her face before continuing.

"I do have an assignment for you."

"Ok," Maria said as her heart pounded furiously in anticipation.

"You must find a way to spend time with Jolene that does not seem suspicious," Jorge said as he carefully studied his daughter. "And you must learn about this new interest in religion that she has. Try to understand why without alerting attention to yourself. My guess is that you will not have to bring it up because she will."

"She does all the time," Maria reminded him. "Like, what is that about?"

"This is what I would like to know," Jorge admitted. "Maria, you must understand that Jolene, she is our weakest link. I fear that she will talk to the wrong person about the *familia*, out of stupidity or possibly, a new man in her life."

"Do you think that is what she is doing?" Maria asked with interest.

"I do not know," Jorge said. "I have concerns. Jolene, she has always concerned me. Her priorities are often questionable."

Maria thought for a moment and nodded.

"But you must be careful," Jorge insisted. "Find a way to spend a day with her."

"The mall," Maria automatically thought. "To Christmas shop. I don't want you or Paige to see what I buy you. I thought it would be fun."

"Good!" Jorge nodded, a smile lit up his face. "That is very good, Maria."

"I won't bring up the religious thing," Maria continued in a small voice. "She will."

Jorge continued to nod, his smile grew.

"And I will ask what made her get interested in it," Maria continued. "If she talks about a guy, I will ask his name, what he does….."

"Try to make it fun, Maria," Jorge suggested. "Not like you have her on the witness stand, you know?"

Maria giggled at the idea.

"She trusts you, Maria," Jorge reminded her. "Learn what you can. But be cautious, *Princesa,* because she may be trying to do the same. She may want to know what I am doing too."

"I don't know," Maria shook her head. "I think you're like….helping with a TV show or something about a book."

"What else do you know?" Jorge asked.

"Nothing," Maria shrugged dramatically. "It's just boring stuff, you know?"

Jorge's head fell back in laughter.

"So, you want me to find out what's going on that she's suddenly religious," Maria confirmed. "And if it's because of some guy, and if she's telling him stuff about us."

"Yes, Maria," Jorge grew serious and nodded. "I cannot stress to you how important it is that what happens within this family stays here. We cannot talk to others about anything, as I have told you before. Jolene is the one person that I do not fully trust to not talk."

Maria thought for a moment and nodded. "Yeah, I can see that."

"Now, you must be careful," Jorge repeated his earlier comment. "Jolene, she is a smart lady, so you cannot make her suspicious."

"*Papá,*" Maria sat up straighter. "Remember, I have studied acting. I got this."

Jorge didn't respond, but there was pride in his eyes.

That's when her confidence grew. She could do this.

CHAPTER 29

"So, Maria, she is with Jolene for breakfast then shopping," Jorge said as he moved closer to Paige. Only wearing a towel, his wife leaned toward the mirror over the bathroom sink. She was putting lotion on her face. He could still smell the flowery scent from the shower as it flowed through the room, but it was her naked shoulders that caught his eye. Feeling his desires overriding the topic at hand, he approached her. "Juliana, she is taking Miguel to the park, and *mi amor*, we are home alone."

"We are alone," Paige repeated his words as she looked up, and their eyes met in the mirror. Turning around, she glanced down at his boxers, then back up to his face. "But don't you have to go to a meeting with Makerson or Chase? Someone?"

"I am meeting Makerson at his condo," Jorge's breath increased as he wrapped his arms around Paige and pulled her close. "Whenever I feel like going and Paige, it is early, so I do not want to disturb him at this time on a Saturday morning."

"Are you sure about that," She asked as she leaned in closer and stared into his eyes. "I don't want to hold you up…"

Jorge raised an eyebrow but didn't bother to reply. Instead, moving in to kiss her lips. Pulling her body tightly against him, he felt his excitement immediately increase with the anticipation of some time alone. His hands automatically slid under the towel to explore her body, causing her to let out a small gasp as his mouth moved away from her lips, gently sliding down to explore her neck. His fingers started to move faster, causing Paige's body to weakly fall against the vanity while Jorge's lips moved up her neck, his tongue teasing her earlobe.

"Oh, God!" She cried out as her body suddenly convulsed in pleasure. He moved away to see Paige leaning up against the counter as if to steady herself. Her face was crimson, her eyes full of vulnerability. The towel was opened and slid to the floor. Feeling his arousal at its peak, Jorge removed the boxers he wore and tossed them on the floor. His eyes automatically levitated toward her erect nipples, and he felt desire emerging through every inch of his body as he breathlessly leaned forward.

"I think you need another shower, *mi amor,*" He kissed her before quickly moving away. He reached for her hand and led her to the shower. Turning it on, it didn't take long to adjust the water and the two of them to step in. With two kids, it was always necessary to not waste a moment where pleasure was involved but move quickly to soothe their needs. This time, there would be no rush.

As the warm water flowed over them, Jorge gently pushing her against the shower wall. His hands ran up and down her wet skin, only causing him to want her more as he quickly moved inside of her, letting out a loud groan. Automatically, he reached down and pulled up her hips as she wrapped her legs around him. Pushing roughly inside of her, she gasped loudly as the warm water continued to pour over them. He felt her breasts hitting against his chest, and he thrust into her as she lost control in his arms, her legs wrapped tighter around him, causing Jorge to feel himself floating to the edge. Unable to take it anymore, he finally felt himself release all his tension as he let out an animal-like sound that echoed through the shower. His heart raced as the hot water ran down his back.

"Oh, *mi amor,*" He finally said as she eventually loosened her grip around him and slowly returned to a standing position. He swooped in to give her another slow, soft kiss. "This here was what I need."

"You make it sound like we never do this," Paige said as she looked into his eyes.

"Not like this," Jorge shook his head as blissful feelings flowed through his body, "not this loud."

"We'd scare the kids," She grinned.

"Well, maybe we need to think of something," Jorge thought out loud. "Where we can be...freer to express ourselves because you are like a wild animal, when no one is looking, *mi amor.*"

She raised an eyebrow but didn't reply.

It was while driving to Makerson's condo later that morning that Jorge thought about that conversation again. Hitting the button to call his wife, he grinned to himself as he glanced around at the traffic. For once, it wasn't annoying him.

"Hello," her voice was on the other end of the line.

"Mi amor," Jorge spoke in his usual, confident voice. "I was thinking that I have the perfect Christmas gift for you this year. What about we build a safe room."

"That's the *perfect* Christmas gift?" She laughed.

"Well, what I mean is a safe room that is soundproof," Jorge spoke in a more seductive tone. "You know, in case of emergencies of any kind. It would give us privacy whenever it is needed."

"That *does* sound interesting."

"I was hoping you would agree."

"I like the one Diego has."

"Ours, it will be better," Jorge insisted. "We can occasionally meet... you know, on a whim, it will be exciting. We can be...uninhibited in this here room."

"I like that idea," Paige quietly replied. "Would you like me to inquire with Diego about who did his? I'm going to his house for coffee later."

"This here sounds good," Jorge replied. "But do not tell him all the details, *mi amor.*"

"I wasn't planning on it," She laughed. "I think he had immigrants work on his, and he paid them under the table."

"I am sure he wanted them under the table for one reason or another," Jorge laughed at his joke. "But that is Diego."

"Be nice," Paige laughed with him.

"I am always nice, Paige."

The two ended their conversation, and Jorge made his way to Makerson's building. The two rarely met there, but sometimes on the weekends, it was better. Makerson lived in a luxurious location paid by Jorge for his help and loyalty over the years. He decided this would be one of the lessons he should teach Maria. If they did not have loyalty, they had nothing. He would tell her this when she returned from her Christmas shopping trip with Jolene, where he hoped she would learn some reassuring information. The last thing he wanted for his daughter's second lesson was how to kill a disloyal member, but it was always a possibility.

Arriving at the building, Jorge quickly found a parking spot and made his way inside. Makerson was expecting him and was brewing coffee upon his arrival.

"Good morning," Makerson ushered him in the door as if he was merely a regular guest, dropping by for some Saturday morning coffee and conversation. "I hope you aren't super fussy about your coffee." He pointed toward the kitchen, specifically at a bag on the table, "Being from a coffee family and all."

Jorge merely laughed as he walked inside, watching Makerson closing the door behind him.

Makerson made his way back to the kitchen, where he reached for the coffee pot and Jorge sat down at the kitchen table.

"You just take cream, right?"

"That is right," Jorge replied as he reached in his jacket and pulled out his phone. Turning it off, he looked up to see Makerson return with two cups and placed one in front of him. *"Gracias, mi amigo."*

"No problem," Makerson said as he sat down, pulling out his phone, he showed Jorge that it was off. "Hope it's to your liking."

Jorge took a sip and nodded.

"So, did you have a chance to read chapter one?" Makerson appeared somewhat nervous, something Jorge saw as a sign of caring about his work. "I know you're busy."

"Yes, I read it," Jorge replied as he pulled a USB stick out of his pocket. "Last night, and I liked it."

"Is there anything…"

"Look, this here," Jorge pointed toward the USB and shook his head. "It does not have to be perfect. Remember, we are telling a story, and it was a good story. You talked about how my parents met, how I came to be…you kept it simple."

"It's not too simple?"

"Not for me," Jorge replied. "You talk about my father being strict. About my mother being compliant. About my younger brother, Miguel, my son's namesake, and you know, you made us sound very normal."

"Is that ok, though?"

"Yes, this is what I wanted," Jorge nodded. "I am reluctant to get into the next chapter, though. I do like this first one. Again, you made this story seem much more interesting and pleasant than it was, but the next chapter, that may be tough."

"Is that where you want to talk about your brother's death?" Makerson asked.

"Yes," Jorge looked away. "I do not…I do not know if I should give much detail."

"I know you feel responsible," Makerson showed compassion. "So if you don't want to get too much into it, I can talk about the accident in a general sense."

"No, I think we must be open," Jorge nodded. "But to some, that is when I became *el diablo,* you know."

"It was an accident," Makerson reminded him. "You didn't purposely hurt your brother. You were just kids playing around."

"I know, but my family, they felt otherwise," Jorge reminded him. "Perhaps I should report this in the book."

"We could write it that you *felt* responsible," Makerson reminded him. "It would make you a more sympathetic character. No one is going to blame a 12-year-old kid for hurting his brother."

"Killing," Jorge corrected him as he mused for a moment. "There is a difference."

"It wasn't on purpose," Makerson reminded him. "You thought you were going to have some fun, got on a dirt bike…."

"That I did not know how to drive," Jorge said.

"You were a kid," Makerson shook his head. "We all do stupid shit when we're kids, and the only difference is with you, is it ended terribly. But you can tell that story however you want. You can talk about how it changed your life, made you stronger, made you a better person."

"Oh, *amigo,*" Jorge shook his head. "I am not a better person. If anything, it made me unhinged."

"Again," Makerson reminded him as he reached for his coffee. "We are telling a story. And it's up to you to create the narrative."

Jorge thought about his words, and a sinister grin curved his lips.

CHAPTER 30

"Kill, kill, kill!" Miguel ran through the living room just as Jorge walked in the door. Quickly noting that his father had returned, the toddler swiftly turned around. In his haste, the 2 1/2-year-old fell on his ass, but without missing a beat, he stood up, giggled, and ran toward his father. *"Papi"*

"Miguel!" Jorge reached down to pick him up. "Such words you use! Do you know that word in Spanish?"

The child stared at his father in awe but didn't reply.

"Matar," Maria replied as she walked into the room, her eyes on the child. "He knows Spanish and English words, but he doesn't seem to make the connection between the two."

"He will," Jorge assured her. "I tell Juliana to speak to him in Spanish and of course, most others speak to him in English. He will be completely bilingual like you, Maria."

"I feel like I forget Spanish words sometimes," Maria admitted as she tilted her head and shrugged.

"Maria, you must not," Jorge shook his head. "It is important to know both."

To this, she shrugged again, causing Jorge to be annoyed.

"I need to talk to you," Maria reminded him. "I sent you a text earlier…"

"Yes, and I was in a meeting at that time," Jorge reminded her.

"On Saturday?"

"Maria, you know that I work every day," Jorge said as Miguel wrapped his arms around Jorge's neck to hug him. "This here, it is not new. You are not the only one with things to take care of today."

"But I have news!" Her brown eyes lit up and she tilted her head. "You know, about today."

"Ok, well, then we must talk," Jorge said as Miguel started to wiggle out of his arms. "But where is Paige? Does she need to hear?"

"I already told her," Maria replied. "I want to tell you now."

"But where is she?" Jorge repeated.

"She's on her laptop, upstairs."

"Can you take Miguel to her?" Jorge asked. "Then I will meet you in the office?"

"Yes," Maria nodded enthusiastically and reached for Miguel. "I will be there in a minute."

Jorge watched her walk away and glanced around the room before heading to his office. Once there, he noted that he missed a call on his secure line. That would be Athas. He glanced at his cell phone but didn't see a text or any indication, so he decided to call later. The prime minister hadn't needed anything lately, so chances are he had a problem.

"*Papá,*" Maria entered the room and closed the door behind her. "I have some information for you."

"Now, Maria," Jorge picked up his cell phone and held it in the air. "What do we always do before a meeting?"

"Turn off your phone?" She asked as she rushed across the room to sit down in her usual seat, across from him. "I left mine upstairs."

"Very good," Jorge replied as he tapped on his phone and set it aside. "Marco, he has our phones protected, but it is better to be extra safe. Now, what do you have for me, Maria?"

"Well, before we went shopping," She replied. "We went for breakfast. I thought she might be more chatty that way because, at the mall, we would just talk like clothes, makeup, that stuff, you know?"

"Good point," Jorge agreed and nodded. "This is very smart, *Princesa.*"

"So, I didn't bring up anything," Maria said as she sat up straighter and fixed her skirt. "I decided that maybe it would be better if I was careful."

Jorge nodded for her to continue.

"She started to talk God," Maria said, and Jorge sighed, growing anxious. "And I was like…"

"Maria," Jorge cut her off. "It is not that I am not interested, but I do have to make a call very soon to Athas. So, if you would not mind, can you get to the point of what it is you think I should know."

"Well, she does have a new boyfriend," Maria reported with wide eyes. "And he like runs the church she goes to…I forget which one."

"They are the same, Maria," Jorge shook his head. "I do not need to know at this time. What else did she say?"

"Just how it changed her life, that kind of thing," Maria waved her hand in the air. "I acted interested so she would keep talking, but I really, *really* wasn't interested."

"Jolene, she has the same effect on me," Jorge replied, and Maria giggled.

"I know, right!" Maria rolled her eyes. "She talked a lot about God and religious stuff, and I tried to think of a way to change the conversation to find out more, but I wasn't sure. So, I finally asked her if she thought it was serious, you know, with this guy?"

Jorge nodded.

"She said she thought so," Maria continued. "But it didn't tell me anything about how much she might be saying."

"I know, Maria, it is something you must be careful with…"

"Oh, I was," Her eyes lit up. "And I was trying to think of a way when her phone rang. It was him. They were talking, and I pretended to be playing with my phone, but I listened. At first, they were gabbing about the usual stuff, what she was doing, who she was with, and when Jolene said she was with me, I noticed she paused."

Jorge raised an eyebrow.

"Her face seemed different," Maria said. "And she kind of turned like she didn't want me to hear something."

"Is this so?"

"*Papá,* I heard her mutter something about how she couldn't ask… anyway," Maria paused dramatically. "She got off the phone and asked if I thought you'd donate to his church. They need to fix something…"

Jorge rolled his eyes.

"That's what I thought too," Maria nodded. "But I played along and said, maybe you would. You sometimes give money."

"Not to churches," Jorge said and laughed. "But I do like that you left things open because maybe, this is our way to find out more. Very good, Maria."

"It wasn't much," She shook her head. "But it sounds like he does want your money."

"Does Jolene not have money?" Jorge complained.

"That's what I was thinking too," Maria said as she made a face. "It must be a lot though, or I think she would give it herself to keep this guy around."

Her last comment was abrupt, causing Jorge's head to fall back in laughter.

"Oh, Maria," He finally stopped laughing and slowly grew serious. "This here, it was good work."

"I didn't find out much."

"You did, and you didn't at the same time," Jorge replied. "Maybe there is not much to find in this here case."

"I suspect this guy is only around to get some money," Maria commented. "I get the impression he maybe asked her before, and when my name came up, he brought it up again."

"This here makes sense," Jorge nodded. "You did very good work today. I hope you enjoyed yourself."

"I did," She nodded vigorously. "I did some shopping, but I like trying to find out stuff too. It was fun."

"Now, Maria," Jorge shifted gears. "I was thinking earlier today that one of the top lessons that I must teach you is that loyalty is the most important thing."

"I know," She nodded. "Loyalty above all."

"Exactly," Jorge replied. "This here is why I had you look into Jolene. I do not always feel she is loyal and this, it does make me nervous. If someone does not feel loyal, they have no conscience about what they do to you."

"I understand."

"This here, although it may not seem like much," Jorge continued. "It still is telling. How will she react? Will she be honest with me about her situation, or will she try to manipulate me to give her money?"

Maria listened carefully.

"A loyal person is straight with you," Jorge reminded her. "That is why I got so angry when she taught you to shoot earlier this year. She wasn't loyal to me and my wishes, and she hid it. She was sneaky, and in this situation we just discussed, it could be the same. She has had many warnings about this behavior."

"She was straight with me," Maria considered. "But she seemed unsure if she should talk to you."

"Because she knows I will say no," Jorge replied. "She is trying to think of a way to approach me. We must see if it will be an honest way."

"She tried to get me to go to church with her tomorrow," Maria made a face.

"See, that may be her way," Jorge suggested. "If you went and enjoyed it, then maybe it would be easier to convince me."

"Oh," Maria spoke in a disgusted tone. "I don't like that, *Papá.*"

"I know, Maria," Jorge said in a caring voice. "Neither do I, but...I am very proud of you, you did well in this here first assignment. I have something for you."

Reaching in his desk drawer, he pulled out a hundred-dollar bill and handed it to Maria.

"You're paying me?" Maria appeared surprised.

"Maria, you did work for me," Jorge replied. "You did well, and another lesson to you is that when people work well for you, show you loyalty, then they must be rewarded. I have bought my most loyal people some big gifts as a way to show my appreciation."

Maria smiled and jumped up and rushed around the desk to hug him. He kissed her on the forehead.

"You did well, *Princesa,*" He said as she stood back and smiled at her money. "Hard work, good work, it is always rewarded."

"*Gracias,*" She grinned. "Is there anything else?"

"Not yet," Jorge replied. "But I will keep you in the loop. When you leave, Maria, please close the door."

After she was gone, he called Athas. His tone hardened as soon as he heard the prime minister's voice.

"I see you call me."

"I need a favor."

"What you want?"

"I need Makerson to report on something that shines me in a favorable light," Athas said and took a deep breath. "And I have some information for you. And you're not going to like it."

CHAPTER 31

"I was writing and couldn't stop," Makerson enthusiastically spoke as he entered Jorge's office, a laptop bag slung over his shoulder. Paige was already seated in her usual spot and turned around to greet him with a smile. "I can't wait…oh, good morning, Paige."

"Hi," She responded as Jorge closed the door behind Makerson, and both men headed toward the desk. "I was telling Jorge that I sat down last night and started working on chapter two, and the next thing I knew, it was after midnight. I mean, I'm sure it needs work…"

"I really like the first chapter," Paige replied as Makerson sat beside her. "It was well done, with just the right amount of information."

"Yes, we do not want to say too much," Jorge insisted as he sat down. "But enough to satisfy the people."

"It's hard to stay in those lines sometimes," Makerson admitted as his forehead wrinkled. "But I think that I am finding the right balance, and things seem to flow."

"I've noticed that about writing," Paige nodded.

"So," Jorge jumped in. "I would not normally interrupt you again on the weekend, but I had something important to discuss with you. Something has come to my attention yesterday, and I hope it is wrong, but you must know."

"Oh?" Makerson sat back in his chair, glancing at Paige, then back at Jorge. "Does this have to do with the book?"

"Yes, but not *your* book," Jorge shook his head and made a face. "There is, again, a suggestion that someone else is writing another book."

"What?" Makerson shook his head. "I thought you looked into this before and…"

"I did," Jorge assured him. "But then, some new information, it has just come to me. And from all people, but the prime minister himself."

"Did he hear something in Ottawa?" Makerson appeared confused. "I don't understand."

"Well, he contacted me because he needs your help spinning a story so it does not make him look like an asshole," Jorge said with a mocking tone as he spun a finger in the air while he talked. "But then, he also mention that he hear something about another book."

"Is he sure?"

"Well, that's the thing," Paige said. "We aren't entirely sure…"

"But it looks that way," Jorge cut in. "Some man, he went to Mexico to research me for a book."

"Oh shit," Makerson shook his head. "Do you know who?"

"This is the problem," Jorge continued. "The man, he used a fake passport at the border security. When Athas had the…what is it called, Paige?"

"The Canadian Security Intelligence Service," She replied. "CSIS. They helped us out."

"They help you out?" Makerson's jaw dropped as he glanced at Jorge, who nodded.

"It was part of the agreement when Alec got into office," Paige continued. "Jorge helps Alec, but he has to pulls some strings when we need it."

"Well, this here, it never stops," Jorge shook his head. "Yes, I helped to get him into office, but yet, I am always cleaning up his messes."

"Wait, so this guy went to Mexico to research a book about you?" Makerson attempted to get up to speed. "Then got stopped at border security?"

"Yes," Jorge replied. "They asked him why he went to Mexico. When he say work, they automatically ask more questions."

"You never, *ever,* say business," Paige shook her head. "It's always pleasure."

"Well, it may not be so pleasurable for him when I find who he is," Jorge jumped in. "Because this here will be his last vacation."

"I can't believe he would admit it," Makerson said as he glanced at Paige, who shrugged. "I wonder if he hoped it would get back to you?"

"Well, yes, this has crossed my mind," Jorge replied, then turned to his wife. "And come to think of it, Paige, it must be someone a bit naive to even say this here at the border. Who does that?"

"Not someone who knows anything," Paige shook her head. "That's what I'm thinking."

Jorge didn't reply but nodded.

"What if this isn't true?" Makerson suggested. "I mean, maybe it was just some jackass saying that…."

"Or someone who *thinks* they're doing a book on you," Paige directed her comment at Jorge. "It seems strange this wouldn't come up already if it were a major publishing house. Especially with Marco's research."

"Unless it is not a major house," Jorge replied. "Maybe it is another country they publish with…"

Paige didn't reply. The silence was deafening.

"So, what do we do?" Makerson asked, his face turned red. "That guy's got balls to go to Mexico."

"Well, he would not learn much down there other than rumors," Jorge insisted. "Those close to me, they would shoot him in the head and ask questions later."

"Or at least tell you," Paige chimed in.

"I have reached out to some," Jorge shook his head. "There is nothing."

"Unless it's someone who can stay under the radar," Paige added. "But who?"

"Someone close to you?" Makerson asked. "Close enough that they wouldn't ask questions."

"But who?" Jorge asked. "Who has been to Mexico lately that we know?"

"No one," Paige shook her head. "You know, maybe this is nothing.…"

"Maybe," Jorge agreed. "But we cannot let it go. I want to learn who this person is, even if they did not write a page yet. I do not like someone even suggesting anything at the border."

"When was this?" Makerson asked.

"A couple of days ago," Jorge replied.

"And none of your people down there…."

Jorge shook his head.

"Let's hope it's nothing," Paige said.

"I will have Marco look into it later," Jorge reminded her. "He is with his family today, but tonight, he said he would come talk to me."

"This might be a trick," Makerson said. "Knowing you will react. Seeing what you will do."

"It could be a major publisher, but keeping it quiet," Paige suggested. "Or it could be someone smaller who doesn't understand the risks."

"If he go to Mexico asking too many questions," Jorge nodded. "This here person does not see the risks involved."

"So, is there anything I can do?" Makerson appeared flustered. "I mean…"

"Continue doing what you do," Jorge insisted. "We just want you to be in the loop."

"And be careful," Paige added. "Keep your information secure."

"The laptop I'm using isn't even hooked up to the internet," Makerson said. "I keep a copy in a safe place. I put some information on a USB and bring it to Jorge, that's all."

"I would not send anything to the publisher."

"They're going to…"

"I do not trust their system is safe enough," Jorge said. "You must talk to them, arrange a meeting, to discuss this matter next week."

"Do you want to join?"

"No," Jorge shook his head. "I have too much on my plate. But you, you talk to them and see what they think. We cannot have this where it can be hacked."

"I understand."

"Also, we will be looking to see what we can learn about this here other book," Jorge continued. "I am very disturbed with this information."

"You're not the only one," Makerson assured him. "I guess I'm not surprised, but still."

"They must know to tread lightly," Jorge insisted.

"But if that's the case," Makerson shook his head. "Why tell them the truth at the border? This doesn't make sense."

"That's what I'm thinking," Paige replied. "There's something not adding up here."

"Yeah, if someone is researching you," Makerson commented. "Then they know...you."

"Exactly," Paige nodded. "There's something more going on."

Jorge didn't reply, his thoughts going in many directions.

"I don't like this at all," Makerson said and glanced toward Paige, who nodded.

"We have to talk to Marco," Paige suggested. "See if he can hack into those cameras, see a face. People know that Athas goes to you about everything. I don't have a good feeling about this."

Makerson shook his head.

"It could also be a distraction," Jorge said as he looked around his office. "We must be aware of many things."

"I wonder if you can," Paige turned toward Makerson. "Do some snooping. Just ask around, say that you hear someone else might be writing a book. Be...very casual about it. Don't get into the details."

Jorge raised an eyebrow.

"There's more to this than meets the eye," Paige continued. "And we're going to find out what."

"And take care of it from there," Jorge added. "This here, it *will* be taken care of...."

CHAPTER 32

"This here, is it about your identity crisis again?" Jorge asked Diego as the two men entered the VIP room at *Princesa Maria,* where the group was meeting. They were the first to arrive. "I tell you that it was because…."

"Her and I," Diego cut him off as he found his usual seat. "*That* girl, we hung out the other night."

"What?" Jorge was surprised. "Diego, this here, I never expected from you."

"I know," Diego's eyes widened as he spoke, dramatically waving his hands in the air. "We started to fool around."

"Do tell!" Jorge mocked him then put his hand in the air and sat down. "On second thought, do not tell me, but please, can we get to the point of this conversation."

Diego leaned in, as if in secret, "I liked it."

"Do not get me wrong," Jorge automatically replied. "I do understand this, but since when has this been…something that appealed to you? You are still gay, no?"

"That's the thing," Diego stood up tall. "I might be bi."

Jorge gave him a look.

"I don't know."

"*Now,* in your 40s, *now* you decide this?" Jorge shook his head.

"I know, right?" Diego said as he sat beside him. "But I've been looking into it, and it's not that uncommon. Some people get married to the opposite sex, only to discover they are attracted to the same sex later. So maybe this is like me, only...like, opposite."

"Well, you know what they say," Jorge joked. "Double your chances for a date on Saturday night. I guess."

"But it's confusing."

"Well, Diego, life is confusing for most of us," Jorge attempted to change the topic. "But you know, this here might be better to talk to Paige about....wait, no, do not talk to Paige about this."

"I'm not going to try to pick up your wife!" Diego spoke defensively.

"And here, I was so worried," Jorge mocked him just as the door opened and Chase walked in. "Really, Diego, you might want to tread *lightly* on your new straight feet because you might decide that these may not be the shoes for you."

Chase started to laugh.

"Do not ask," Jorge warned him and Chase put his hands in the air and shook his head. "You do not want to know."

"Maybe I'm getting desperate because I don't want to be alone," Diego considered as Chase sat across from him. "You know, maybe I'm settling."

"This one here," Jorge pointed toward Chase. "If he was suddenly gay, would you..."

"Oh yes!" Diego automatically answered while Chase continued to grin.

"Then, Diego, you are *still* gay," Jorge insisted. "Between him, and this here girl?"

"Oh definitely him," Diego spoke in a lower voice.

"I'm still here," Chase pointed out as he turned off his phone. "I can hear."

"I am just making a point," Jorge reminded him.

"And you have," Diego wrinkled up his nose and shrugged. "Maybe I will keep things with this girl, casual, you know."

Jorge and Chase exchanged looks as the door opened. This time it was Marco, followed by Paige and Jolene.

"I was about to text you to let us in," Paige pointed toward the main bar. "But I saw staff here, so they let me in."

"I told them to keep an eye out for you," Chase replied. "no one else though."

"Good thing," Jolene piped up as she took her usual place at the table, beside Chase. "We do not want any person wandering in, you know?"

Marco appeared concerned as he sat down. Once everyone was seated, Jorge spoke.

"So, we know the situation here," Jorge said as he glanced around the table. "We have some work ahead of us. We must learn who is responsible for this here other book, if there is *in fact*, another book for sure."

"Sir," Marco shook his head. "I am not seeing anything. At least, not with any publishers."

"There are so many though," Paige shook her head. "If there *is* a book, it could be published anywhere."

"We don't even know if this person has a publisher yet," Marco added. "My understanding is that no one has proposed such a book, other than the one you are currently doing, sir. So it is hard to say where this is coming from."

"Again, this could be a distraction," Jorge reminded them. "It may be something to set off alarm bells, putting me on a wild goose chase."

"But why?" Paige wondered. "Distraction from what?"

"This is what concerns me, *mi amor*," Jorge replied. "I must be anticipating anything."

"Ok, let's take it one step at a time," Chase suggested. "Marco, you can't find anything?"

"No, sir," Marco shook his head. "I have even hacked into CSIS, security cameras at the border, but nothing. It is difficult without a specific time and date to know who this person is, but I am still looking."

"It's funny Alec didn't tell you sooner," Paige turned her attention toward Jorge.

"I think he tell me as soon as he knew," Jorge replied as he glanced at his wife. "He was told that same day."

"It's very cryptic."

"*Mi amor*, there are so many layers before information gets to him," Jorge reminded her. "As usual, everything is more complicated with the government than it should be, you know?"

"So, what do we do now?" Jolene piped up.

"I am not sure what to do," Jorge admitted as he glanced around the table. "Marco, I suppose you can keep looking, and I may talk to Athas again, see if he has learned anything new."

"Sir, this man was in Mexico," Marco said as he leaned forward on the table. "I am wondering if you have talked to enough people there? Is there anyone you may have forgotten?"

"I have talked to many," Jorge admitted. "Some, they are not easy to find."

"Maybe I should go down there," Diego suggested. "Do some snooping around?"

"Is that a good idea?" Paige asked. "Remember that trap we were talking about?"

"No, Diego, stay here," Jorge said and paused for a moment. "You know, I am thinking, this person who went to Mexico...there are only a couple of places where they would focus on. If I spread the word that I am searching for information and plan to pay, maybe this will bring me the truth."

"Some want money," Diego reminded him. "Some want to get the fuck out of Mexico and move to Canada."

"If I get the right information," Jorge replied. "This is possible."

"So, you're going to send out word in your old stomping ground that you're willing to pay for information," Chase nodded. "That should work."

"I have done much for those communities," Jorge replied. "I think they will help and if you are doing a story about me, that is where you would start, because that is where I started."

"I do think sir," Marco nodded. "That this might work."

"It may be a long shot," Jorge pointed toward Marco. "It does feel like someone is covering their tracks well."

"Sir, I will continue to look," Marco spoke earnestly with worry in his eyes. "This is the first time I was not able to learn anything when I hacked."

"It's someone keeping things low to the ground," Paige insisted. "On purpose."

"They know Jorge has resources," Diego added. "They know not to cross him."

"Maybe, it is someone close to you?" Jolene asked. "Maybe an old relative in Mexico?"

"This here has crossed my mind," Jorge replied. "But most of my relatives, they know better. I do not think they would admit being related to me unless a gun was to their head."

"We don't know it wasn't," Chase replied and took a deep breath. "I'm still not convinced there is a book. This could be all bullshit."

"But if this is the case," Jorge thought for a moment. "We must know why. There has to be a reason."

The meeting ended shortly after, with everyone filing out of the room with their thoughts. Jorge and Paige were left behind, where they exchanged looks.

"What do you say, *mi amor?*"

"It wasn't anyone here," Paige quietly replied as she paused for a moment. "I watched them all closely. There are no signs."

"That is what I think as well," Jorge confirmed. "Even Jolene, she seemed hellbent on learning who is behind this."

"Unless someone is being tricked," Paige commented. "I don't know where to start. Where do we look?"

"As I said," Jorge thought for a moment. "Maybe talk to Athas again. Perhaps he was able to learn more. I encouraged him to dig a little deeper. As I said in the meeting, there are so many layers to these things. By the time he receives the information, I suspect it is filtered."

"Do you really trust CSIS to tell Alec everything?" Paige asked wryly.

"I do not trust CSIS at all," Jorge confirmed as he stood up straighter. "Or the government, in general, but I also wonder if a man would be so stupid as to tell the border person that they are writing a book about me?"

"That, in itself, is suspicious," Paige confirmed. "It's way too clumsy for someone writing a secret book, but then again, they may crumble under the pressure."

"If he crumbled under their pressure," Jorge raised an eyebrow. "Can you imagine how he will react when I find him?"

Paige grinned. She knew.

CHAPTER 33

"In fairness," Alec Athas' voice echoed through the office. Jorge exchanged looks with his wife as he leaned back in his chair before looking back at the phone. "You've made a lot of enemies since you came to Canada. Do you think maybe one of them is writing a book for revenge?"

"This here is a good point," Jorge pondered the thought.

"We've been focusing more on the publishers," Paige reminded her husband. "Assuming someone was going up against the book Tom is writing."

"Well, that is a possibility," Athas appeared less defensive when replying to Paige. "I'm not saying that's wrong, but if it were me, I would focus on Jorge's enemies. Big Pharma, he burnt them in the first year of the series and affected their bottom line. Then the police, last season…which slides into government, right? Now, it's what? The media? They might even be attacking before the next season is off the ground. They've already seen what he's done to the others."

"I humiliated them," Jorge spoke in a sinister voice, with a hint of pride mixed in. "This is true."

"It's just a thought," Athas replied. "But as for my end, the only information I got was what I told you. I'm trying to learn more, but they aren't forthcoming."

"You're the goddam prime minister," Jorge complained. "If they are not forthcoming with you, then who are they forthcoming with?"

"They are secretive," Athas confirmed.

"Fucking useless twats like most of the government," Jorge muttered.

"We have a lot of that," Athas confirmed. "Trust me, I see that more and more every day."

Paige laughed.

"Ok, well, thank you, Athas," Jorge replied as he leaned over his desk. "Please let me know if you learn more, but it does sound like they keep you on a *need-to-know* basis."

"One more thing," Paige jumped in. "Do you think CSIS is spying on us?"

"I have told them your family is off-limits," Athas spoke sternly. "But I can't be certain that they listened. They aren't necessarily known for being completely credible."

"They've been caught a few times," Paige confirmed to Jorge. "Ok, thank you, Alec. Please let us know if you hear more."

Ending their conversation, Jorge and Paige shared a look in silence.

"So this here," Jorge pointed toward the phone. "Should we worry?"

"Let's hope not," Paige replied. "If they can justify that you're a threat to Canadian's security, they might think they have a case to investigate."

"I'm only a threat if the fuckers get in my way," Jorge replied as he leaned back in his chair. "I hope Athas would have some power in that situation."

"I sometimes wonder if he has that much power," Paige replied. "Certainly not as much as I think he expected."

"That makes two of us," Jorge sniffed. "Well, at any rate, I am not running scared. We may not have the most moral operation, but we are clean, and we are careful."

"That we are."

"What is the time, *mi amor?*" Jorge reached for his phone to turn it back on. "I have a meeting with Jolene today."

"Do you think she knows something?" Paige asked with interest.

"I think she wants money for her church, like Maria said," Jorge grinned. "You know, Maria has been asking what her next task is, so this here is good. She wants to make an effort. Maybe I should send her to find out who is writing this book. She might be smarter than all of us."

Paige laughed as she rose from her chair.

"Let me know when Jolene is here."

"I will."

"Never a dull moment," Jorge shook his head as he glanced toward his bulletproof window.

"You never have a free moment to be dull," Paige confirmed as she walked toward the door. "So much for slowing down."

"I'm working on it, *mi amor,*" Jorge teased.

After she left, Jorge quickly checked his phone. Hoping that Marco had more information, he instead found no new messages. Jorge thought about Paige's comments on CSIS and wondered if there was a reason to worry. Worst case, he could uproot the family and move again, but did he want to do that? It would be easy for them, but the children were another story. Their lives were in Toronto, but maybe, their lives could be somewhere else.

A text alerted him that Jolene had arrived. He sat back, turned off his phone, and waited for her.

"Jorge," She loudly spoke as she walked in the room, her loud heels clicking as she walked. "I need to talk."

Jorge didn't reply but pointed toward the chair on the other side of the desk.

"It is not about what you think," She said as she sat down.

"Oh, Jolene, and what is it I think?"

"You think I have information on your book," She confirmed as she sat her large, red handbag on the chair beside her and crossed her legs. "But I do not know who does this."

"Then, what can I do for you, Jolene?" Jorge asked with disinterest.

"I know you like to help people," She started gently. "You know because you are a wealthy and giving man."

"Who do you want me to give money to, Jolene?" Jorge jumped in. "Make this quick. I got a lot of stuff to do today."

"The church," She replied.

"No."

"But you did not…"

"I do not need to hear anything," Jorge cut her off. "I do not give money to churches."

"But you are Latino," She shook her head. "We believe in God. We have faith."

"No, Jolene, *you* have faith," Jorge shook his head. "Me, I do not. There is no way I could be the man I am today if I did."

"But, the church, it needs some serious renovations," Jolene continued to plow through with her request. "It is a beautiful church. You should come see it."

"I have no interest in seeing a church," Jorge argued. "Tell me about your new boyfriend."

"The minister and I are dating." She looked skeptically.

"Exactly," Jorge cut her off again. "You want money for your new boyfriend."

"It is not for him," Jolene argued. "It is for the church."

"Right," Jorge nodded. "Are you sure?"

"Yes, the church, it is in terrible condition."

"That does not mean money will go to the church," Jorge reminded her. "How well do you know this man?"

"He is a man of God."

"He is a *man*."

"But if you meet him…"

"I do not want to meet him."

"But, please, can you listen?"

"Jolene, I lost interest as soon as you said you needed money," Jorge spoke harshly this time. "What about you? I pay you well. You want to give your money, go ahead, but why should I give mine?"

"But your company could?"

"I do not mix business with religion," Jorge spoke abruptly. "And you should not mix business and personal relationships. Just because this guy is a good fuck does not mean he should get my money for his church. Now, are we done here?"

Jolene glared at him.

"Jorge, you are a mean man," She finally commented and stood up. "Your soul, it will pay for this."

"My soul, Jolene, it is already fucked," Jorge snapped as he stood up. "And speaking of fucked, go jump on this minister's dick while you still can because once he learns you got no money for him, he is history. I promise."

"You are so wrong!" She pointed at him, then grabbed her purse and flew to the door. "You will see, Jorge. He is a good man."

Jorge didn't reply but watched her leave. Laughing to himself, he sat back down and turned on his phone.

These situations with Jolene were so predictable. She rushed in and took over, then was surprised when she didn't get her way. This minister wanted money more than he wanted Jolene. She would see.

As soon as his phone came alive, it beeped. It was a message from Marco that they had to talk. Intrigued, excited that maybe he had some new information, Jorge hit the call button and leaned back in his chair. Marco answered on the first ring, his voice sounded dismal, drained, and it gave Jorge a moment of pause.

"Marco?" Jorge asked. "Is everything ok?"

"Sir," Marco paused for a moment. "We must talk."

"Ok," Jorge sat up straighter. "Do you want to meet me?"

"Sir, I will need you to come to my house," He spoke in a quiet voice. "If that is ok?"

"Yes, I can," Jorge replied, assuming that he was home alone with the children and couldn't leave. "I can be there in a few minutes."

"Please, come as soon as possible."

"I will, *amigo*," Jorge jumped up from his desk and headed for the door. "I am on my way."

"Also, can you maybe ask….Chase to join us."

Surprised, Jorge agreed.

"I can," He replied. "Is this…"

"I cannot say more now," Marco spoke with no emotion. "We will talk more when you get here."

"I am on my way."

CHAPTER 34

The glow of Christmas lights met Jorge and Chase as they walked up to Marco's front door. There was a combination of sparkling lights, oversized candy canes lining the short driveway, and a life-sized, smiling snowman perched beside the front door. Jorge grinned and turned toward Chase.

"This here, it is fun for kids," Jorge mused as he reached for the doorbell, giving Chase a sideward look. "But Miguel, he would be terrified of that snowman."

Chase nodded and laughed, just as Marco answered the door. His face was pale, his eyes full of anxiety, as he quickly stepped aside and ushered them in.

"Thank you, sir," He finally spoke in a quiet voice as the two men entered the house. "I did not know what else to do."

"Marco, what is going on?" Jorge jumped right in. "Do you have information on the book?"

"No, this is not about the book," Marco made a face. "Please follow me into the kitchen."

Jorge glanced at Chase, who appeared confused, but both men walked behind Marco into the next room. Once in the kitchen, Marco moved aside. That's when Jorge saw the blood coming from behind the island in the middle of the floor. Reaching for his gun, he calmly walked around to the other side.

"It is too late, sir," Marco said as he glanced at Jorge's gun. "I…I think he is dead."

Jorge didn't say anything but calmly looked at the large, white man on the floor. Blood was pouring out of his head. It was running like a river on the ground, with splatters on the nearby wall and some of the appliances. He nodded his head and looked back at Chase, who appeared slightly ill. His eyes returned to the man, noting a large, ceramic Santa ornament nearby. It had a crack in it.

"So, Marco, was this here a break-in of some kind, or did you let him in?" Jorge attempted to understand the situation. "I assume this here man was not trying to sell you a vacuum or talk to you about Jesus?"

Marco grinned in spite of himself.

"No, sir," He sheepishly replied. "I come home, and he was here."

"So, he broke in?" Chase glanced around as if to see where this man had entered the house. "Your family?"

"They are out," Marco nodded vigorously. "Thankfully, they will be gone for a few hours, visiting with family, shopping, doing things with the children."

"Make sure they continue to stay away," Jorge instructed. "Call your wife. Be fucking calm. See what's going on. Do not let on anything is wrong. Just check in."

"I will," Marco nodded.

"Do that now," Jorge continued as he knelt to check the man's pulse, "then we will talk about what happened here."

"Ok, sir," Marco appeared quite vulnerable as he left the room, turning on his phone.

"Is he dead?" Chase asked in a low voice.

"He is," Jorge replied as he stood back up. "I do not like this. We must get the cleaning crew over here. You know who to call, what to say, then contact Andrew, get him to the crematorium."

"Ok, but how are we gonna discreetly get this fucker out of here?" Chase asked. "That's the worst part."

"No shit," Jorge shook his head. "And this man, he is not skinny. It makes me wonder how he got in the first place."

Marco returned to the room. His eyes glanced at the man on the floor, then back at Jorge.

"It is ok, sir," Marco said with some relief in his voice. "They will be some time. They are a bit out of town, and she said not to expect them home till seven tonight.

Jorge glanced at the nearby clock, then at Chase, who was on the phone. Ushering Marco aside, he spoke in a low voice.

"What is it that happened?" Jorge asked quietly. "He was here when you got home?"

"Sir, as soon as I arrive home, I hear something," Marco replied. "I could tell something was wrong."

"And you found him in here?" Jorge tilted his head back and toward the body, as Chase continued to make calls in the background. "In the kitchen?"

"Yes, sir," Marco nodded with fear in his eyes. "He said that I was 'Jorge Hernandez spy' and I said, 'I do not know what you mean. I do IT at his company' and he claims he saw me with you before, so he knows I am more than IT. He said he knew I was a hacker and I tell him, I would not know such things."

"You didn't question how he got in your house?"

"Yes, sir, but I was so angry," Marco shook his head, and Jorge noted his small status and wondered how intimidated he must've felt. "I say, 'you cannot be in this house, how did you get in?' And he said, 'well, maybe I am a hacker too'. I did not understand, but sir, he came at me. Fortunately, I had extensive training in martial arts when I lived in the Philippines, and well, I got him on the floor, and sir, I was scared. I did not know what he would do. So I hit him, just to knock him out, but I was very angry and...I thought, what if my children were here...."

Jorge could see that he was getting agitated as he spoke and put his hand on Marco's shoulder to calm him down.

"*Amigo*, you do not have to explain this here to me," Jorge insisted. "I am hardly someone who is going to tell you that this was wrong. I would have done the same thing."

"Yes, this true," Marco nodded as Chase finished his calls and approached them. "It happened so fast. But to answer your question, I do not think this was about the book."

"Well, you did the right thing," Jorge insisted as he turned toward Chase. "Are we set?"

"Everything is in place," Chase nodded and looked at Marco. "This should be cleaned up before your family gets home. Probably long before."

"Should we call Paige and Diego?"

"I hope it's ok," Chase shrugged. "I already did."

"This is fine," Jorge nodded. "They will want to help."

"Andrew said he can't get the crematorium free for a couple of hours," Chase wrinkled his nose. "The guy running it is around but has a meeting later so, we can get in then. Andrew has to be there anyway. Another body is coming in, a legit one, I mean."

Jorge grinned. "Well, this body on the floor looks legit to me."

"Sir, I cannot tell you how much this means," Marco spoke nervously. "If it was not for you, I do not know what I would do."

"Well, if it were not for me," Jorge replied. "You would not have this here problem."

Marco's cheeks turned pink, and he smiled.

"I wonder if this guy has anything on him," Chase said as he approached the body. "A phone?"

"I can hack his phone," Marco nodded vigorously.

Chase searched his pockets and Jorge turned toward Marco.

"Do you got any old blankets or towels you don't want?" He gestured toward the body. "We can keep the blood from spreading more."

"Oh, yes, sorry, sir," Marco shook his head. "I have been so scared, I just…"

"Do not worry, Marco," Jorge insisted. "This here, it is not my first rodeo, but I am guessing it is yours."

"Found this," Chase announced as he held up a phone. "This might help."

"Any ID?"

"Nope," Chase shook his head, "a gun, though."

Jorge turned toward Marco, who looked ill as he stopped in his tracks.

"This here," Jorge pointed toward the large Santa ornament on the floor beside the body. "You did the right thing. This man, he was dangerous. He was not just looking for information."

Chase nodded as he stood up with the phone in hand.

"Sir, I will get the blankets for this," Marco spoke nervously. "Then I will look at the phone....from here, it looks like one of the ones that are easy to get into."

"I got into it already," Chase was sliding his finger over the smartphone. "He didn't even have it locked."

"What a gangster," Jorge sarcastically spoke as Marco scurried away. "Dumb fuck did not even have a password."

"He has a lot of numbers in here," Chase confirmed. "Family photos, his banking, wow...like his whole life is in this phone."

"When he had a life," Jorge muttered as he leaned in. "Marco, he will get to the bottom of this here. But you know, turn off the wifi or whatever else makes it traceable. We do not want anyone to know where he is."

"Sir," Marco was saying as he returned to the room with a large, dark blanket. "I can fix it so that it seems like the phone is across town."

Impressed, Jorge nodded.

"Do that, take it offline," Chase suggested, "and study what you can, then destroy it."

"Sir, I will do so," Marco nodded vigorously. "Trust me. I know what to do."

"The man, he is a genius," Jorge said as he took the blanket from Marco's arms and headed toward the body. "This here, it is a nice absorbing blanket. The cleaners should be here soon."

"What are the cleaners?" Marco asked as Chase passed him the phone. Grabbing it, he began to tap on the screen.

"They're the guys who clean the messes," Chase replied. "We take the body away. They make it shine. Do you got something we could take the body out discreetly? Like carpet, something big you want to get rid of?"

"I have a large box in the basement," Marco thought for a moment. "Oh, this here phone, it is already set up to look like this here man is in the other end of town."

"Not surprised at that," Jorge said as he started to walk back toward them. "Do whatever you got to do."

"The box?" Chase attempted to pick up on their conversation.

"Yes, sir, I have a large box that the fridge came in," Marco said as he headed out of the room. "It was supposed to make it so that it wasn't dented, but sir, they still dented it."

"People got no pride in their work these days," Jorge shook his head. "Get it. This here is perfect."

After Marco left the room, Jorge and Chase exchanged looks, then turned their attention towards the dead man on the floor.

CHAPTER 35

His heart was still racing, long after Jorge Hernandez and the others left. Later, when his family returned home, Marco somehow managed to keep a calm exterior, even though he was shaking like a leaf inside. A man had broken into his home. He had a gun. What if his family had been home? What if his children had discovered this stranger in their kitchen? Marco couldn't stop thinking of the things that might've happened under different circumstances.

"We had a good day," His wife smiled, her eyes so trusting. Marco smiled back but quickly looked away. "Too bad you couldn't come with us. The kids had so much fun!"

"I know, but you know," Marco shrugged good-naturally. "Mr. Hernandez, he needed my help with some issues with our system, so I could not say no. He has done so much for us."

"He is a good man," She said as she crossed the room and grabbed a bottle of water from the fridge. "He has been very generous to our family. When you think of how little we had when we came to Canada."

Jorge had discovered Marco working at a hotel doing a customer service job, below his actual abilities and qualifications. This was common with so many immigrants that came to Canada. Most, however, felt it was worth the sacrifice to give their children a better future. Now, because of Jorge Hernandez, Marco could give his kids every opportunity they wished for, and his wife was able to stay at home with the children. He had much to be thankful for, but that day had shaken his security and made him wonder.

"He is a good man," Marco repeated her comment as he watched his wife take a drink of water. "I have to go meet him to discuss the changes I made today. Also, talk to him about some upgrades that we will have to make to our systems."

"Well, you should rush along then," She waved her hands toward the door. "You must not keep your boss waiting."

"I will be back as soon as I can," Marco promised as his spirit rose to its usual level. "I promise."

"Oh, Marco, did you clean here today too?" His wife was sniffing the air. "It smells very fresh! The floors look cleaner."

Marco halted for a second but quickly got back on track.

"Ah, yes, I spill coffee," Marco laughed self-consciously. "You know me, such a klutz, looking at my phone, not paying attention."

To this, she laughed, taking in his lie with no question. He felt guilty.

"Go, go see your boss," She insisted with laughter in her voice. "We are fine here. You must keep this man happy. He is good to you."

"He is," Marco's mind swept over the day. Jorge Hernandez had quickly resolved the situation. He made sure the body was removed and disposed of and blood cleaned up. He even had Clara sweep the house for listening devices and cameras. He arranged for an alarm installation the next day. Marco would tell his wife later.

"Tell him I said hello."

"I will."

Marco felt ill when he got outside. Nervously looking around, he made his way to his SUV and jumped in behind the wheel. Guilt flowed through him, and Marco felt nauseous driving across town. His mind continued to replay everything that happened that day. He hated lying to his wife, but then again, there was already so much she didn't know. It was for her safety, and until that day, Marco had never worried. He covered his tracks well. At least, he thought he had.

Making his way toward one of the wealthier neighborhoods in the greater Toronto area, Marco felt his heart racing when he finally drove into Jorge's driveway. His boss lived in a large house, what his children referred to as 'the mansion', but it was probably modest in comparison. However, there was no denying that it was a beautiful home.

Marco walked up the driveway, feeling his anxieties returning, along with the memories of the day. For the first time, he wondered if it was worth it. Was it worth it to put his family in danger?

He rang the doorbell.

"Marco!" Paige said as she opened the door, her voice calm, her smile sincere. "Come in."

Behind her was Jorge's 14-year-old daughter, watching him with interest. Although she was small in stature, appearing like any other teenage girl, there was something in her eyes that resembled her father. It was a piercing, dark glint that many would probably miss, but he didn't.

"Hello Maria," He spoke courteously, wondering if she would someday be his boss. There were rumors. "How are you today?"

"Good," Her face lit up even though her eyes remained curious. "Are you here to see *Papá?*"

"Yes, we had some things to take care of," Marco found his words, sounding more nervous than he intended. "It has been a....a busy day."

"Just go right in," Paige spoke with kindness. "I know he's waiting for you."

"Thank you," Marco said, taking a deep breath as he walked away, feeling a cold sweat come over him.

"Marco!" Jorge said as soon as he saw him in the doorway. "Do come in! Shut the door behind you, if you do not mind."

"Of course, sir," Marco spoke graciously, following instructions. "I... again...today..."

"Marco," Jorge shook his head as the IT expert walked across the room and chose a chair on the other side of the desk. "You know, you are *familia,* and you also know what that means to me."

"Thank you, sir," Marco spoke graciously. "I do appreciate this."

"But you are worried," Jorge said as he studied him carefully. "I know, Marco, you have had a very difficult day."

With that, Jorge reached in his drawer and pulled out a bottle of tequila. He pushed his chair back and pulled open another drawer, and pulled out two shot glasses.

"Marco, I could be wrong," Jorge said with a grin. "But you might need this right about now."

"Sir, I do not know what I need about now," Marco joked, feeling relief swoop over him as if he could finally let everything go. "Sir, I know that you are used to this…"

"Marco," Jorge cut him off, shaking his head as he poured them each a shot and slid one toward the Filipino. "You do not have to explain. I understand. But let us first have a quick shot to relax. It has been a long day."

Marco couldn't disagree and reached for the glass, wasting no time knocking his back, feeling the burn down his throat. He made a face. To this, Jorge Hernandez laughed.

"It is like fire, this here one," Jorge pointed toward the bottle. "Would you like another?"

"Not right yet," Marco shook his head. "I have made the mistake of drinking this too fast before."

Jorge laughed again. He grabbed his shot and knocked it back.

"Marco, this here," He pointed toward the bottle. "This is the best tequila out there. I do not indulge often, but sometimes, it is necessary. Today, that would be one of those days."

"Sir, I cannot get over that this man was in my house," Marco started to confess. "I know you want to get a security system, but I still worry."

"Marco, you tell me what you need," Jorge said as he moved his chair forward. "And I will get it for you."

"I do not know, sir."

"Look, the security system," Jorge thought for a moment. "It is not perfect, but it gives you some power. That is a help. Do you need a gun?"

"With small children, sir," Marco shook his head. "I would rather not."

"Not that you need a gun," Jorge observed as he glanced around the room. "You killed a man twice your size with a Santa ornament."

"Well, it was the first thing…"

"You cracked that motherfuckers head open like a piñata," Jorge continued as his head fell back in laughter. "Oh, I do not think you have to worry."

"Sir, it is my family," Marco said. "That is why I worry."

"Well, Marco, as I said, tell me what you need."

"I am thinking of creating a fake address," Marco said. "Make it look like I live at another house, but continue to have a post office box so it will not matter."

"That is a good idea," Jorge nodded. "But if you want to move, Marco, this is also possible. Maybe in my neighborhood. I have been thinking there is safety in numbers. I would like to own more houses in this area, so I know my neighbors, you know?"

"That is an interesting idea, sir," Marco nodded. "But I guess regardless, I will always worry now."

"But at least, we know how the man got in," Jorge pointed out. "Your wife, she left that window in the back door opened. And when she go out and left it opened…"

"I know, sir," Marco paled. "I must talk to her about that."

"This is what you do," Jorge corrected him. "You tell her that you have heard there are break-ins in your area, and you decided to get a security system. Tell her all windows must be closed when the alarm is on. It must be on at all times when you are out, even when she is home alone with the children. That you will feel safer. Meanwhile, if you suspect a problem, you got us."

"Thank you, sir," Marco spoke graciously, starting to feel a bit lighter as the alcohol hit him. "I do appreciate. I do not mean to seem…"

"Marco, you had a bad day," Jorge reminded him. "You are one of my best people, and you do not have to apologize. This here, it is fine. Meanwhile, we must learn about this man, who he is, and why he was at your house."

"I got that, sir," Marco spoke in a low voice. "But it is not because of the book."

"Oh?" Jorge was surprised. "Then what did you find out, Marco?"

"This man," Marco spoke apprehensively. "He comes to my house today, looking for me, not because of you. He knew I was a hacker for you. This social media company had invited me to work for them before, and I said no. He wanted to force…intimidate me to change my mind."

"All of this for social media?" Jorge was confused. "You mean these sites where people show pictures of themselves and say stupid things?"

"Well, that is the thing, sir," Marco spoke calmly. "These companies, they are very powerful. They create the narrative. It is unsettling."

"Really?" Jorge was intrigued. "I guess this here is something I knew, but I have always chose to keep away from them. So, this man today, he wanted to?"

"He wanted to blackmail or intimidate me to work for…one of the more sinister companies," Marco replied, shaking his head. "People, they do not realize how much information these social media companies have on them. And they are powerful. They can completely raise someone up or shut them out."

Jorge sat back and thought about his words. He remained quiet for a moment, causing Marco to fear that he had made a mistake not telling Jorge sooner. What if Jorge thought Marco was considering it? What if he thought Marco had kept it hidden? His stomach started to tighten as he looked down at his feet.

"Sir, I am sorry I did not mention this sooner, but…."

"So, how does one start a social media company?" Jorge cut him off, almost as if he hadn't heard Marco at all. "Because if this is where all the power is, then I want in."

CHAPTER 36

"You want to start a social media site?" Paige asked as she climbed into bed beside her husband. Appearing exhausted, she shook her head. "Jorge, what were we saying about you keeping a lower profile? Do you remember that discussion?"

"*Mi amor,* I know, but these here social media companies, they have so much power," Jorge spoke enthusiastically. "They control the narrative and…"

"And anyone who goes against it gets de-platformed," She cut in and shook her head. "And they steal people's information, their data, they sell it….it's all very…sinister."

"But do you not see," Jorge said with excitement lighting up his eyes. "This is where I can come in. I will allow anyone to say anything, I will not censor opinions, but I will make sure that those who need to be heard, get the most attention."

Paige tilted her head but didn't say anything.

"I know, *mi amor,* I know," Jorge sunk into the bed and turned his head toward her. "You wish for me to keep under the radar."

"Well, I thought we agreed on this many times," She shook her head. "And it's not that you can't do it because you *can*. And it's not that I want to stop you from doing what you want, but I fear that it brings too much attention to you. This has been my fear all along. We don't want to invite the wolf to the door."

"If the wolf comes to this here door," Jorge reminded her. "He will be slaughtered."

"Well, my fear is someday he will slaughter us instead," Paige reminded him. "And we've had some close calls. And speaking of close calls, Marco looked very scared today. I hope you are looking after him."

"Of course, *mi amor,* I am putting a security system in his house tomorrow," Jorge said as he moved closer to her. "And, we took care of him today."

"But you forget that he isn't us," Paige gently reminded him as she turned toward her husband. "He's not used to this…..kind of situation. It shook him up. He's worried about his family. You don't want him to second guess his decision to work for you."

"Of course not," Jorge agreed. "We talked about it. I reassured him it would be ok. His wife left the window open. That is how the man got in. I cannot believe she would do that in this here city, but what do I know."

"She's a little naive," Paige said and took a deep breath. "He did seem better when he left."

"He was," Jorge insisted. "You know me. I smooth things over."

"Just remember," She looked into his eyes. "This isn't Marco's world. This is our world. What he dealt with today would be equivalent to Maria dealing with the same thing. Not everyone is like us."

"I know, *mi amor,* I know," Jorge nodded. "Sometimes, we get desensitized. I understand but, I think you have underestimated Marco. He is stronger than he may seem. It is normal that he is shaken. This here, it is ok. He was fine when he left tonight."

"Just look after him."

"*Mi amor,* you know that I always look after my people."

She gave him a solemn look but didn't reply.

The tide had turned by the next day, and Jorge was riding the current. Before his family got out of bed, Jorge was already on the road. He had an early meeting with Makerson. The two had agreed that the VIP room at *Princesa Maria* was probably the best location to have a private conversation regarding the book. It was too risky to broach the subject in most public places.

"I started to hear rumors of another book again," Makerson confirmed as the two men sat down, both with a coffee in front of them. "But nothing I can sink my teeth into…just rumors."

"It depends where these here rumors come from," Jorge reminded him. "It could be gossip bullshit, or there might be something to it."

"That's the thing," Makerson said. "It's mainly around the office. But when I ask more questions, it always leads to nowhere. Maybe someone is trying to fuck with me because they know I'm working on your book."

"Well, if they fuck with you, they also fuck with me," Jorge reminded him as he raised an eyebrow. "We continue to look because we hear the same rumors too, but so far, nothing."

"Athas wasn't able to learn anything else?"

"Athas is pretty much useless most of the time," Jorge admitted as he shook his head. "They keep him on a need-to-know basis. I am sure of it. This here, it can be a problem."

"A problem I'm sure you can solve," Makerson suggested. "But maybe they were bullshitting him too."

"But what is the point?" Jorge shrugged. "I do know. Marco, he is looking into it, but so far, he has turned up nothing."

"Well, for now, maybe we should assume there's nothing," Makerson suggested. "And focus on our book."

"So you have another chapter for me?" Jorge was intrigued. "You are a machine."

Makerson laughed and shrugged, his face turning pink.

"Sometimes, my thoughts are clearer," Makerson admitted. "And I sit down and write. The next thing I know, I have another chapter completed."

"I am impressed."

"Well, you might want to read the chapter before you say that," Makerson spoke sheepishly. "It's the one about when your brother died."

Jorge didn't reply but merely nodded as Makerson passed him a flash drive that contained his work.

"The process of writing it was easy," Makerson continued. "But the actual content was another matter. I hope I was able to capture the day. I know it's not something I can even imagine, but I feel like I was able to put myself in your shoes, and I…I just can't imagine."

"It was…the worst day of my life," Jorge admitted as his eyes inspected the flash drive. "The only thing that I can ever imagine being worse would be to lose my children or my wife. But the odds are good, that I will be gone long before any of them."

Makerson didn't reply but gave a sorrowful smile.

"We do not want to think about death," Jorge continued. "But it is unavoidable. We do not know when or how. It is just one of those things."

"I don't dwell on it," Makerson admitted. "But I don't think anyone would be the same if they experienced what you experienced. I mean, the tragedy with your brother but then, how your parents treated you afterward. I wasn't sure how much to put in the book."

"It is fine," Jorge said after some thought. "People must know that my parents, they were very brutal with me. I do this not to get sympathy but because it is true. My goal is to show how I have risen when I could have easily sunk. That is what they wanted."

"Do you really think that's what your parents wanted?" Makerson asked quietly. "They wanted you to die too?"

"I know that is what they wanted because they told me," Jorge confirmed and watched shock cross over Makerson's face. "I know, this is hard for me to understand, now that I have children. If my daughter were to….well, it would break my heart, but I would never blame her. I would not beat her and tell her that she does not deserve to be alive."

"I don't know what to say," Makerson spoke quietly. "I'm sorry you had to live through that. I can't imagine."

"It is fine,' Jorge shook his head. "I have lived with it many years and dealt with it to the best of my ability. Maybe it was said at an emotional moment, but I never forgot, and I will not protect my parents in this book. Do not worry about adding it to the chapter."

Makerson nodded and looked down at the table.

"All our experiences," Jorge continued. "The good and the bad, they help make us who we are. Again, I could have decided to die that day too. It was obvious that my parents, they blamed me. I made the decision to be powerful, to be strong, to be bigger than life because when you are bigger than life, no one fucks with you."

"And that's you now."

"And that is me now," Jorge repeated, nodding his head. "And speaking of power, I am playing around with the idea of starting a social media company."

Makerson's eyes grew in size.

"I do not know yet when or if it will happen, but I am thinking about it."

"That's a lot. You do a lot," Makerson appeared to be concerned.

"That is what my wife says," Jorge laughed. "She says I do too much, and I must step back."

"Maybe she's right," Makerson considered. "You have a lot of balls in the air."

"I always have," Jorge confirmed. "And for many years, this caused me to strive, but maybe she has a point. Maybe I should take some time to smell the roses."

"I think it's well deserved."

"But this here, it may not be for me," Jorge added as he glanced around the room briefly, looking back at Makerson. "But first thing is first; we got to finish this here book."

"The publisher is very happy with what we have so far," Makerson confirmed. "They're looking at a potential release date."

"This is good."

"So, we got to keep going. I want to work on the next chapter this weekend."

"You do that," Jorge nodded. "And I will continue to search for whoever is also writing another book about me."

"You know," Makerson considered. "Maybe you need to find a way to lure the snake out of the grass."

"I like how you think," Jorge grinned and raised an eyebrow. "Do you have any ideas?"

Makerson thought for a moment and grinned.

CHAPTER 37

"Diego, I do not care if your dog pisses on your beloved lime trees," Jorge cut off his longtime friend and associate, causing laughter around the table. "This here is not abnormal. After all, it is a dog. This is what they do."

"But not my Priscilla," Diego sat up straighter as he gave the others a warning look. "She is *not* usually like that! And it isn't just *one* of my lime trees. It was a couple. I want to get a real Christmas tree, and I'm worried. What if she pees on it too?"

Jorge let out a sigh and ran a hand over his face before looking up at his table of associates and doing a quick run-down. They were only missing one. His wife wasn't there yet.

"Diego," Jolene jumped in. "Christmas, it is not about trees and presents and all this superficial stuff. It is about family and Jesus."

Across the table, Jorge noted that Chase rolled his eyes, while beside him, Marco had a grin on his face as he tapped on his keyboard. Jorge glanced to the head of the table, where Diego was glaring at his sister. Jolene kept talking.

"It is sad that you worry about such things, Diego," She shook her head. "I was talking to Pastor…"

"Ok, this here is enough," Jorge cut her off. "I do not call meetings to talk about dogs pissing on trees or Jesus. I am here to talk about business and important matters. About my book, the pot shops, the production house…"

Turning his head the other way, Jorge glanced at Andrew, who was doodling on a piece of paper, and Tony, who gave him his full attention. Makerson gave him a sympathetic smile and shrugged.

"Where's Paige?" Diego asked.

"Good question," Jorge took out his phone and turned it back on.

"I think I hear something now," Makerson glanced toward the door.

A small knock followed and Chase jumped up to answer it. Jorge's wife entered the room, glancing around the table, her face was pink.

"Sorry I'm late," She said as she made her way around the table to the seat beside her husband. "Miguel was…I had to deal with the daycare again."

"Oh, *mi amor*, what now?" Jorge let out a sigh as he turned his phone back off and slid it in his pocket. "Not the kill thing again, is it?"

"You're kid's killing already?" Andrew swung his head around, his abrupt comment causing everyone to laugh. "Isn't he like a baby or something?"

"He is a baby and he just yells the word kill," Jorge attempted to explain and realized there was no way to make his child sound normal, no matter what he said.

"He overheard a conversation," Paige attempted to explain while Andrew raised his eyebrows in response. "And now, he yells the word kill all the time."

"I can only imagine the conversation he heard," Diego muttered.

"Anyway, it wasn't that today," Paige shook her head. "He bit another kid."

"Is that how you started too, Jorge?" Andrew asked innocently, to which he received a glare.

"We might have to talk about putting him in another daycare," Paige muttered as she moved her chair in.

"Wow, your house must be nuts crazy to grow up in," Andrew shook his head. "Mac & cheese and a little murder on the side."

"We don't feed our kid Mac and cheese," Jorge corrected him at the same time Paige shook her head and said, "We avoid processed food."

Andrew gave them a strange, humored look and glanced toward Tony.

"My kid, he is two," Jorge continued. "He is not a murderer, so can we stop this foolish conversation? We have more serious things to talk about here today. And please, everyone, turn your phone off. If you did not already."

"Did you find out who write this book about you?" Jolene spoke up as everyone followed instructions, showing Jorge their dead phones. Jolene grabbed her phone and showed him it was off. "Diego said someone else is writing a secret book about you? Is this true?"

"We are hoping not," Jorge said with a nod to show he saw the phones. "But there are a lot of dead ends."

"Sir," Marco jumped in. "I thought I had something earlier today, but it went nowhere. I do not understand."

"Would they use some kind of code in emails?" Paige suggested.

"I do not know," Marco shook his head. "I feel like I'm going in circles."

"Maybe that's on purpose," Chase suggested and Makerson nodded. "Maybe to distract you from something else."

"This is possible," Jorge agreed. "One of the reasons why I have this meeting today is because I would like to ask everyone to be vigilant. Keep your ears to the ground, notice if anything seems strange. If anyone is asking too many questions, anything."

"I think someone's yanking your chain," Andrew agreed. "I don't think there's another book."

"I heard there was someone in Mexico doing research," Jorge informed him. "My sources say no. Not that there are many left back there that know anything."

"Would it be a family member?" Tony asked. "Maybe?"

"No," Jorge shook his head. "My family in Mexico is all gone and the relatives left behind, they do not talk about me."

"You make a lot of enemies, Jorge," Jolene quietly reminded him. "In Mexico and here, and probably other places too."

"I am aware of this," Jorge nodded. "There are some powerful people who know about me, but they all have something to lose because they are associated with me. I go down, they go down. That is the rule. Many others have died. It is difficult to say."

"My guess," Diego jumped in. "It ain't anyone in Mexico. They know better. Someone might have gone there to ask questions, but I doubt they got any answers."

"And why would they even admit that at the border," Paige added. "That's the part I can't understand. Maybe it's not true at all."

"Yes, but we cannot assume that either," Jorge said as he loosened his tie, suddenly feeling it was much too tight. "What if we let it go and this here book shows up someday?"

"It can't happen without someone talking," Makerson assured him. "I mean, there are too many people involved in the process."

Jorge took a deep breath and closed his eyes for a moment.

"Like I said the other day," Makerson reminded him. "You got to lure the snake out of the grass. Maybe get the word out that you might be interested in doing two kinds of books. One authorized, which is by me, and another one with the whole story, unauthorized. You're just looking for an author."

"Yeah, if they think they can get it right from the horse's mouth," Andrew looked up from his doodles. "They are gonna want to talk to you."

Jorge thought about it but didn't comment.

"I can't really get it around the publishing world," Makerson added. "My story is that you are telling me everything but, maybe someone else can get the word out."

Marco raised his eyebrows. "Sir, I could start a rumor online. That would be easy."

"Yeah, that way," Andrew said. "They're going to come looking for you, and that's when you trap 'em."

Jorge noted that everyone seemed to agree. He looked into Jolene's eyes to see if there was any deception, but there wasn't. He glanced at his wife, who appeared skeptical.

"No? Paige?" He asked.

"I'm worried," She admitted. "Like, I keep saying, I don't want the wolf at the door. But then again, there may be no other way."

"I can start that rumor around the production house," Tony suggested. "Maybe say that new series about the cartel boss, or hint, it might be your actual story. Toronto is a big city, but a small city too when it comes to rumors in the entertainment industry. It should spread quickly."

"Yeah man," Andrew agreed. "You gotta do this. We can all be on high alert if anything seems out of sorts."

"I can say at the production house," Jolene jumped in. "Like I misspoke. It would make sense that I slip the tongue."

Andrew almost choked on his laughter. Across the table, Marco looked down and covered his face. Chase shook his head and gave Jolene a side look. Makerson made a face. Paige made an annoyed sigh that was barely audible to anyone but Jorge.

"You know, I say..."

"I understand," Jorge put his hand up in the air. "Yes, Jolene, go slip your tongue and see what happens."

This time Diego laughed.

"I can say," Jolene ignored everyone. "I can accidentally call it Jorge's story or something...you know. We will do it."

"I think that's a good idea," Chase nodded. "If a few people get the idea out there, it will get back to whoever this is, and even if they don't want to work with you, they might slip up because they want to get this book out faster."

"And sir, I will be watching," Marco pointed toward his closed laptop. "I have a few places I am checking closely."

"Then this here is the best we can do," Jorge confirmed. "It is vital to all of us, that this book, if there is a book, it never sees the light of day."

Jorge noted everyone's expression. They were in this together, and they needed to remember that fact.

"But wouldn't they fear lawsuits?" Chase asked. "I mean, you could sue anyone who says anything they can't prove."

"It don't matter once it's out there," Andrew said as he continued to doodle. "It gets tongues wagging."

"A rumor is one thing," Jorge insisted. "A book is another."

"And get Athas to do something," Andrew continued. "What the fuck does he do all day? Plus *you* got him there."

Jorge glanced at his wife who appeared expressionless.

"Well, this here is a good point too," Jorge nodded. "He has much to lose if this book comes out because he is closely tied to me. I must remind him of this fact."

"I'm sure he knows," Paige insisted. "He's the one who brought the information to you about the border."

"Yes, but I do not think he is digging as hard as he could be," Jorge replied and looked toward Andrew. "And to answer your question, what the fuck do any of those politicians do all day?"

"Exactly," Andrew replied. "Put the goddam fire under him. If the most powerful man in the country can't find out, who can?"

"You are correct," Jorge nodded. "Except, it is not *him* that is the most powerful man in the country, and I *will* find out."

CHAPTER 38

"With the money we pay for that fucking daycare," Jorge ranted as they made their way to the SUV. "You would think they could do a better job looking after our son."

"Well, they do have a lot of kids to contend with," Paige tried to be fair as she got in the passenger side while her husband jumped in behind the wheel. "I can't imagine watching that many kids at once."

"No, but *mi amor,* that is not *your* job," Jorge gently reminded her as he hit the button to start the vehicle. "They have a lot of staff, and they know that Miguel...he is very...hyper, and that is something they should be watching, no?"

"I don't know, honestly," Paige shook her head as they drove off. "This is a whole new world to me. Maybe I'll ask around about other daycares."

"Marco's wife," Jorge suggested. "They have kids."

"They're on the other side of the city," Paige said. "I'd rather Miguel be closer."

"We will figure out something," Jorge insisted. "I know this here is frustrating, but I think this is a sign that this is not a good daycare. There are others. We will get him in one."

"It's not that easy," Paige reminded him. "There are a lot of other kids trying to get in too and not enough spots. Maybe I should keep him home for now. Apply at some that look good and wait."

"Maybe," Jorge agreed. "He might need more one-on-one attention. And this was so he could interact with other kids. Maybe, you know, get him in playgroups or something else."

"That's what I'm thinking," Paige nodded. She looked out the window as they drove home. "I can't imagine being in a situation where I needed daycare because I worked and there wasn't anything available. I wonder what those parents do."

"I do not know," Jorge replied "Back in Mexico, families come together to help one another, but it is different here."

"I worry, you know," Paige continued. "He's aggressive for his age. He's only two."

"He is getting closer to three, and he's a Hernandez," Jorge shrugged. "We develop faster. I did."

"Did you bite kids at his age?" Paige asked her husband. "And hit them?"

"I do not know," He laughed. "I certainly made up for it later."

She laughed and shook her head.

"You know, this here will be fine," Jorge reminded her. "He is not the first kid to bite, and he is not the first kid to be aggressive. I am not sure why he is this way. I am guessing it is in his blood."

"I don't want him kicked out of every daycare and then school when he starts," She firmly reminded him.

To this, Jorge laughed. "Look, Maria, she was bad. Even here in Canada, you have seen her get in trouble, and she's still in school. I think you are worrying too much."

"Did she bite other kids?" Paige asked. "Push them?"

"Well, not at his age," Jorge shook his head. "But she wasn't in daycare at his age either. But in Mexico, she got in trouble. She was bullied a lot because of me and fought back."

"She was bullied," Paige reminded him. "She wasn't *the* bully."

"I know, *mi amor,* but if I have to choose," Jorge shrugged. "I do not want my kids to be the victim, you know?"

"Can't it be somewhere in the middle?" Paige asked as they got closer to home. "Does it have to be one or the other?"

"No," Jorge shook his head. "But most of us, we fall into one category or the other at times, do we not?"

"Fair," Paige agreed, and the two fell silent for the rest of the drive home.

Once there, Paige went upstairs to check on Miguel. When Jorge got to his office, he sat behind his desk and took a deep breath, then closed his eyes. Even if he didn't say much to his wife, Jorge did worry about Miguel. He worried about both his children, but for different reasons. There were some things you could teach them and others that were not so easy. But it would be fine. Everything would be fine.

Grabbing his secure line, he called Athas. Chances are he wouldn't be in his office at that time of day, but he had to try. There was no answer. He texted him with caution to let him know they needed to talk. Five minutes later, the secure line rang.

"I was around," Athas admitted, "just away from my desk."

"We gotta talk about something," Jorge got right to the point. "I gotta find out who is writing this other book about me or if it is even true. It is important to put a muzzle on them."

"I wish I knew," Athas replied curtly. "But like I told you before, I don't have that information."

"Then I suggest you find it," Jorge snapped at him. "Remember, you have very close ties to me. If they take me down, you will be right behind."

"I know," Athas seemed to drop his original attitude. "Look, the information came from the border personnel. I didn't get names, images, nothing."

"Do you trust the person who told you the information?"

"No," Athas replied. "Jorge, I don't trust anyone here and not CSIS. They hide a lot from me."

"So, who tell you this information," Jorge pushed. "Someone walked in your office and…"

"That's the thing," Athas cut him off. "No one walked into my office to tell me. It was a report sitting on my desk."

"You did not think that was random?"

"No, because it was with some other reports, also on my desk," Athas explained. "Anything that sets off an alert comes to me. But I still don't get a lot of information."

"Get the head of CSIS and tell him or her to get the fuck in your office and push," Jorge insisted. "Ask some questions."

"I can't just demand this information," Athas corrected him. "As I said, they keep me on a need-to-know basis."

"Then tell them you *need to know*," Jorge pushed. "Athas, you are the fucking prime minister! It is time you stop being a pussy and become a lion."

The laugher outside his office alerted Jorge. He knew that laugh and took a deep breath. Turning his chair around, he continued in a lower voice.

"I am not fucking around, Athas," Jorge insisted. "Find out something for me and stop playing their games. Make *your own* fucking rules."

With that, Jorge abruptly ended the call and turned his chair back around, and glanced at the door. Standing up, he quietly made his way across the room and swung the door open to find Maria on the other side. Her face was full of horror when realizing he caught her eavesdropping.

"Maria!"

"*Papá,* I'm sorry, I came to see you and…"

"And you were listening at the door," Jorge cut her off. "You know this here will not be tolerated. You better not be doing this all the time!"

"I wasn't!" Maria insisted as Jorge gestured for her to come into his office. "I was here to see you, and I happen to hear…."

"Maria, this better be good," Jorge snapped as she entered the office and he closed the door. "You do not, *ever,* listen at the door around here."

"I don't!" She continued to insist. "I wanted to talk to you, but you talk so loud that I heard what you said, and…"

"This better be the truth," Jorge spoke abruptly while secretly worrying what else she heard; whether it be work-related or more intimate encounters, the last thing he needed to worry about was having his daughter's ear stuck to the door.

'It is, I swear!" Maria continued to plead.

Jorge took a deep breath and shook his head.

"Please sit down," He pointed toward the chairs in front of his desk. "I hope you are not lying."

"I'm not," Maria said as she walked toward his desk and sat down.

"You never do that again," Jorge continued to snap as he returned to his chair. "We do not listen at doors in this house."

"I told you, I wasn't."

"What are you here for," Jorge he got right to the point. "just tell me."

"I wanted to ask my next assignment."

"You do not have one yet."

"But you were yelling at Alec on the phone."

"How much did you hear?"

"You called him a pussy and told him to be a lion."

"And that was between him and me," Jorge reminded her. "It has nothing to do with you."

"But why were you mad at him?"

"I am mad because he can get some important information for me," Jorge replied. "And he is not."

"Can I help?"

"This here is not something you can help with, *Princesa.*"

"But tell me," She whined. "Maybe I can."

Jorge took a deep breath.

"You know that Makerson, he is writing a book on my life?"

"Yes," Maria nodded and lowered her voice. "I mean…like not your real life, right?"

"Kind of," Jorge shrugged. "I cannot say much, but…"

"Propaganda?"

"Maria, it will be mostly true, but obviously, limited."

"Ok, I understand."

"There is someone else that may be writing a book about me," Jorge continued. "That may be damaging if it is released."

"Oh," Maria nodded, as a look of understanding crossed her face.

"So, Athas, he give me this information," Jorge continued. "But not enough that I can find out who. I was yelling at him because he has a powerful position, and he has access to this information."

"Oh."

"So, I am pushing him to do his job," Jorge continued. "Or something to help me out."

"I can help."

"Maria, this is not for you," Jorge shook his head as he calmed. "I appreciate your offer, but this could be dangerous."

"I don't care."

There was a determination in her eyes that was undeniable. Jorge smiled, and she smiled back.

CHAPTER 39

"So, as you can see," Tony continued as he and Jorge walked through the production house, making their way to the office. "Everything is running pretty smoothly. Things always come up, but the shows are all in some stage of production. We have a smooth-running machine, so far."

"This here is good," Jorge nodded in approval. "I am glad. So new shows will be coming soon?"

"The first episode of *Eat the Rich* will be out shortly after Christmas," Tony confirmed as they walked into the office and closed the door. "Which is the perfect time because everyone is staying home because it's cold and they're broke. The other shows will be in the spring or summer, but yeah, I mean, things are coming along, and streaming services are demanding Canadian content."

"Canadian content that is good," Jorge reminded him. "There is a lot that is bad."

"Limited budgets," Tony reminded him as they both sat down.

"Whatever it is," Jorge shook his head. "We must be competitive, internationally."

"I think we're on the right track."

"And Jolene, she's less controlling?"

"For her," Tony nodded. "She's not always around. I assumed you had something for her to do."

Jorge rolled his eyes.

"I take that as a no?" Tony showed concern.

"Tell Jolene if she wants a job," Jorge pointed toward the wall. "She has to be here."

"In fairness, she does do some work from home."

"In fairness, what she does at home is probably not work."

"I try to get along with her."

"You're her boss," Jorge reminded him. "She is no different from any other employee. If she does not contribute, then tell me. I will move her somewhere else. Is she even here today?"

Tony shook his head no.

Jorge pulled his phone out of his leather jacket and turned it on.

"Well, this here bullshit," Jorge insisted. "Is about to change."

She answered with the first ring and sounded half asleep.

"Jolene, where the fuck are you?"

"What?" Jolene sounded sleepy. "Where was I supposed to be?"

"At work!"

"Oh, I go in later…"

"It's working hours," Jorge corrected her. "You come in now! Every time I come here lately, you are not here. If you want a job, start coming to work, or you're going back to the crematorium."

"But I…"

Jorge hung up on her.

"Problem solved."

"That's probably my biggest problem here," Tony admitted. "Although, I sometimes feel like she contributes a lot less than others."

"I might move her anyway."

"So, did you find out who's writing the book?" Tony asked in a low voice.

"Me, I am still looking," Jorge shook his head. "Nothing. I got everyone on it, including Athas, but he can't seem to shake the right trees, so I might have to shake them for him."

"Jolene started the rumor that the cartel show we're doing next year is about you," He said and shook his head. "Nothing came out. I haven't heard a thing. No one has, but on the plus side people are keeping it quiet."

Jorge thought for a moment before finally speaking. "I do not know. I am finding nothing. I have my best people on it. Nothing, as if there never was a book."

"That's strange," Tony leaned back in his chair. "So, whoever knows is keeping quiet or there really is no book."

"That is what I do not understand," Jorge replied. "I am going in circles here because nothing makes sense. I am not sure what to believe."

"Well, if I can do anything," Tony reminded him. "Please let me know. I keep wondering, but I don't understand."

"That makes two of us."

Jorge left shortly after and headed to *Princesa Maria* to check in with Chase. Glancing at his phone to see if Marco or any of the others were trying to contact him, he was disappointed to see nothing. He knew they were trying their best but couldn't understand why no one was turning up any information. Had Athas been wrong?

Chase was walking around with a clipboard when he arrived.

"Hey," he looked when Jorge entered the club and turned off his phone. "What's going on?"

"I am doing my rounds," Jorge replied as he headed behind the bar. Grabbing a bottle of tequila, he poured himself a shot and knocked it back.

"So, it's that kind of day, is it?" Chase asked as he watched him.

"You know, every day, it seems to be that kind of day," Jorge admitted. "There is always something. My son, he is no longer welcomed at daycare. My daughter, she asks a lot of questions. Jolene, she does not want to go to work unless it suits her. And I cannot find out who is writing this fucking book about me."

"Well, the thing with kids," Chase attempted to tackle the list of issues. "There's always something. I don't even live near my kids, and I'm always dealing with it, to some degree. I mean, Miguel is hyper, and they want kids practically sedated in schools because it's easier for the teacher to contend with."

"They want *all* of us sedated," Jorge corrected him as he leaned against the counter. "So we will *all* be easier to contend with."

"Well, that's true," Chase agreed as he walked closer to the bar and sat the clipboard down. "As for Maria, she's curious. She wants to be a part of the family business, and she asks a lot of questions. Even to me, but I tell her to go to you."

"What does she ask?" Jorge tilted his head. "Do I want to know?"

"Most recently," Chase thought for a moment. "She wants to know how you *really* met Paige and why she knows so much about self-defense and this whole world if she just started being a part of it a few years ago."

Jorge cringed.

"I didn't say anything."

"She will ask me eventually," Jorge predicted. "My daughter, she wants to grow up too fast. But this has always been the case."

"Since I met her," Chase agreed.

"It is interesting, though," Jorge admitted. "Watching these children and seeing what kind of people they become."

Chase nodded with sadness in his eyes.

"But, it is also stressful," Jorge shook his head. "I wish Maria wanted to be a doctor and had no idea what or who I was. I sometimes wish that Miguel was a normal, calm child. But they would not be themselves if that were the case."

"You can't make them into the people you want them to be," Chase reminded him. "They become the people they are."

"They will one day run all of this," Jorge said as he walked around the bar and sat on one of the stools. "This here, it will be their world. I am interested to see what they do but concerned that they will not be prepared."

"I think they'll be prepared," Chase insisted. "I mean, you have them on the right track. That's all you can do, and your businesses are legit. You have no connections to Mexico anymore, right?"

"No," Jorge shook his head. "All ties were severed, with that man, who had thought he was coming to Canada to kill me last year. He is dead, and so is my connection to my former life in Mexico."

"So, it's not someone from that world who would be writing this book?" Chase asked as he sat beside him. "I mean, you said that the guy was coming to Canada. Was he a Canadian citizen or a Mexican coming here to investigate you?"

"My understanding," Jorge said. "He was Canadian coming back from Mexico. This here, it does not make sense. There should be a trace somewhere, but there is nothing. I fear I will wake one day to find a book is out about me and my life. That would be my worst nightmare."

"Accusations in a book mean nothing," Chase reminded him. "It might be someone trying to make money. I think you'll find that person before anything happens. Also, any smart publisher should know that at the very least, they'd have a massive lawsuit against them."

"At the very least…"

"Exactly," Chase grinned, "at the *very* least."

Jorge left shortly after, turning his phone on as he walked to the SUV. A message popped up from Paige.

When you get home, someone is trying to contact you.

Athas.

Jorge jumped in his SUV, hopeful that he was about to learn some new information. He had shaken Athas tree and maybe, it worked. Perhaps he was able to learn some more information from CSIS.

He was barely home and in the door when Paige met him.

"Your secure line was ringing," She said as he rushed toward his office. "Alec messaged too."

"I will call," Jorge said as he made his way to the office, grabbing the phone before he even had time to sit down.

"Hello," Athas answered right away.

"You got something for me?" Jorge asked.

"I might," Athas replied. "I'm not sure it is much."

"Give it to me."

"I don't think it's a book," Athas said in a quiet voice. "I just had the CSIS guy here, and he was vague, but when I pushed, he admitted he wasn't sure if it was a book, or an article, or something else. He was complaining that his staff dropped the ball on this one."

Jorge rolled his eyes.

"But it mightn't be a book," Athas confirmed. "So, you might be going down the wrong track altogether…."

"So, this here opens the field."

"It could be anything," Athas continued. "An article…investigative journalism…I know that's not much help, but…"

"It gives me more," Jorge said as he thought for a moment. "I will talk to my people."

CHAPTER 40

"Sir, I feel so bad," Marco followed Jorge inside the *Princesa Maria* with his bicycle by his side, a laptop bag swung over his shoulder. Despite the colder temperatures, he remained strong against any elements he faced. "You did so much for my family and then the most recent…"

"Marco," Jorge cut him off and stopped walking, turning toward the Filipino. "This here, it is fine. I will explain what I learned today, and it may help. And it was my pleasure to take care of your security."

"It does mean a lot, sir," Marco continued to appear worried, shaking his head. "That system you installed gave me peace of mind, and also, that security expert you sent was able to point out the vulnerable areas in my house."

"Well, that there was Paige," Jorge shook his head. "She knows people. We had him take a look at our house too, and found a few things we could also improve. When it comes to safety, especially when children are in the house, nothing is too much."

Marco nodded, and with that, the two men walked into the empty bar.

"They must all be here by now," Jorge observed. "I am running a bit late."

"Me as well, sir," Marco said as he propped his bike against the nearby wall and removed his helmet. "Today, at the office, it was one thing after another. That new assistant of mine must learn to take on more responsibility. I am trying to be patient, but I do not have time for all her little questions."

"Just be careful," Jorge reminded him as the two men crossed the bar, heading to the VIP room. "Check her carefully and her work. We do not want any surprises."

"I always do," Marco assured him. "I monitor all employees carefully."

"If only we could clone you," Jorge grinned as he reached for the door to open it. To this, Marco giggled.

Inside the room, Jorge found his wife already there, involved in a conversation with Diego. Chase sat in his usual spot with no expression on his face. Tony and Andrew were having a separate discussion about a show they were working on, and a quick survey of the room let him know who was missing.

"Where the fuck is Jolene?" Jorge interrupted everyone as he glanced around. "I told her the time of this here meeting."

"Probably with her new boyfriend," Andrew abruptly spoke while turning around. "She's either talking to him, with him, or he's dropping by to pick her up for lunch. He looks like a douce to me, but whatever."

"Well, at least she is showing up for work now," Jorge commented as he sat down. "This here is something new."

Diego groaned and shook his head.

"Hey, Diego, this here is not your fault," Jorge assured him. "We cannot control our families. Trust me. No one knows that better than me."

"Speaking of which," Paige turned her attention to Chase. "I heard Maria is asking a lot of questions about me. About my past and where Jorge and I met."

"Online dating," Jorge spoke flippantly, causing the others to laugh. "I filled out this here application, and they say she was perfect for me."

"Yup, that's exactly how it happened," Paige spoke in a soft voice, going along with the joke.

"Although, these days, it is our son who is bad," Jorge shook his head as he turned off his phone. "We have to find a new daycare."

"Good God!" Andrew shook his head. "As for Jolene, don't count on her showing up. She doesn't show up for *our* meetings either."

Jorge exchanged looks with Diego, who shrugged.

"Like, what is she doing with that guy all the time," Andrew went on to say. "She must have her ass worn off by now."

To this, everyone laughed.

"Look, she is, a lost cause," Jorge replied. "I know she has helped us in the past, but it seems she is getting less and less involved with the *familia*. Her priority is this here man. I do not know. I expect loyalty above all, and if she can't even make it to a fucking meeting, then we might have a problem."

"Maybe she's involved with this book," Diego spoke in a low voice.

"Sir, I have checked that a million times," Marco shook his head. "Also, I have checked this man she is with, and there is nothing that suggests this at all."

"So, he's just a good 'ole boy?" Chase challenged.

"Usually," Marco continued. "If you check even text messages, emails, something usually slips out, but he is clean."

"This here does not leave the room," Jorge reminded everyone. "We do not talk to Jolene about any of this."

He gave Diego a warning look. His response was to raise his hands in the air as if to surrender.

"She's very insecure and needs that assurance from someone," Paige suggested. "If a boyfriend is in the picture, it's going to be him. If no one is in the picture, she looks to Jorge for approval. Almost like he's her parent or something."

"Yeah, well, she might need some more parenting," Diego suggested. "Because we didn't get much growing up. Just bible shit thrown at us for everything."

"I guess she has, you know, gone back to that," Jorge said and took a deep breath. "Either way. I do not wish to talk about Jolene all day. We have more important matters to discuss and we must address them now. I need you all to be aware of some new information."

"Did you find out who's writing the book?" Chase asked as he leaned forward.

"No," Jorge replied. "However, I was talking to Athas that suggested that it may not be a book, but an article by an investigative journalist, something of this sort."

"It's possible," Chase agreed. "Maybe we're on a wild goose chase looking for a book and maybe there is *no* book."

"It would certainly not seem to be," Marco added. "Not with everywhere I looked."

"Unless, it's kept well under wraps," Tony threw in from the end of the table. "That's not unheard of either, so we might not want to drop that idea entirely."

"Either way," Jorge continued. "It might be part of a show, an article, a book...this here opens things up, but at the same time, makes it more difficult to narrow it down."

"I thought the person at customs said it was a book," Paige reminded him. "You know, maybe it was someone researching you to write a fiction book, did you ever consider that?"

"I feel like we're going in circles here," Andrew jumped in. "Like getting nowhere. Whoever got this shit going on, they got it buried, *deep*. And they got it buried deep for a reason. Some shitbag is keeping this under wraps because he knows you are capable of finding what the fuck you look for."

"Except this time," Jorge commented wryly. "I am not having luck."

"Sir, this might help," Marco replied. "See, before, I thought you might be the main focus of a book. What if you are one of several in a book or like Paige said, it is fiction."

"That seems like a long way to go to research fiction," Chase shook his head. "I mean, to write fiction, you might not want to get in Jorge's crosshairs."

"And they're covering it up too tight for someone who doesn't know what he's capable of," Andrew threw in. "This ain't no newbie."

"That's true too," Paige agreed. "Maybe it's part of a book, or maybe there was a misunderstanding, and it *is* part of a documentary of some kind. I mean, you do documentaries on other people and piss them off. Maybe someone is attacking back."

"I can look at this too, sir," Marco said as he pulled out a notebook and started to write a list. "I can look at all these possibilities."

"I find it hard to believe they're able to hide it so well," Chase shook his head. "Usually there is a paper trail of some kind."

"But I may not have looked in the right places," Marco suggested. "If I am looking at books featuring Jorge, then my focus may be wrong."

"I don't envy your job," Diego said to Marco. "How the fuck do you even know where to start?"

"Well, I had previously started with major publishing companies," Marco explained. "then to smaller ones, then more independent. I look for Jorge's name in emails, keywords like cartels, Mexico….I have searched through some of his enemies."

"Fuck, that could take forever," Diego shook his head.

To this, Jorge laughed.

"Yes, they might not have his actual name, and what if the emails are encrypted?" Paige asked. "Maybe you aren't seeing them."

"I have not found many such emails," Marco disagreed. "When I look, I find that most people are wildly careless in their emails."

"People, they are stupid," Jorge reminded his wife. "It often amazes me how naive they can be."

"But this will be my focus today," Marco said as he turned toward Jorge. "Can I work from here? I have too many interruptions from my new assistant at work."

"Of course, Marco, work from wherever you wish," Jorge insisted. "And if this assistant is too much of a pain in the ass, fire her."

"I do not like to do that," Marco spoke sadly. "She is young. This is her first job out of college."

"Just watch her carefully," Paige suggested.

"Watch everyone carefully," Jorge added. "I do not care who they are. Someone must know something, somewhere."

After the meeting ended, Paige glanced up at Jorge and Marco, who remained. The three exchanged looks.

"I have a thought," Paige spoke with some hesitation. "And I don't want you to be mad."

"Paige, I could never be mad at you," Jorge assured her.

"I was thinking," Paige continued and glanced at Marco then back at Jorge. "Maria is asking a lot of questions lately. What if someone is working on her? What if someone she thinks she can trust is looking for information? What if she is confiding things? I don't like to say it, but it has crossed my mind."

Jorge fell silent and looked down, took a deep breath, and looked up.

"I hope not," Paige continued. "And I don't think so, but we might have to consider it."

Jorge hesitated before nodding slowly.

"Sir, I can look…."

"Yes, Marco, please do," Jorge exchanged looks with Paige. "I know she takes our family very seriously, but you are right. This here is a possibility."

Paige reached out and squeezed his hand.

CHAPTER 41

"Nice of you to show up at work today!" Jorge snapped as he walked into Jolene's office, causing her to jump. "Our meeting yesterday, you did not think was important enough to make an appearance?"

Jolene opened her mouth to respond, but before she could, Jorge slammed the door closed and continued to speak to her in a loud, abrupt tone.

"What the fuck, Jolene?" Jorge continued as he crossed the room. "Why do we keep coming back to this, again and again? I got to tell you, this here, it makes me not trust you."

"Jorge, it was important," Jolene started to speak up as if to compete with his boisterous voice. "I had a doctor's appointment."

"And you could not tell me about this?" Jorge shrugged as he stood over her, his eyes glaring. "You could not let me know that you had this here appointment? Was it a secret? Are there any other secrets, Jolene?"

"I am trying to have a baby, and I need special treatments," Jolene snapped. "Ok, is this ok with you? Do I have to get some special permission to live my life?"

"I do not care," Jorge shook his head. "I do not care what it was for. This here is not the point. It is the fact that you are, in general, always doing what you want, when you want, and this here concerns me."

"I have to plan around my ovulation," She attempted to explain. "And sometimes, this means I am a little late because you have to…"

"Jolene, this here it is too much information," Jorge put his hand in the air and finally sat across from her. "Please, do not get into the details, but is this not something you should have told me before? You give me no explanation and disappear. How do I know it is true?"

Jolene made a face, grabbed her purse. She took out a small plastic device and threw it on the desk.

"What the fuck is that?"

"It tracks my ovulation," Jolene attempted to explain. "So it tells me…"

"Ok," Jorge cut her off. "I got it, but Jolene, this still does not explain why you did not tell me sooner."

"Because it is private."

"So you show up to work when you want?" Jorge asked as he shrugged his shoulders. "Do not show up to meetings? Give no explanation?"

"I did not think it would matter."

"It does."

"I will tell you next time."

"I think it is time you go back to the crematorium."

"I hate the crematorium," Jolene shot back. "You do this to punish me."

"Jolene, you are no good here," Jorge waved his hands in the air. "You do nothing but try to tell Tony and Andrew how to do their job. They say you are not helping them. They do not even know when or if you will show up to work. I think it is time you go back. There are less critical deadlines for the work you would do there, and also, you can keep an eye on the new manager."

"You do not trust him?"

"I do not *know* him," Jorge leaned in. "Therefore, I do not trust him."

"I think I am a much better fit here," Jolene attempted to explain. "I contribute *much*. I do *plenty*. Those boys do not like me because I…."

"Because you are bossy even though you are not the boss?" Jorge attempted to finish her sentence.

"No, because I do good work," Jolene insisted. "I do a lot of work to help them."

"Oh, is this so?" Jorge shot her back some attitude. "Is this true? Is this the hill you wish to die on, Jolene?"

She sat back and made a face.

"Go back to the crematorium," Jorge said as he stood up. "And I mean, immediately. As in tomorrow, and I will send a message that you are to return. He did need some help, so this here, it works perfectly."

"It does not work well for me," Jolene complained.

"Then leave the *familia*," Jorge snapped, his eyes darting in her direction. She fell silent, her eyes filling with fear. There was only one way you left the family, and Jolene knew this well.

"I will go back to the crematorium," She finally replied. "tomorrow."

Jorge didn't reply but turned to walk out of the room, but he stopped and turned around.

"Oh, and because you missed it," He studied her. "The meeting was about how someone is writing, or maybe producing, something about me that is not very flattering. Whoever it is, is being careful to keep undercover, but eventually, I will find that motherfucker and well, Jolene, you know how this story ends."

She nodded but didn't reply. Jorge studied her face before turning and walking out of the office, closing the door behind him.

Finding Tony on his way out, he quickly filled him in on Jolene's upcoming departure.

"Honestly," He stood, leaning against a nearby chair. "Jolene is more of a hindrance lately than a help. She's not exactly reliable, and basically, she makes a few phone calls to verify things."

"This here, I know," Jorge nodded. "I think this will be the best for everyone."

"Andrew will be ecstatic," Tony continued. "There's a lot of animosity between him and Jolene."

"That goes way back," Jorge confirmed with a grin on his face as he remembered. "And is justified. She will still be at the crematorium, but he's rarely there."

Leaving the production house, Jorge made his way across town to Makerson's condo. As he drove, he thought about his recent conversation with Paige. What if Maria was getting pulled into a situation by someone she trusted? His daughter knew not to discuss family matters, but could she be manipulated? As much as Jorge wanted to believe his daughter was powerful, he did have concerns. It wasn't her vulnerability so much as her fragile, emotional side. It was a cause for concern and something both he and Paige had dealt with in the past. He was anxious about what Marco would find out.

Once arriving at Makerson's, Jorge pushed these thoughts aside to focus on the progress with the book. So far, he was impressed with how quickly and accurately the young writer was with this project. It was impressive.

"Hey," Makerson met him at the door and moved aside to let him into the condo. "I just finished another chapter. I took advantage of my afternoon off to get some work done."

"Wow," Jorge shook his head. *"Amigo,* I do not understand how you write so fast, but it is good. I enjoy every chapter I read, and you write it…I do not know how to explain."

"I try to tell a compelling story," Makerson nodded as he pointed toward his kitchen table. "at least, that's my goal. Do you want a coffee?"

Jorge thought for a moment and nodded.

"Sure."

Makerson went ahead to pour them each a cup, while he continued to talk.

"I was a little worried when I started," he confessed. "I mean, I never wrote a book before, but I don't know, once I get started, I can't stop. It feels very natural."

"Maybe you will become a great author," Jorge suggested. "It might be easier than working at a newspaper."

"I like the paper," Makerson confessed as he sat Jorge's coffee in front of him, to which he nodded. "I like the pace. I like the feel, but yeah, I didn't realize until I stepped away some, how much it's burning me out."

"I can relate," Jorge confessed. "With me, it is the same…the pot shops, the production house, all of this is exciting, but you get very caught up in things, and there is a point where you have to step away. Even if temporarily. It is like getting caught up in a hurricane. When the hurricane is over, you are left exhausted, but at the time, it's quite exciting."

"I'm enjoying the process," Makerson nodded. "But we got to be careful with the next part that I'm working on. I have to understand your...account of your teenage years. I have a vague idea of what they were."

"Yes, well, this here, it will never make the pages of this book," Jorge grinned as he took a drink of his coffee. "I have some notes I brought with me today, and of course, we have talked about it before."

"Your teenage years were very...."

"Terrible," Jorge said. "My parents, they hated me, so I did my own thing, however for the book purposes, I worked harder to meet their approval."

"That's when your father started his coffee business?"

"It was growing," Jorge nodded. "By the time I was 18, it was going full force."

"And you?"

"For the book purposes," Jorge grinned. "Helping him, despite his disdain for me."

"I know we talked about it before," Makerson nodded. "I can't imagine living like that. I mean, with your parents."

"What I believe," Jorge said as he clasped on to his cup of coffee. "is that if you are disowned or unappreciated by your own family, you find a replacement. This is human nature. It might be a group of people, maybe others in the same situation as you, or maybe you start your own family. It could be a situation more like mine. The point is that you look for your tribe. We need that connection."

Makerson considered his words and slowly nodded.

"I could get more into that story," Jorge shook his head. "But for this here book, we've already discussed what must be said. Make it interesting, relatable. That is all I ask of you."

"That's what I hope to do," Makerson confirmed before switching gears. "Any news on the other book?"

"We are still working on it," Jorge confirmed. "But whoever it is, is being careful. It may not even be a book but an article or something else."

"I've looked into my sources too," Makerson said and took a deep breath. "If it's legit, it's carefully hidden, and in the publishing world, that's surprising. Usually, someone talks."

"We continue to work at it," Jorge said. "This here, it keeps me up at night."

After going through some information with Makerson, Jorge was on his way out when he turned his phone back on. By the time he was back in the SUV, he had a collection of messages. The top one was from Marco. He had to see him.

CHAPTER 42

"Ok," Jorge said as he entered the VIP room of *Princesa Maria* to find Marco sitting at the table, laptop opened. "Give it to me. What is my daughter doing now? Do I want to know?"

"Oh, sir, give me a moment," Marco replied and rushed to turn off his phone and laptop. Only after they were powered down did he begin to speak. "Sir, I was looking through her texts and messages, and I did not find much. At least not yet."

"No?" Jorge was surprised, slowly relaxing as he sat down. "So, this here is not about Maria?"

"Sir, most of what she has in her texts and emails are normal for her age," Marco shrugged. "She does worry a lot about her appearance, but there is nothing that truly alarmed me, and certainly nothing about the... family business."

Jorge sat up straighter, impressed that his daughter was listening to him.

"So, this here is not about her?" Jorge asked. "You are not trying to protect me because Marco if there is anything, I got to know."

"No sir," Marco responded with a smile. "No, that is not why I called you here today. As I said, I do not see any reason to be alarmed. I am surprised how little she is on these social media channels. I also noted that her online searches are regarding guns, self-defense, this kind of thing, but I think given the circumstances…"

"Yes, this makes sense," Jorge nodded. "She wants to learn, and even though I wish she would focus on something else, I guess there could be worse things."

"Sir, there could be *much* worse things," Marco confirmed. "She talks in her messages about other kids in school, and believe me, it is scary what some her age are doing. So, in comparison, I would not be so concerned. Her research might alarm some…"

"But not me?" Jorge jumped in before throwing his head back in laughter. "Yes, Marco, this here sounds right. I mean, no, I would rather she did not get involved in any of this. I guess I am not in a position to complain. At least her time is not being wasted on frivolous bullshit."

"There are some gossip sites," Marco confirmed. "A lot of videos on hair and makeup, but I would not be concerned by anything I have found. I mean, it would seem to me that she takes this family very seriously and that she is focusing on that."

Impressed, Jorge nodded. He felt pride erupt in his chest, but Marco's next comment broke the spell.

"There is something of concern though," he continued with a lower voice. "And you are not going to like this."

"What?" Jorge shook his head. "I guess it would be too good to be true that my daughter, she…"

"No no, sir, I do not mean Maria," Marco quickly corrected him. "As I said, I do not see any reason to be alarmed. I have not finished checking but so far, I am satisfied that you should not be concerned, either as a father or regarding your organization."

"Then what?" Jorge felt his body tense again. "Who is betraying me? Is it Jolene?"

"Sir, I do not know for sure," Marco took a deep breath. "There are some messages I am seeing that concern me."

"Oh?" Jorge raised his eyebrows. "What is she saying?"

"She talks a lot to this minister, but sir, is this her boyfriend?" Marco asked as his forehead wrinkled. "Because what I saw today, it does seem to be another man. I am a little confused. I thought the minister *was* her boyfriend, but then there is mention of another man."

Jorge sat up straighter.

"It is very confusing," Marco continued as he took out an iPad to show it to Jorge. "There are a lot of messages from this other man she calls 'Rico' but the priest, his name is 'Ricky' so I thought this was the same but now, I see messages that give me the impression they are two men."

"Rico….it is a nickname…." Jorge attempted to explain. "It could mean a few things, all of which Jolene likes."

"See, this here is how she has him listed in her phone," Marco continued as he shook his head. "I did not originally catch on for some reason because the messages to both are very…sexual."

"Oh?" Jorge was vaguely interested. "So, she is fucking both Ricky and Rico?"

"Well, Rico, as you said, could be a nickname," Marco reminded him. "I am uncertain if this is his real name. It seems that she is trying to get pregnant, sir?"

"I did hear this," Jorge sighed in frustration. "This is why she does not bother to show up to any meetings or work unless she feels it."

"Well, sir, these two men, they keep her pretty busy," Marco said and immediately started to laugh. "I can see why she has no time."

Jorge couldn't help but grin as he scanned over the messages.

"I see why you got the two mixed up," Jorge shook his head. "She says the same to both."

"I know, that was what fooled me," Marco continued. "I thought, why would she tell him this same stuff again. I must admit sir, I should have caught this sooner, but with Jolene, it is always such silliness."

"She has no substance," Jorge complained. "I know in a pinch, she helps us and I know she has saved Paige's life, but overall, Jolene is about Jolene."

"So does she want to get pregnant and not know who the father is?" Marco made a face. "This seems very irresponsible."

"No, you do not understand," Jorge corrected him. "She wants to get pregnant, period. She does not care about what happens with these here two men. She will, in the end, pick the ones she prefers and use the baby as leverage."

"I hope they are similar enough in appearance," Marco shook his head and let out a loud sigh. "Anyway, this, I do not respect."

"Jolene is difficult to respect any day," Jorge reminded him. "So, we know who the minister is..."

"Yes, that has been confirmed," Marco nodded. "I know this for sure."

"But Rico?"

"That is a mystery, sir," Marco shook his head. "Originally, I thought this might even be his real name, but then she remarked in one message that...you know, I will not get into it. The point is that her messages, they are confusing, sir."

Jorge made a face.

"Can you look up the number, Marco?"

"I have tried, but it is like it isn't listened with a phone company."

"Would it not have to be?"

"That is what I do not understand, sir," Marco shook his head. "All numbers, burner phone or not, are listed with some company. This is also why I am confused."

"But money talks," Jorge reminded him. "But why does he not wish to be listed with a phone company?"

"We must figure this out," Marco concluded.

"Is there anything about us?" Jorge asked as he bit his bottom lip. "Anything to set off alarms?"

"Until today," Marco shook his head. "No, they just talked about hooking up mostly. However, today, there were some remarks."

"Oh?"

"They were talking about how you interrupted them?" Marco said with wide eyes. "You yelled at her for not being at work?"

"Yes, because she was supposed to be at work," Jorge nodded and began to laugh. "This interfered with her fucking schedule?"

"*Literally,* her fucking schedule, sir," Marco said, and both men began to laugh. "Sir, he commented how you interrupted them because he had... something 'mind-blowing' prepared for her that morning. I will not get into the details..."

"Please," Jorge shook his head. "I do not want to know about Jolene's sexual escapades. So, they talk about how I interrupted them and what?"

"He said something like 'Oh, you can't piss off the powerful Jorge Hernandez'," Marco continued.

"At least one of them gets who I am," Jorge said as his eyes narrowed.

"She said, you were her boss, *technically*," Marco slowly continued. "So, she had to show up to work."

Jorge rolled his eyes.

"Then this Rico man, he says," Marco slid his finger up the screen before squinting and continued. "'I hear you do not piss off this man or you might end up in a body bag' and she responded, 'I will not end up in his body bag.' He asks why and she said, 'Because I won't be his puppet like everyone else.'"

"Oh, is this so?" Jorge asked as his blood began to boil. "This is what she thinks and *says* to a stranger?"

"Sir, I do not know if it *is* a stranger," Marco looked up from the iPad. "He talks almost like he knows you…which concerns me."

"What else you got, Marco?"

"He goes on to say, 'Maybe it's time to cut the strings' to which Jolene responds, 'If I cut the strings, he will cut my throat'."

"It is tempting," Jorge confirmed. "Some days more than others, it is tempting."

"Sir, I do understand," Marco nodded, his eyes widened. "She is too much. Even here, the way she talks."

"What else?"

"He says, 'If you are scared, we will find you a way out.'"

Jorge said nothing. His face turned to stone while fury ran through his veins.

CHAPTER 43

"Just relax," Paige instructed with her hands in the air, attempting to calm her husband. "Jolene is not worth getting this angry about."

"I know she is not worth it," Jorge confirmed as he paced back and forth in his office. "But this here, it is too much. What is she telling this man, and who is he? If this is what she says in a text, what kind of pillow talk do they have after he fucks her?"

"Ok, well, maybe this is all she has said," Paige reminded him. "She knows better than to talk too much."

"But *mi amor,* she already has," Jorge reminded her, and Paige looked down. "What Marco showed me, it says that she is a problem."

"Well," Paige seemed at a loss for words. "So, this man knows you are dangerous."

"Which she confirmed," Jorge nodded as he walked toward Paige, "It is either she has told him about me, or he already knows me, but either way, this here is a problem. What if it is the man who writes this book or article about me?"

"Ok, well, we don't know that," Paige spoke calmly. "But we are going to get to the bottom of this."

"Marco, he continues to look, but Paige," Jorge shook his head. "I am ready to go over there and kill her right now."

"Kill who?" Maria's voice came from outside the door, as she pushed it open and walked inside. "Who are you killing?"

"Maria, what did I say about listening at the door?" Jorge snapped, which didn't seem to phase his daughter.

"You said not to do it, but I wasn't listening at the door," Maria corrected him. "I came to tell you something, and the door was open ajar, so I couldn't help but hear you."

Jorge took a deep breath and attempted to calm himself, but his heart was racing.

"Maria, this....you misunderstood," Paige stumbled over her words. "People exaggerate. He didn't *literally* mean he was killing anyone."

"Fine, whatever," Maria brushed it off as if she didn't care. "But who are you talking about?"

"Maria...I..." Paige started, but Jorge was quick to cut off his wife.

"Jolene," Jorge replied to his daughter. "I do not trust her."

"I know, you never trusted her," Maria nodded. "What did she do this time?"

"Maria," Paige suddenly had a thought. "Do you know who someone named or nicknamed Rico is? Has Jolene ever mentioned him? Or having two boyfriends?"

Maria thought for a moment.

"This here is important," Jorge calmly reminded his daughter.

"I know she talked about the minister guy," Maria made a face. "I forget his name, but she mainly talked about him. But *Rico* might mean..."

"Yes, yes," Jorge nodded vigorously. "So, any other man that you got the impression she had...."

"A sexual relationship with?" Maria attempted to finish the sentence, causing Jorge to cringe.

"Anything," Paige jumped in. "Maybe she mentioned someone you even know? I mean, we have to consider everything."

"I don't think it would be anyone we know," Maria reminded them. "Chase hates Jolene...and I mean, *hates* Jolene. He keeps it professional because he has to and because of Diego. What about that newspaper guy or the television guys? And wasn't she dating Alec Athas once?"

Jorge checked his wife's reaction, but she had none.

"I can't see it," Paige said and shook her head. "She didn't exactly make his life easy."

"That is not Jolene's thing," Jorge added. "I will find out."

"Who else?" Maria shrugged. "She doesn't talk to that reporter guy."

"Makerson?" Jorge shook his head. "I cannot see."

"Who else?" Maria thought. "Marco? I don't think so."

"No," Jorge thought for a moment.

"And Andrew hates her too," Paige added. "That's obvious, and Tony?"

Jorge thought for a moment and finally shook his head.

"She would be at work more if it were him," Jorge said. "And he *is* at work all the time."

"What about that guy she used to date that was married?" Maria asked. "Where is he now?"

"Keeping as far away from Jolene as possible," Jorge insisted. "Trust me on that. I check in with him often. He is in Mexico."

"I don't know then," Maria said. "It's probably no one in your inner circle. That's what I think."

"I think she's right too," Paige nodded. "And although she has said too much, we still don't know if this guy is writing a book."

"Regardless," Jorge shook his head. "She has said too much."

"We have to find out who this Rico is…."

"Yeah, because *Papá,* she is not going to tell a *minister* about you."

"This guy could be fishing for someone else," Paige thought out loud.

"Do you want me to find out?" Maria volunteered. "I could find an excuse to get her to spend time with me."

"No," Jorge shook his head, his heart suddenly filling with pride. He leaned in and kissed her on the top of the head. "Maria, you have helped more than you realize already. Your *Papá* does not always think with a clear head when he is angry."

"I know," She nodded and smiled. "No one does."

"Maria, you said you had something to tell us?" Paige asked as she watched Jorge lovingly run his hand over his daughter's hair.

"I got the top grade in the class for my presentation on countries of the world," Maris beamed. "Of course, I had Mexico, which I know lots about so, I talked about that. Another girl wanted to do Mexico, but *I* am

Mexican, so I said *I* should do it, and the teacher let me, and I got the best project in the class."

"Wow, *Chiquita,* this here is good!" Jorge leaned in and kissed the top of her head again. "I am very proud. I am glad you are taking what I said seriously, and you are working extra hard to do well in school."

"Well, it's like you said, *Papá,* you have to be thinking ahead of the other guy," Maria repeated a comment from earlier that week. "And you can't do that if you're dumb."

"Well, Maria, you aren't dumb," Jorge smiled. "But I am very proud of you. You are proving yourself more than a much, much older woman in this *familia.*"

"In fairness, *Papá,*" Maria shrugged as she swung around. "It wasn't much of a stretch."

To this, Jorge threw his head back in laughter.

"Anyway, if you need my help," Maria continued as she blushed. "I can."

"Maria, unless you know of this other man," Jorge shook his head. "I do not know what else you can tell me."

"Are you having someone follow her?" Maria asked, and Jorge's eyes widened. Paige exchanged looks with him.

"You know what, Maria," Jorge replied, somewhat thrown off course. "I did not even think of this."

"Yeah, well, if you just found out," Maria attempted to explain. "And when you're so angry, you can't think straight. Paige taught me that the best strength is keeping a clear head."

"That's right," Paige nodded with a smile. "That's what I always tell you."

"That's how the other guy wins," Maria went on. "If you are upset or stressed, you miss things or opportunities."

"Well, Maria, I do think you are showing a lot of promise," Jorge was dumbstruck. "For 14, I cannot believe...I mean, I *can* believe, but this here is impressive."

"I take my lessons very seriously," Maria reminded him. "I wasn't just saying that I want to move up. I meant it."

"I see this," Jorge nodded and glanced at Paige. "Well, I think that tells me everything."

"I would suggest someone like Chase," Maria went on to explain. "He can keep calm and easily fit in anywhere. He needs a car she won't recognize, but he can watch her house."

Jorge nodded, again impressed.

"I think you're right," Paige nodded.

"Or you," Maria directed her comment at her step-mother. "But if she's talking to this guy a lot, guaranteed she's gonna be with him soon, right?"

"This here is right, Maria," Jorge replied. "I will go talk to Chase now."

"Maybe he can grab the guy on the way out," Paige muttered. "So *we* can talk to him."

"You ladies, you are clever," Jorge grinned from ear to ear. "I'm heading to the *Princesa Maria* to talk to Chase."

"Do you want me to do anything?" Paige asked as he headed for the door.

"Be on standby," Jorge suggested. "Because we might need your help."

"Do you need my help?" Maria asked excitedly.

"No, you," Jorge pointed to her from the hallway. "You did good work today, Maria. Take the evening off and order some pizza."

Enjoying a final moment of joy in his daughter's eyes, he turned and headed for the door. If Jolene thought she was going to get away with this shit, she was sadly mistaken.

CHAPTER 44

"Fuck!" Diego put his head in his hands and looked down at his desk before his eyes shot back up. "Are you fucking serious? What if this Rico guy is writing the book? Or knows who's writing the book, or it's *a cop?*"

He said the final word with disgust as his eyes narrowed at Jorge, who sat across from him.

"Diego, you know the police, they do not scare me," Jorge shook his head with humor in his voice. "I *own* the police."

"Yeah, but not *all* the police," Diego leaned forward on his desk. "We gotta be careful."

"Diego, I do understand," Jorge insisted. "But we gotta step back here and look around. This man could be anyone, or he could be no one. Have you seen or heard Jolene talk about this Rico guy?"

"I don't talk to Jolene about that shit," Diego confirmed. "Look, she's my sister, but you know, it's just not something I talk to her about. Her dating life has been and always will be a motherfucking mess. If she's not chasing a married guy, it's someone she scares off."

"Jolene, she has her good points, but Diego," Jorge gave him a warning look. "This time, she may have crossed the line. She does not listen to me. She rebels like a child, and there is nothing that I hate more than an adult who acts like a child. It is more frustrating than an actual child misbehaving, and God knows, I got lots of that already."

"But in her defense," Diego twisted his lips together. "Maria, she did good today."

"She did great," Jorge confirmed with a smile. "I am very proud of her. She has come a long way. I do not wish this lifestyle for her, Diego, but if it must be, I feel better knowing that she is smart about it."

"She could teach Jolene," Diego shook his head and sigh. "Are we gonna have to…"

"I do not know yet," Jorge replied and thought for a moment. "Chase, he is gonna get this Rico piece of shit, we talk to him, and then we take it from there."

"Are we going to the club or crematorium?" Diego asked bluntly.

"I am not sure yet," Jorge replied. "But I gotta tell you, the comments I read today between the two of them, the ones Marco showed me. They did not leave me with a warm, fussy feeling."

"Ok," Diego took in the information and paused for a moment. "Whatever you need me to do, I can do it. If you want, I can search her house?"

"She is home now," Jorge replied. "It is interesting how she did not bother to go to work half the time. This is becoming a habit. I knew right there that there was a problem. Jolene used to whine that she had nothing to do. Now, she shows up occasionally."

"And she wants a kid?" Diego asked and watched Jorge nod. "She can't have one. Remember that time she lost a baby? The doctors told her if she tried again, it would be the same. Plus, she's getting a little long in the tooth."

"Diego," Jorge laughed as he moved ahead in his chair. "We are *all* getting a little long in the tooth."

"Speak for yourself," Diego twisted his lips and squinted his eyes.

"You do not have children," Jorge replied as he stood up. "If you did, you would age much faster."

"I got Priscilla."

"Priscilla, she is a fucking dog, Diego," Jorge headed for the door. "This is not a child. She sleeps all day and pisses on your lime trees."

"I got her to stop doing that," Diego corrected him.

Jorge turned and gave him a smile before opening the door.

"Let me know if you need help," Diego called out as Jorge left. To which, he only waved.

Once in the elevator, he turned his phone back on and checked the messages. Nothing from Chase yet, which meant he was still watching Jolene's house. It was getting late in the day, so chances are this Rico guy would be showing up soon.

He called Paige.

"How did it go?" She asked, knowing he had gone to see Diego.

"Good," Jorge confirmed as he made his way out of the building, glancing around at his surroundings before spotting his SUV. "I do not think anything surprises him at this point."

"I don't think anything surprises any of us at this point," Paige replied. "She's unstable."

"Well, I have not heard back from Chase," Jorge continued. "Did you have your pizza?"

"Yup," Paige said with laughter in her voice. "Full bellies all around. Even Miguel did pretty good."

"Good," Jorge grinned to himself as he got into his vehicle. "I think I will stop at the production house. Maybe give Andrew a heads up and also, see what they may have heard."

"It's a long shot."

"It is the only shot I have now," Jorge replied. "Until I have a chance to see this Rico man."

"Probably tonight."

"I expect so," Jorge said as he started the SUV. "Unless it is the minister's night."

"I guess she's doubling up her chances of getting pregnant."

"Yes, well, according to Diego," Jorge said. "It is unlikely to work. Her doctor told her this."

"As if Jolene ever listens."

"Exactly," Jorge agreed. "I will be home soon, *mi amor.*"

As he drove to the production house, he made a mental note to call Athas when he got home. Chances were the Canadian prime minister had nothing to do with Jolene anymore, but it was always worth checking out.

Andrew and Tony were finishing up their day when Jorge arrived at Hernandez Productions. Both appeared surprised to see him.

"Hey, thank *you* for finally firing Jolene's ass," Andrew bowed to Jorge when he arrived. "I had about enough with her."

"That makes two of us," Jorge replied as the three men went into Tony's office.

"Three," Tony added. "If she did actual work, or could be relied on…"

"Yeah, well, you know," Jorge took out his phone and turned it off, as did the others. "She was not fired, so much as moved to the crematorium."

"Yeah, well, I can throw her in the fire there," Andrew quipped, causing Tony to laugh. "But here, I got nothing."

"Well, your wish might come true sooner than you think," Jorge replied as he leaned against the chair, and the two men watched him with interest. "To make a long story short, she is talking to a man that may know too much."

"Really? The priest?" Andrew asked.

"Minister," Tony corrected him.

"Whatever, man, it's all the same bullshit," Andrew shook his head. "He does the confession thing."

"That's also a priest," Tony corrected him again.

"Whatever…"

"That is the thing," Jorge said and shook his head. "We think there are two men. A 'Rico' and a 'Ricky'."

"Fuck, can't she do two guys with a different name, at least?" Andrew complained. "I mean, come on!"

"Well, Rico, it is a nickname, and in Spanish, it can mean rich, or it can mean something a little more sexual…"

"Yeah, ok, I don't gotta know," Andrew made a face, and Tony laughed. "So she is talking to this guy, you mean?"

"We have uncovered some stuff where she has said a little too much to this man. The one she refers to as Rico."

"Do you know who it is?" Tony asked.

"I am wondering, would you have any idea?" Jorge asked. "Anyone stop here to see her?"

"Just that priest guy," Andrew said. "I mean, minister, whatever…"

"Yeah, that's the only one that comes here," Tony confirmed, then thought for a moment. "Well, then again…."

"Is there someone else that comes to see her?" Jorge asked with interest.

"Not comes to see her," Tony replied. "But there's a guy that works here…"

"Oh?" Jorge asked. "Do tell."

"Well, he doesn't really 'work' here, but he's the custodian."

"Just say he's the janitor, man," Andrew corrected him. "He cleans the bathrooms and stuff. He's super buff, so she's probably nailing him. Yeah, I can see it. I saw them talking before with her tits out."

"Her tits were *out?*" Tony asked in shock.

"Not *out* literally, I mean, she had them stuck out like she does when she wants guys to look at them."

"Oh, gotcha," Tony grinned. "Yeah, I saw them talk too."

"He's not here all the time," Andrew added. "I mean, like once, twice a week. He's not our employee. He's through the company we got hired."

"What's his name?"

"Oh, fuck, I dunno…" Andrew shrugged. "I never talked to the guy, and honestly, I didn't give a fuck."

"He's young," Tony added. "Like probably your age, Andrew?"

"I don't fucking know," He shook his head. "He's kinda under the radar. I never would've thought of him if you hadn't mentioned it."

"Can we find out?" Jorge asked.

"For sure," Tony said as he reached for his phone. "I can call now and see who it is….make up some shit why I'm asking."

"*Perfecto.*"

CHAPTER 45

"Ricardo Rubio," Jorge repeated the name to both Diego and Paige, as the three of them stood in his office, and looked at the photo. "Never heard of him in my life, but he is Mexican. He's here to go to school, but he has a couple of jobs too."

"That seems reasonable," Paige said with concern on her face.

"So, she is like his sugar mama or something?" Jorge asked them.

"This is the first I heard of the guy," Diego said as he made a face. "She's got a Ricky and Ricardo…."

"Sounds confusing," Paige said and took a deep breath. "Have we heard anything from Chase yet? Are we sure it's the same guy?"

"I suspect it is," Jorge confirmed. "Chase is still watching Jolene's."

"But wait, what's this kid studying in university? Not like fucking writing or journalism or some shit like that?" Diego asked. "Cause if he is…"

"Nah," Jorge shook his head. "It is science-related. I cannot remember. I got Marco checking on him now. He's gonna call when he finds anything. He started to when I was there, but there was not much. Just that he is a student, works part-time as a janitor and washing dishes at a restaurant, that is it."

"No ties in Mexico we should know about?" Paige asked.

"Nothing," Jorge shook his head. "Unless Marco learns something else. It sounds like he is clean."

"I would question that if he's with Jolene," Diego grunted.

"Well, he is young and horny," Jorge laughed. "Jolene is trying to make a baby with anyone who comes along, so you know…."

"That's more information than I had to know," Diego made a face.

"He is young," Jorge began to laugh. "He got more ammo than the old minister she is dating if you know what I mean."

"Anyway," Paige attempted to turn the conversation around as Jorge laughed at his own joke. "So, she met him at work, and yet, you would think she'd be interested in showing up once in a while."

"I am guessing she did when he is there, which is two, three times a week," Jorge shrugged and made his way to the desk. "But her interest in ever coming to work is limited. She is in baby-making mode, and nothing else matters."

"I don't understand," Diego shook his head. "I mean, I do, but…."

"I kind of doubt he's writing a book," Paige threw in. "I mean, he might know your reputation because he's from Mexico. I know that's still not what you want to hear, but it also is better than the alternative."

"You did have a reputation in Mexico," Diego reminded him. "You were notorious."

"To some," Jorge admitted as he sat in his chair, and they followed his lead, sitting across from him. "But it was mostly gossip."

"Depending on where he was from in Mexico," Diego reminded him. "It might not just be gossip to him."

Jorge considered the point and shrugged.

"Let's not be too quick to throw him to the wolves," Paige suggested. "I think we need to be fair. He's just some kid. What does he know about anything?"

"He might know too much," Diego suggested.

"We will talk to him first," Jorge assured him. "See what he got to say for himself."

"At least he's Mexican, and not some *gringo* making these comments," Diego said, then turned toward Paige, "No offense."

To this, she merely shrugged, "None taken."

"Paige, she is officially a Latina as far as I am concerned," Jorge winked at his wife.

Paige laughed.

"So we wait?" Diego asked.

"Maybe we should go see Marco?" Paige suggested. "Rather than sitting around here?"

"We might have to go to the club too," Diego thought out loud. "I mean unless Chase needs us."

"I have a feeling that Chase," Jorge shook his head. "He will not need us. Let's hold on for now and wait."

"You know," Paige suddenly spoke up. "If this kid is young, we might be able to work with him, if we want him to talk."

"You think?" Jorge asked. "I mean, I do not know."

"Hey, he might be looking for an opportunity."

"He did not sound like he would want an opportunity from me in the messages Marco show me," Jorge insisted as he tilted his head. "He was totally on her side, but then again, Jolene is letting him fuck her, so he might say anything she wants to hear."

"That's how men work," Diego informed him. To this, Jorge shared a look with Paige and laughed.

"Ok, yes, well, maybe this here is possible," Jorge agreed. "He is young, strong, no money, new to Canada. He may appreciate an opportunity to work for me, but can we trust him?"

"Start him small," Diego suggested.

"Well, I threw that idea out there," Paige said as she exchanged looks with both men. "But it depends what we think when we meet him. We might hate the guy or, end up he knows too much and...."

"It is a possibility," Jorge considered. "I will see how I feel when we get him."

The three continued to talk, then have some coffee and leftover pizza. Finally, the phone rang. It was Marco.

"Sir," he spoke in a quiet voice as if someone was around. "My wife, she is here to pick me up, but so far, I am finding nothing. He has not been in trouble before. He is smart, judging from his grades, and honestly, nothing sets off any alarms other than his conversations with Jolene."

"That might be enough," Jorge commented. "But then again, we will see."

"I will look when I get home," Marco continued. "But I am not seeing anything to be alarmed about."

"*Gracias,* Marco," Jorge spoke respectfully. "I do appreciate it. If you wish to look a bit more, but if nothing shows up, then take the night off to enjoy with the family."

"We are going to the Christmas concert with the children," Marco spoke excitedly. "But if you need me…"

"No, this is fine," Jorge shook his head. "I am fine. Please, go and enjoy the evening with your family."

Ending the call, he shook his head.

"Nothing?" Diego asked.

"It appears no alarms are going off," Jorge replied. "at least not yet."

"That's reassuring," Paige nodded. "I don't think there's anything with this guy, but we'll see, won't we?"

The next call was from Chase about a half-hour later.

"Look, he's in there," he spoke in a low voice. "But, I don't know if he will be leaving anytime soon. I'm wondering if we don't just….meet here?"

"I like how you think," Jorge nodded. "This might be best. I do want to speak to both, so why not bombard them. Maybe they will be in a vulnerable situation?"

"I guarantee it," Chase replied.

"We will be there soon."

"What's going on?" Diego asked as soon as the call ended. "We got them?"

"They are together, in the house," Jorge replied. "We're going to bombard them and find out what the fuck is going on."

"I'll text Juliana," Paige replied smoothly. "She can keep an eye on the kids."

"Well, Maria is here," Diego pointed toward the ceiling, indicating she was upstairs.

"I would feel better if there was an extra set of eyes on the children," Jorge confirmed. "You know…"

"Yeah, this is true," Diego nodded as he reached for his jacket. "Especially if you're getting close to anything."

"Even if we aren't," Paige replied. "I feel better if she knows we aren't home, to keep her eyes and ears opened."

"Only you guys would have a nanny with a fucking gun in a diaper bag," Diego quipped as the three headed toward the door.

"Well, who would ever look in an innocent-looking immigrant lady's diaper bag?" Jorge teased.

"Someone who knows she works for Jorge Hernandez," Diego spoke abruptly, causing both Jorge and Paige to laugh.

The three barely made it to Jorge's SUV when an excited Maria came running out of the house.

"Maria, is everything ok, *Princesa?*" Jorge asked as his daughter approached him.

"I want to come too."

"Maria," Jorge shook his head. "School-night, and it is…work related."

"I know, Juliana said that," She insisted. "I want to come."

"No, Maria," Jorge shook his head and leaned in to speak in a low voice. "It could get dangerous. You must stay home."

"I can bring a gun."

"Maria," Jorge laughed "Look, we are going to talk to Jolene and her boyfriend…"

"Which one? She seems to have a lot," Maria quipped, causing Jorge to laugh, as he glanced toward Diego and Paige, who were in the SUV.

"Maria, I do agree with this here, but you know," Jorge thought for a moment. "You know, on second-though, maybe this is a good idea. If you are with us, she may see it as a friendly visit. Innocent and be unsuspecting."

"She won't think you'd bring me if you were going to give her hell," Maria insisted. "I promise to be careful."

Jorge thought for a moment, weighing his options.

"Maria, things, they may get dicey," He continued to speak in a low voice.

"I know," She nodded. "I will keep back, I promise. As much as Jolene can be dumb, she isn't dumb enough to hurt me."

Jorge leaned over and kissed her on the head.

"I appreciate your interest, Maria, however…"

"I will go back in the SUV," She rushed to add. "Her defenses will be down when she sees me. Once you're in, I will go back to the SUV and wait. I promise."

"You promise?" Jorge asked skeptically.

"I promise. I will keep watch out there."

Jorge thought about it for a moment.

"Ok, Maria, I am trusting you," Jorge agreed. "Text Juliana to tell her."

She smiled and reached for her phone.

CHAPTER 46

"But *Papá,"* Maria spoke with a maturity in her voice, which was somewhat shocking to Jorge. "Paige does make a good point. If this guy is young and in Canada as a student, he might jump at a chance to do anything to stay here. That might be an asset for you."

"Maria," Jorge glanced in the rearview mirror at his daughter's face. "I do appreciate this, but it is hard to say until we meet him. Remember, he *is* with Jolene."

"She's got a point," Diego agreed as he twisted his lips and nodded toward Maria. "You got the connections to make it happen. Some people will do anything to stay here and get the hell out of Mexico."

Jorge gave him a warning look in the rearview mirror.

"I mean, no offense…"

Paige grinned on the passenger side but didn't say anything.

"Well, Diego, some people, they do enjoy living in Mexico," Jorge informed his friend. "Just like some, they like living in Colombia."

"There's a lot of poverty in both places," Diego reminded him. "Corruption, a chance at getting shot. At least in Canada, we don't gotta worry about this stuff so much."

"Speak for yourself," Jorge reminded him.

"Papá," Maria spoke up. "I sometimes miss Mexico, but I feel safer here."

"That is all I care about," Jorge smiled and glanced in the rearview mirror at his daughter. "I want my kids to be safe."

"Miguel will always be safe while I'm around," Maria spoke smoothly and glanced out the window. "I will protect him."

"I know this, Maria," Jorge nodded as he turned onto Jolene's street. "I know I can count on you."

There was a relaxed tone that filled the SUV as they parked close to Jolene's house. Jorge turned to look at his daughter.

"Now, Maria, you are only to come in at first," Jorge reminded her. "You are not to stay. You come back to the SUV, keep an eye out for us, and keep your cell phone off."

"It's off."

"Oh shit," Diego dug his out and turned it off.

"Good thing there is not a tracking device on those things or anything," Jorge quipped.

"Like it's weird that I might go see my sister?" Diego reminded him.

"It depends what you go to see her for," Jorge said under his breath and glanced at Paige. "We are getting to the bottom of this shit now."

The four of them got out of the SUV. They quickly met with Chase, who came out of the darkness.

"Anything?" Jorge asked.

"I think it's him in there," Chase confirmed. "The guy in the picture, but I can't say for sure."

"It is dark," Jorge nodded. "He was young?"

"Oh yeah," Chase nodded. "He looked to be."

"We should get in there," Paige glanced around. "We don't want too much attention from the neighbors."

Approaching her walkway, the three of them followed Maria, who rushed ahead to ring the doorbell. It took some time, but Jolene finally answered, wearing only a robe. She appeared stunned to find the group waiting on the other side. Not missing a beat, Maria quickly broke out in song.

"*We wish you a Merry Christmas...*"

"Oh," Jolene attempted to hide her discomfort, but Jorge could see it. "You sing door-to-door to people for Christmas?"

"Yes," Paige nodded, as the youngest member of the group continued to sing. "It was Maria's idea...the rest of us aren't great singers."

"You not going to invite us in?" Jorge asked, just as his daughter stopped singing. "Come on, Jolene, you can't be sleeping this early."

"I was...a..."

"Maria, go get the gift you have in the SUV," Jorge gave her a warning look, but shouldn't have been surprised when his daughter didn't listen but looked behind Jolene.

"Oh, who's that?" She asked innocently, pushing past Jolene. "Is this your...boyfriend, Jolene? The priest guy?"

"Minister," Jorge corrected her as the group followed his daughter inside, looking at the couch where a shirtless Latino sat. He resembled the picture Tony sent Jorge earlier. Ricardo glanced at the young girl, then to the others, his eyes landing on Jorge Hernandez. He froze.

"Maria, you were going to go outside to get..." Jorge attempted to reason with his daughter, again but to no avail.

"I left it at home," Maria brushed him off, as Paige closed the door behind the group, and Jorge glared at his daughter, who ignored him. "So, Jolene, is this the boyfriend you told me about? The church guy?"

"What?" Ricardo suddenly came out of his daze, his eyes glancing between Maria and Jorge. "Who is the church guy?"

"What is going on?" Jolene ignored his question, her focus on the group. "Why you here?"

"Jolene, enough is enough," Jorge shook his head. "Who the fuck is this guy, and is he writing a book about me?"

"What?" She appeared confused. "He is my friend, and why would you ask this?"

"Book?" Ricardo shook his head with fear in his eyes. "Why? I do not understand. Jolene?"

"Tell me what the fuck is going on, Jolene." Jorge snapped at her. "I am tired of your games. You are hiding something. Is this the guy writing a book about me?"

"I do not write book, *señor*," Ricardo attempted to jump in, his voice shaking. "I struggle with the *inglis,* so I cannot write book."

"He does not write book," Jolene shot at Jorge. "Why would you say this? You interrupt and..,"

"You can fuck him later, Jolene," Jorge shot out and heard his daughter laugh. He immediately wished he hadn't made that comment as he glanced at her. "Back in the…"

"I'm not leaving, *Papá,*" She stood her ground.

"What is this?" Jolene shook her head. "Why you bring your daughter to this?"

"Jolene, I asked you a question," Jorge snapped at her. "Who *is* this man?"

"*Señor,*" The young man nervously stood up and cautiously approached Jorge. He extended his hand. "I am Ricardo Rubio. I know about you. You are a legend in my country. You are Jorge Hernandez."

Jorge eyed him suspiciously and shook his hand, showing no warmth in his expression.

"I do not know about this book," Ricardo said as he let Jorge's hand go. "But I do not write this. I have problems even writing my papers at school in *inglis* and have some help from a tutor, so no, I do no write book. I would not have time with school work, if I wanted to, but you definitely should have a lovely book wrote about you."

Diego laughed.

"Diego," Jorge shot him a look. "Let the man speak."

"I know why you all here," Jolene complained. "You gang up on me."

"Jolene, we are here because we wanted some truth from you. For a change," Jorge raised his voice. "Who's writing the fucking book, Jolene?"

"I do not know," Jolene attempted to sound strong, but there were tears in her eyes.

"You better tell me the fucking truth, Jolene," Jorge yelled. "Because you know, I do not like it when people lie to me."

"I promise," Jolene began to cry. "I do not know or I would tell! But it is not Ricardo."

"Ah, so he is your boy toy?" Jorge glanced at Ricardo, who tilted his head, listening to Jorge carefully. "Someone, to help you get pregnant?"

"Pregnant?" Ricardo suddenly appeared very alert as he rushed to Jolene's side. "What? You say you cannot get….are you, were trick me? What is this?"

"If you aren't using a condom," Jorge informed him. "She is tricking you. She wants a baby."

"I…no, this…"

"Jolene, tell the truth for once in your fucking life," Diego jumped in. "What is going on here?"

She clamped her mouth shut as tears rolled down her face. She looked away.

"You say you cannot get pregnant," Ricardo appeared confused as he confronted Jolene. "You say, you are on pill or something?"

"And you are not the only one," Jorge threw in. "She has a minister boyfriend too."

"What?" Ricardo appeared hurt as his face turned red. "You have another man in your life? And you try to trick me to have a baby?"

"The good news is Jolene," Jorge glanced at her. "She's old, so the eggs, they are dried up, just like she is…"

"My eggs are fine!" Jolene shot back. "You are a terrible person."

"I am not the one lying to this man here," Jorge pointed at Ricardo, who was glaring at Jolene, clearly humiliated.

"Jolene, you're a cougar," Chase suddenly jumped in. "And I don't have a problem with a woman dating younger men, but you…you're different. You *prey* on them."

"She preys on everybody," Diego corrected him. "This guy, he's a kid, Jolene. What the fuck is wrong with you?"

"She wants a baby," Jorge snapped. "She don't care who she uses."

"I do not want this," Ricardo said as he shook his head as he moved away from Jolene.

"Rico, it is not like that," Jolene attempted to explain. "They do not understand."

"I think I understand," Ricardo said as he grabbed his shirt off the couch. "What they say is true."

"It is not," Jolene started to cry. Then with her misery abruptly turned to anger, she shot back at Chase. "I may be a cougar, but cougars, they have sharp teeth and claws, so be aware."

"Do not threaten Chase," Jorge laughed her off. "Jolene, this here, it is gross, but fortunately for you, I am going to let it go. There is nothing here that says to me that you have betrayed the family. This guy," Jorge stopped to point at Ricardo. "He is another story."

"I do not betray."

"Me, no," Jorge shook his head. "And Jolene, you do not want to either."

His dark glare caused her to shrink back and assess the situation around her.

"I would suggest," Jorge continued. "That you clean up this mess and maybe think about going to work tomorrow morning, for a change."

"You ruin my life, Jorge Hernandez!" Jolene spoke dramatically.

"Jolene, it is *you* that ruined your life," Jorge corrected her and gave her one final warning. "And you know, this here could end up a lot worse."

With that, he turned around and gestured for the others to follow him toward the door.

CHAPTER 47

"That was weird, *Papá,*" Maria spoke honestly as the five of them headed down Jolene's walkway toward the sidewalk. "I mean, she was sleeping with two different guys at once and trying to get pregnant? That's gross."

"Lots of things about Jolene are gross, *Princesa,*" Jorge put his arm around his daughter, while the general feeling amongst the group was heavy. "But at least, we know this man, he is most likely not involved in the book about me."

"No, I don't think so," Maria insisted.

"He's clean," Diego agreed, who glanced at Paige, who nodded.

"Just another one of Jolene's victims," Chase muttered.

"There are a lot of those," Jorge replied as he glanced toward his SUV.

Jolene's door opened, alerting Paige, followed by the others. Ricardo was walking out with a look of defeat on his face. He appeared embarrassed, as he approached the group.

"Mr. Hernandez, I am very sorry," Ricardo spoke up as he approached him. "I have great respect for you."

"Oh, is that right?" Jorge shot back. "What I hear is that you tell Jolene that she will end up in a body bag if she does not listen to me? That I am the 'almighty' Jorge Hernandez? That she should try to get away from me?"

Ricardo put his head down in shame.

"That is what I thought," Jorge said as he started to turn away.

"Wait, no," Ricardo said and shook his head. "You do not understand. That is not how I mean it."

"It sure seems that way," Chase commented as he crossed his arms in front of his chest. "You might want to explain yourself better."

"Maybe we should take this guy somewhere to talk," Diego glanced around. "more private."

"I can go," Ricardo seemed apprehensive. "But what I mean, it is that I respect you. You *are* very powerful in Mexico, and yes, you are known to be dangerous. I do not say that disrespectfully. It is just a fact. But you are also a good man."

Jorge eyed him suspiciously, while the others moved in to listen.

"One year, when I was quite young, where I live, we lost our church. It was burned down by another cartel, and you had another one built for us. You brought presents for us children...." He looked away as his eyes began to water. "It would be so little for you, but it was so much for us. So, *por favor,* I do not mean disrespect. I do not know what you seen or heard, but I did not mean it like that, *señor.*"

Jorge took a deep breath and looked at his daughter, who watched him in awe, while the others shared a look of surprise.

"*Papá,* you did this?" Maria asked in a small voice.

"Maria, these places in Mexico," Jorge began to speak. "They are very poor, and yes, there are times we...we must help. If we do not, who will?"

"Not the government," Ricardo shook his head. "It was very beautiful what you did. My *madre,* she said many prayers for you."

"Now we know how you survived this long," Diego muttered, causing grins all around. "I always wondered how Jorge Hernandez made it to 40... now we know, his mother's prayers."

"It certainly was not *my* mother's prayers," Jorge grinned, causing everyone to laugh. Everyone, but Maria, who continued to look in admiration of her father. He put his arm around her, and she wrapped her arms around him.

"It was an honor to meet you, *señor,*" Ricardo spoke respectfully as he glanced toward the street. "But I must go home now. I can catch the bus at the corner."

"I can drive you," Chase offered. "Unless there's anything else, Jorge?"

"There is one thing," Jorge turned toward Ricardo. "Why is it your phone, it is not listed anywhere?"

"I do not know," Ricardo shook his head. "It was one Jolene give to me."

"I think it would still be listed," Diego watched him carefully.

"I do not know," Ricardo repeated. "I do not have money so she said she would get me one. I do not know where."

Jorge gave Chase a look and nodded. "Yes, Chase, please take him home. I do think I may have more questions for you, Ricardo, so we should meet very soon again."

"I would like that," Ricardo nodded. "But *por favor,* if Jolene, she with child…"

"We'll let you know," Paige assured him.

"It's a long shot," Diego jumped in. "A very long shot."

"She's desperate," Paige confirmed.

"Ok, then we are done here," Jorge said and nodded. "Until we meet again…"

"Yes, *gracias,*" Ricardo followed Chase while the others loaded into Jorge's SUV.

"That's pretty cool, what you did," Diego said after they were on the road. "I knew you did shit like that, but wow…what are the chances of meeting this guy?"

"It may not be true," Jorge reminded him. "I did help a community with a church, yes, this is true, but I want to have Marco look into it some more. If he confirms it, then I will trust him, but we are not quite there yet."

"But what Jolene did," Paige spoke in a low voice, shaking her head. "That was terrible."

"A lot of what Jolene does is terrible," Jorge said. "And me, I am not a saint, but that is….crossing a line."

"I think she is *loco,*" Maria spoke up. "Who tries to get pregnant with two different guys? *Gross.*"

Jorge laughed.

"Well, Maria, this here, it happens," Jorge said and took a deep breath. "I am not pleased that you stayed in the house when you promised to leave however, you did good. But I prefer you listen in the future."

"I was going to," Maria insisted. "But when I got there, I sensed I should stay."

"She might've kept things under control," Paige offered. "I think emotions would've run much higher if you hadn't been there, Maria."

"This is true," Jorge agreed. "I think it is ok. Everything, it will be fine."

"Jolene will be miserable for a few days," Diego said as he glanced around at the streets as they passed people who waited outside a nightclub. "But that's deserved at this point."

"I do feel a bit bad for her," Paige said. "But the way she went about it, it's playing with people's lives."

"That man was upset," Maria observed. "He was very upset."

"He was tricked," Diego added. "Gotta feel sorry for him."

"But you know," Jorge decided it was time to move forward with this conversation. "He has learned the truth. Jolene has been forced to deal with it, and in the end, we still do not know who is writing this book."

"Maybe there is no book," Diego suggested.

"I wish this was true," Jorge replied. "But I feel something is going on behind the scenes."

"Maybe check to see if Alec knows anything more," Paige suggested. "I'm not sure what else to do at this point. Marco isn't finding anything. Makerson, Tony, they're not hearing anything."

"This feels like a dead end," Diego said and shook his head.

Jorge thought as they drove along, everyone falling silent. By the time they got home, he had an idea. Going to his office, Jorge sat alone, contemplating what was next. He picked up the phone and decided to touch base to see if anything new had come up. The first person he called was Makerson.

"Hey Jorge, I was just finishing another chapter."

"It is going well?" Jorge asked.

"Yeah, I managed to smooth some things out about your teenage years, so it looks polished," Makerson said with kindness in his voice. "Did you find out more about…"

"No, I was going to ask you the same."

"Nah, I got feelers out too," Makerson admitted. "I don't know."

"We will find out."

"We will."

"I wish you a good night."

He then attempted to contact Athas. As expected, there was no answer on his secure line, so Jorge called his cell.

"This is unexpected," Athas answered the phone. "Did you catch the culprit yet?"

"No, I was hoping you had some thoughts on that."

"I do not," Athas said. "Maybe that guy gave up? Maybe he was writing a book and changed his mind."

"Let us hope."

Jorge ended the conversation and leaned back in his chair. Maybe there was no book, but he couldn't shake the feeling there was. He sent a quick text to Marco.

I have something I need you to check out. Meet me first thing tomorrow.

Will do, sir. Do you need anything before then?

No. Good night, Marco.

Jorge didn't think Ricardo was a threat. He would check him out to be sure, but he certainly wasn't writing a book. He still didn't trust Jolene. She was a cat that was coming up to her last of nine lives.

A knock at the door interrupted his thoughts.

"Come in."

Expecting Paige, he was surprised to see Maria.

"Should you not be in bed by now?" Jorge asked, and she merely shrugged. "What can I do for you tonight?"

"I wanted to say what you did for that man's town was cool," Maria said as she plopped down on a chair across from him. "And that guy tonight, I think he's ok."

"I agree."

"I have a weird feeling, though," She continued.

"You do?" Jorge was curious. "About him?"

"No," She shook her head. "About this book thing."

"What is that?"

"Like, I feel like you aren't talking to the right people," Maria said as she crossed her legs, appearing more adult.

Humored, Jorge nodded and listened.

"Paige said once that if you aren't getting the right answers, maybe you're asking the wrong questions or, you're talking to the wrong people."

The grin on Jorge's face suddenly disappeared as a thought crossed his mind.

CHAPTER 48

"It did not take long, sir," Marco replied as Jorge glanced up from the laptop. The two men sat in the VIP room at *Princesa Maria*. "He has no history, and yes, he did say those things I show you before to Jolene, but other than that…"

Jorge nodded as he leaned back in the chair.

"He is clean, sir," Marco confirmed, pointing out a few things on the screen. "He comes from a poor community, where you helped build a church. His parents have a lot of children. He is here because an organization provided money for his scholarship. He is lucky because there were a lot of others trying to have this same opportunity."

"And he studies sciences?" Jorge confirmed.

"Yes, I understand he wants to become a doctor, sir," Marco confirmed. "He also is studying hard to improve his English. But that is all. I see nothing concerning. Previously, my only concern was the remarks he made to Jolene. At the time, their conversation set off an alarm for me."

"That makes two of us," Jorge nodded. "I am at the end of my rope with her. I feel that we always come back to this same place with Jolene, and I cannot trust her."

Marco moved away from the laptop and watched Jorge as he spoke, nodding his head.

"Sir, what you tell me about last night," Marco said as he closed the laptop. "It does give me a reason to be concerned too. There are a lot of secrets with this woman."

"I have no doubt she hides a lot," Jorge replied. "But, unfortunately, I do not think the person writing my book is one of them. I was hoping to find this here information, but I did have an idea last night."

"Oh really?" Marco raised his eyebrows. "Is there something you want me to look up?"

"Not yet," Jorge shook his head. "I do not think the person doing this has a record anywhere because they know that I would find it."

"So, not Jolene?" Marco spoke in a low voice.

"No, I do not think it is someone in my life," Jorge shook his head. "But someone who knows that I would go to great lengths to find them, so they hide in the shadows."

Marco appeared worried.

"But I must talk to someone first," Jorge rose from his chair. "And Marco, thank you for finding this information. If I need something else, I will be in contact."

"If you need *anything*," Marco nodded. "Please message me right away."

Jorge left the club and headed for his SUV. He felt heavy, concerned with what he was about to do next. It wasn't going to be an easy day.

Once on the road, his thoughts were dark. Paige had been right so many times when she suggested that unless he got out of the spotlight, there would always be a chance that someone would try to take him down. He had a bad feeling about the devil waiting at the door.

He made his way across town. Parking in front of an older-style house, Jorge sat in his SUV for a few minutes before getting out and heading up the walkway. Even then, he hesitated before ringing the doorbell.

The door opened, and Mark Hail stood on the other side. He appeared surprised.

"Jorge, I wasn't expecting you," He seemed curious as he stood aside. "Come in."

"I will not be long," Jorge said as he entered the house, glancing around. "I must talk to you about something."

"Sure," Mark nodded and gestured toward the kitchen. "I was having some coffee before I headed out. Want some?"

"No, I am fine," Jorge shook his head as he followed the constable into his kitchen. "Actually, no, I am not fine."

"Oh," Hail turned on his heels. "So, coffee then?"

"No, my stomach, it is not good," Jorge replied as he glanced around the kitchen. "I need to speak with you about an important matter."

Appearing curious, Mark grabbed his cup from the counter and sat across from Jorge at his table.

"This, here, it is new," Jorge touched the table as he sat in the chair.

"Yeah, nothing fancy," Hail replied. "I got a long way to go before this place looks anything close to modern."

Jorge grinned and nodded.

"So, what's going on?" Mark appeared intrigued. "I haven't seen you in a while."

"Well, I am trying to find out something," Jorge admitted as he launched into his story. "Recently, I learned that someone might be writing either a book or...something about me. CSIS informed Athas that someone was coming into the country, saying they were in Mexico because they were researching me, but provided no further information."

"Did you find out who?"

"That's what I am working on," Jorge admitted. "But I am, you know, not finding anything because whoever does this is hiding well."

"Wouldn't there be a publisher or something?" Hail tilted his head.

"You would think, but no," Jorge shrugged. "There is nothing. So then, I think, maybe it is part of a series, a documentary, something else but still, we find nothing."

"Are you sure it's even a real thing?" Mark asked. "Or maybe, they found out who you were and backed away from the idea?"

"I think of this too, but I cannot...I cannot shake the feeling," Jorge admitted. "So, I think, who are my enemies? Who have I pissed off?"

Hail's eyebrows raised.

"I know," Jorge nodded. "This list, it is long."

"I didn't say that," Hail replied. "But you do have some enemies, including in the police, and you *know* a lot of their secrets too."

"This is what I am thinking," Jorge said.

"Well, it's not me," Hail spoke earnestly. "And most of those guys I work with, I'd be surprised if they can even spell their names, let alone write a book."

To this, Jorge laughed.

"Are you wondering if it's an investigation?" Hail asked. "I mean, maybe they're saying it's a book, but..."

"This has crossed my mind, yes," Jorge replied. "I do not think it would be your department..."

"But someone higher up, maybe the RCMP?" Hail nodded. "What about Athas? Can he find anything?"

"Athas would probably be more than happy if I was thrown in jail," Jorge laughed. "Who knows?"

"I can look into it," Hail said with a shrug. "But I dunno if I'll get anywhere. I don't think this would get leaked to Athas actually, unless he knows more than he said"

"This, I cannot see," Jorge shook his head. "I helped you all eliminate a problem earlier this year for both the police and RCMP. Would your department be working with the RCMP?"

"I don't know that the RCMP work *with* anyone," Hail snuffed. "They are above us, and they make sure we fucking know it, but I can check into a few things when I go to work today."

"This here, it would be helpful."

"But, you know, if that was the case," Hail continued. "They would find your weakest link and take that person aside to work for them. Think about who that might be in your organization. Because if the police are involved, that's the route they'll take."

Jorge considered his words as he left. It was when Maria pointed out the previous night; sometimes you're looking in the wrong places.

He went home. Glancing around, he noted the house was empty. Maria had gone to school, Paige was at the office, and Juliana took Miguel to the park.

Without giving it a second thought, Jorge unlocked the basement apartment door and walked downstairs. The place he had provided for Juliana to live was comfortable, not dark and dank like most apartments situated underground, but well lit up and slightly elevated compared to others. But this was the last thing on his mind. He was on a mission.

Glancing at his phone, he noted the time and knew Juliana would not be home for at least a half-hour. He had no time to waste.

He started in her bedroom since that was the place most people hid information. He carefully searched her drawers, closet and even found her secret hiding place behind a box. There was nothing.

Taking a deep breath, he sent Marco a text.

I need your help.

Just give me a name and number.

Keying in her information, he waited a moment.

Searching.

Gracias.

Jorge continued to look around, finally locating her laptop in the kitchen. It was still on. Glancing toward the door, he started to flip through everything; her emails, pictures, documents, anything. It felt like a useless endeavor until something caught his eye.

Jorge's phone rang. It was Paige.

"*Hola.*"

"Can you come by the office?"

"Now?" Jorge was surprised.

"Yes, it's kind of important."

"Oh…yes, I will be there soon."

"Make it as quick as possible."

"I will, *mi amor.*"

Jorge continued to look at the laptop, finally taking a picture of what he found.

Glancing around, he made sure that everything was in order before he left the nanny's apartment. Feeling drained, he made his way back upstairs.

CHAPTER 49

Sitting in traffic, Jorge glanced at the array of Christmas decorations and lights that stood out against the bleak morning. Watching as people rushed along, shopping bags in their hands, it suddenly occurred to him that the holidays were quickly approaching. The sound of a Christmas carol seeped into his car, but nothing could lighten his soul today. He was dead.

The days of enjoying an electrical charge of anger as it roared through his veins were gone. While the challenge of taking on an enemy had once filled him with passion and fury, it now weighed him down. He was getting tired of always fighting. It no longer empowered him so much as depleted his energy. Maybe he was just old.

Traffic was slow, but Jorge eventually found himself sitting in the underground parking for the office. Warily, he got out of the SUV and headed for the elevator. He remained quiet, deep in thought as he made his way up to the floor which housed the *Our House of Pot* offices. Now that he was no longer CEO, he rarely dropped in. It was now Diego's domain.

Scanning his card at the door, he walked inside, quickly saying hello to the receptionist, before making his way to the conference room. He found Paige, Diego, and Marco waiting for him. Swinging the door opened, he went inside.

"So what's going on?" Jorge jumped in with less enthusiasm than usual. "You guys got all my answers?"

"We definitely have some, sir," Marco appeared skeptical. "This here, I do not like."

"I was in Juliana's apartment…"

"You were in her apartment?" Paige asked. "You mean, looking for something?"

"Well, Paige, it did cross my mind…"

"Oh, sir," Marco shook his head. "This is not about her, sir."

"That is what I was hoping," Jorge said as he thought back to his nanny's laptop.

"I did find one email…."

Marco and Jorge exchanged looks.

"You too?" Marco asked.

Jorge nodded.

"What?" Paige asked as Diego pushed his reading glasses to the top of his head and listened to their conversation, exchanging looks with her. "What are you talking about?"

"We will talk about it later."

He noticed Marco looking away without replying.

"Is she…did she do something?" Paige guessed, but Jorge didn't reply.

"Sir, we should talk about what I found," Marco cut in, giving an apologetic look at Paige. "It is rather important."

"What you got?"

"When you said to look up Juliana," Marco replied as he tapped a few keys. "I did not find anything, but then, it occurred to me, sir, her accounts were all easy to sign in to, so what if someone else saw this too? Maybe as a way to learn something about you. I checked to see, and it did not appear anyone was hacking her account, but then, I decide to dig a little deeper…"

"Do you mean…"

"Sir, I discovered that someone was trying to hack your phone," Marco said and began to shake his head. "This person made several attempts through your cloud. Fortunately, I have everything very secure, so this person was not able to."

"It's unnerving," Paige spoke calmly.

"But this, it is fine," Marco continued. "As I say, they were not able to get in, but it does give me the ability to trace them through their IP address. They cannot tell, but I have located the area that this person lives, and hacked them. When I did so, I found something of interest."

He paused, which caused a knot in Jorge's stomach. Marco was usually straightforward, so his hesitation was a reason for concern.

"Please, Marco, just tell me," Jorge insisted. "So I can prepare. Is it someone wanting to hurt my family? My children?"

"No, sir," Marco was quick to shake his head. "Sir, there is a book."

"There *is* a book?"

"But, it is about many people," Marco said as he turned his laptop around, showing the title in large, strong letters.

PSYCHOPATHS RULE THE WORLD

"What the fuck is this?" Jorge laughed. "This here, this is *the* book."

"You are one of many that are in the book," Marco revealed. "You are listed in the chapter about cartel leaders."

His words drifted off as Jorge stared at the screen. They all fell silent while the others watched his reaction.

"What?" Jorge shook his head in disgust. "I don't get *my own* book?"

"Jorge," Paige gave him a look. "I don't want you to think…"

"That he's *not* a psychopath?" Diego finished her sentence with a grin on his lips.

"Look, you know these words," Jorge pointed to the screen. "They do not hurt my feelings, but I am a little insulted that I do not get my *own* book. I must share it with these…..who is in it?"

"Sir, they talk about people like serial killers, cult leaders, dictators….."

"Company CEOs," Diego added. "You know, besides you, but the *really* ruthless ones who don't let their employees pee more than once a day, that kind of thing."

"This is not you," Marco rushed ahead to assure him.

"Ok, this here, I do not care," Jorge shook his head. "Please tell me that this has not gone to press yet? That it is not out?"

"No, he's in the process of finishing it," Paige confirmed. "Which is good because from what Marco found, no one else has seen it. The author is very secretive about his work."

"Then we gotta get this here author," Jorge insisted. "I am not fucking around. This book, it will not get out there, and if it does, my name will *not* be in it."

"What are you gonna do?" Diego asked. "Me? I would show the fucker what kind of psychopath you can be!"

Jorge shot him a look.

"Sir, I am normally not for violence, but…" Marco started.

"Me neither," Jorge spoke innocently, causing them all to laugh, then he grew serious. "So, you can get an address?"

"I have an IP address, and I'm working on narrowing down the location and confirming," Marco said as he typed into his laptop, shaking his head. "It is very rural, sir."

"Can I talk to you?" Paige said to Jorge, pointing toward the door.

"You can use my office," Diego said as he looked over Marco's shoulder.

Jorge nodded but didn't reply. He followed Paige out of the conference room and into Diego's office, where she closed the door.

"What's going on with Juliana?" She asked. "Do you think she's part of something? We can't have her around the kids if that's the case."

"No," Jorge replied. "It is nothing like that."

"Then what is it?" Paige pushed. "What did you see?"

A knock at the door interrupted them, causing Jorge to dodge the question.

"*Sí.*"

Marco opened the door and stuck his head inside.

"I do not mean to interrupt," He said, glancing at Paige, who smiled and looked down. "But I have found this man, the address."

"Thank you, Marco," Jorge said as he gently touched his wife's arm, giving her a pleading look. "We must go now."

"Marco, can you do me a favor," Jorge said as he followed him back into the conference room with Paige behind him. "Can you go to see Chase and let him know? Have him meet us there, in case we need…help…"

"I can do that," Marco pointed toward the laptop and turned it around, showing an image of a slim, middle-aged white man wearing glasses. "This is him, sir. He lives alone in rural Ontario."

"Tell me everything you know," Jorge said as he leaned in to get a better look. "Who the fuck is this Gerald Myers guy?"

"Sir, I cannot seem to find much on him yet," Marco quickly filled him in. "I did see his research, and he seems to have a particular…fascination with people he considers psychopaths, but his focus was on you."

"He probably knew that if he wrote a whole book about you," Diego jumped in. "You'd find out, but this might get under the wire."

"Sir, it almost did," Marco commented with concern in his eyes. "He was scheduled to meet his agent soon with the first draft. The only reason I found him was because I saw where he was trying to hack you. He was very careful."

"He covered his tracks well," Jorge said and took a deep breath. "The fucker knew who he was messing with, so he thought he'd slip it in the book."

"And create enough interest," Paige suggested. "To maybe write a book focusing on you later, once this got out."

"This here is possible," Marco nodded. "It is clear from what I see that you are the person he was most interested in researching. His file on you is quite large."

"Wow, I would say," Diego leaned in as Marco scanned through the file while Jorge glanced at his wife. She was worried.

"Anything else?" Jorge asked as his heart raced.

"I'm doing a search, sir," Marco quickly tapped. "I'm looking for emails to his agent."

"There's a lot of those too," Diego said as his eyes scanned the screen.

"Sir, it says right here," Marco pointed at the laptop. "That he has some 'very revealing information about a Canadian businessman who has conned us since day one and made himself a hero', but he refuses to tell his agent who, instead indicating it would be a surprise."

Jorge shared a look with his wife, who appeared anxious.

"This book," Jorge pointed toward the screen. "Will never see the light of day, and this fucker, never will again either."

CHAPTER 50

The media. It has made us laugh and cry. Sometimes, it provokes us to push for change, while other times, it has misled and manipulated us. The media is a powerful source of information, which we often blindly follow. We get caught up in frivolous stories and controversy, often missing the bigger picture. And sometimes, the bigger picture is nothing more than the information the very powerful decide that you shouldn't know.

Jorge Hernandez was more than familiar with the media. It had always been a top priority for him to have a pristine image under their bright lights. However, years of reality shows and limited interest in investigative journalism created an atmosphere where he could get by with a charming smile and carefully chosen words. But this book could potentially change that forever.

As they made their way to Gerald Myers' home, Paige read passages from *Psychopaths Rule the World*. Even she, at times, appeared shocked by the words she read, while in the backseat, Diego was unaffected. Jorge showed no reaction. The anger he felt increased as they neared the community. His heart pounded furiously. There was no way that Gerald Myers was going to live.

Paige suddenly stopped reading.

"What?" Jorge asked in an abrupt tone, quickly catching himself. "Paige, I am sorry, I did not mean to snap, but when you stop reading, I fear…"

"I stopped reading because the vein in your forehead is about to pop out," Paige calmly replied. "Not because anything here is too shocking for me to handle. It's not like you've ever hidden who you were back then, who you are."

"Mi amor," Jorge took a deep breath. "This here, cannot get out. So much of it is not true, but no one will believe what I say and what if Maria, she sees this?"

"She won't be seeing this," Paige assured him. "No one will. This isn't the first dragon we've had to slay. We can handle it."

"And Makerson's book," Diego piped up in the back. "It's gonna come out next year and this will be long gone."

"Are we sure the agent does not have it?"

"No one does," Paige reminded him. "Remember, Marco checked it and he plans to keep looking. This Myers guy is pretty careful about what he does. He knows that if anyone else reads it, there's a chance that you'll get your hands on it. And as it is, we only got it because he was attempting to hack your phone."

"The fucker got a little too close to the fire," Jorge snapped as he stayed focused on the road.

"And he's about to get burned," Diego reminded him. "He probably felt pretty safe because you hadn't found out anything and pushed his luck."

"But what if," Jorge shook his head. "Even if we get this guy, who is to say that someone else is not going to do the same thing. Who did he talk to? What if, after Makerson puts out the book, we find out someone else is going to counter it."

"I think we need to leave something that sends a message," Paige suggested.

"How about deleting the entire book," Diego suggested as he fixed his tie. "But leave the title for everyone to find. As if he was just starting it."

"That might work," Paige said. "If there's a bloody body…"

"I think we need to get rid of the body altogether," Diego suggested. "But leave some blood."

"I like that," Paige looked back at Diego. "That's just enough to send a message."

"But will it work?" Jorge worried. "I do not know."

"It could be a suicide," Diego suggested. "He could leave a letter."

"I want to bash this fuckers head in," Jorge insisted. "This here will not look like no suicide."

"Maybe you could hold off for the greater good?" Paige asked.

Jorge didn't reply.

"You know, maybe you need to retire," Diego suggested. "Focus on training Maria. Do something to counter any potential bad images that could come out. Do charity stuff. I dunno."

Jorge considered his words but didn't reply. He continued to drive, thinking about everything he'd discovered that morning.

By the time Jorge arrived in the rural community where the author lived, he was already thinking about the future.

Things were about to change.

They were especially about to change for Gerald Myers.

After passing the small farmhouse where the would-be author lived, Paige was the first one to speak.

"I don't think he's home," She observed. "He's registered to have a truck, but I don't see it."

"No garage," Diego said as he leaned toward the window. "I think we need to hide the SUV, get into the house, and wait for him to get home."

"There's a hiking trail nearby," Paige said as she studied a map. "We can park there and walk over."

"Who the fuck goes hiking in the winter?" Diego asked.

"You'd be surprised," Paige replied as she glanced at her husband, then Diego. "Not that either of you is dressed for it."

"Expensive shoes made of imported Italian leather, hiking," Diego sat up straighter. "I don't fucking think so."

"We aren't *really* hiking, Diego," Jorge explained. "And you know, we could be those religious people going door-to-door."

"They tend to sometimes park away," Paige nodded. "Someone might see your vehicle if it's too close."

"We do not want to alert suspicion either way," Diego glanced around as they slowed down by a sign that told about the hiking trail. "Not that there seems to be anyone else living out here in the boonies."

"Diego, you consider anywhere that doesn't have a subway to be the boonies."

"It *kinda* is," Diego spoke condescendingly.

"Some commute to the city, so aren't necessarily here during the day," Paige jumped in. "It's a drive, but it's cheaper to live here than Toronto."

"Ok," Jorge said as he parked the vehicle, slightly out of sight. "Let's just do this."

The three got out of the SUV and headed toward Gerald Myers' house. When they heard a car in the distance, Jorge felt anxious, hoping no one would spot them. That was the thing with small towns; people noticed when a stranger was in the area.

"I think it's Chase," Paige commented as the vehicle got closer. Fortunately, she was right. He slowed the car down and rolled down his window.

"Where you guys parked?"

"Over there," Paige pointed back. "At the hiking trail spot."

Chase nodded and drove away. A few minutes later, he was jogging to catch up with them.

"Buddy home?"

"Nope," Diego said. "We gotta get in fast."

"Clean?" Chase asked next.

"Not if this one has his way," Paige muttered as she pointed at Jorge.

"If you heard what she just read to me," Jorge pointed at Paige. "You would not be clean either."

"Bad shit?"

"There's a lot of," Paige thought for a moment. "Accusations about Jorge's life when he lived in Mexico. How he got to the top, the body count..."

"Yeah, there's stats for each of these guys the book is about..." Diego started.

"Each?" Chase cut him off. "How many people are in the book."

"It's called *Psychopaths Rule the World,* and can you believe it's not *just* about Jorge?" Diego quipped. "He's fucking insulted that he had to share the pages with other people."

"Each one has stats and facts," Paige went on to explain. "What they are worth…"

"And they had this wrong too!" Jorge complained. "I am worth more than what they say!"

"Anyway," Paige said, and Chase nodded in understanding. "We're getting the book and ending this."

"Ending him," Jorge added.

A faint sound of music grew louder as they approached Gerald Myers' property. A scatter of awkwardly placed decorations filled the yard. It was like a winter wonderland despite the lack of snow.

Once they got to the house, they put their gloves on and checked the windows to confirm no one was home.

"No cameras?" Chase asked as *Silent Night* played around them.

"No one has cameras around here," Diego said. "Marco, he looked."

They got in the house quickly, with Paige's crafty skills, and located the office right away. Notes, some of the chapters, and a laptop were sitting on the desk.

"It's a cute little house," Diego suddenly spoke up, looking around. "Like a cottage."

"We are not here looking for real estate, Diego," Jorge said as Paige sat in front of the computer and began to work.

"Gone," She said.

"And that's it?"

Reaching for a hard drive, she plugged it in and hit a few buttons.

"Gone here too," She repeated.

"Any other copies?

"Good question," Paige shook her head. "This was too easy."

A noise from upstairs alerted them. Everyone reached for their gun.

"It could be a pet," Diego whispered. "So don't shoot and ask questions later."

Another, louder noise grabbed their attention. It sounded like a scream.

"That's not a fucking dog, Diego," Jorge said as he rushed ahead. Upstairs, with the others behind him, he tried to open the door where the sound was coming from, but it was locked. Backing up, Jorge kicked it opened to find a young Filipino woman, naked and tied to the bed. She had dried blood on her chest, thighs, and face. She was crying hysterically.

"Please, help me," She cried. "Please before the Mr., he come back."

Shocked, Jorge froze. He exchanged looks with the other men, who appeared stunned by what they were seeing. Paige rushed ahead to untie the woman, who was hysterical. Grabbing a blanket, Paige wrapped it around the shaking woman as she helped her up. Paige picked her clothes off the floor then led the hostage to an adjoining bathroom.

"Who is this fucking monster?" Paige whispered as she passed the horrified men.

"He be back soon!" The woman continued to cry hysterically. "He will kill me. He say this, please…"

"Lady," Jorge spoke up. "We will protect you, but you never repeat anything that happens here today."

"I never tell," She assured him as tears dripped off her chin. "Never, you, you are all my angels."

Jorge felt a wave of light flow through his body when she looked into his eyes, before looking back at the ground.

"Come," Paige helped her toward the bathroom as the music stopped and another song began to play. "Let's clean you up."

"Holy fuck!" Chase said as he looked between Diego and Jorge. "What the actual *fuck!*"

"And he writes about *me* being the psychopath," Jorge shook his head just as the sound of a car door shutting captured his attention.

"Let us hide. He will come up to see his victim."

Only the Christmas music could be heard, as the group held their guns. The sound of a flushing toilet in the bathroom caused them to be on high alert. A pounding on the stairs indicated Gerald Myers was on his way to the check in on his hostage. He was barely in the room when Chase and Diego pointed a gun at him, and Jorge came from behind and put a gun to the back of his head.

"Well, now, it is interesting that you write a book with me in it," Jorge commented. "And yet, you do not talk to me to find my side of the story."

Gerald Myers had a look of panic on his face when Jorge walked around him. A gun was held directly to his forehead.

"Now, I have a young woman in that bathroom," Jorge gestured toward the adjoining room; even from behind the doors, the woman's sobs and screams could still be heard. "I am thinking that she would have quite a story to tell the police about *you*. We might have to compete for that psychopath title that you decided suited me and a few others."

Gerald Myers continued to stare in shock.

"So you are going to tell me," Jorge instructed. "Where are all the copies of the book?"

"There….there's one on my computer," Gerald stuttered. "And there..there…there is one..one on an external hard drive."

"Where else?"

"N..n… nowhere else," He managed to put his words together. "T… that is all."

"Why the fuck you got a woman tied to your bed?" Chase yelled across the room. "What the fuck is wrong with ya?"

"She…she s..s..was so young," Gerald continued to stutter. "And…a…."

"Oh, enough of this shit already," Jorge cut him off. "Where are the other copies of the book? Does your publisher have any? Safety deposit box? Tell me, or I will cut your balls off in front of the little girl in there…" Jorge pointed toward the bathroom. "And you seem to be the fucking expert on me, so you know I *will*."

"No!" He shook his head. "No other copies."

"You swear?"

"I dunno," Diego said. "He could be just saying that. I would start cutting and see what's left of him…"

"No, no, please!" Gerald's teeth began to chatter as he spoke. "No, there are no others…"

"Call your fucking agent," Jorge instructed. "Call him now, put him on speaker. Ask him if he got the copy you sent. Say anything fucking else, and I will not only kill you but find your entire family and fucking kill every one of them. And you know I am more than capable."

This final threat was all Gerald needed to carry out the command. Within minutes, he was on the phone with his agent, who confirmed they had no copies and seemed confused by the call. Gerald ended it by saying he was about to send them something.

"I'm satisfied here," Jorge nodded. "But as I said, if there are other copies, I *will* find and kill everyone you love."

"I...I...I know," He nodded. "Please, I..."

Jorge shot him in the head, and his body slumped to the floor.

Suddenly all he could hear was the music from outside. A haunting version of *I'm Dreaming of White Christmas* broke the silence, and the three men looked at each other, then down at the crimson blood that collected on the floor.

There was one less psychopath in the world.

Check out the rest of the Hernandez series and learn more about Mima's books. Go to <u>www.mimaonfire.com</u>

Printed in the United States
by Baker & Taylor Publisher Services